THE
OXYGEN
FARMER

THE
OXYGEN
FARMER

COLIN HOLMES

CamCat
Books

CamCat Publishing, LLC
Ft. Collins, Colorado 80524
camcatpublishing.com

Hardcover ISBN 9780744306675
Paperback ISBN 9780744306699
Large-Print Paperback 9780744306729
eBook ISBN 9780744306736
Audiobook ISBN 9780744306743

Library of Congress Control Number: 2023939397

Book and cover design by Maryann Appel

5   3   1   2   4

for
Mitchell

I think he would have liked this one.

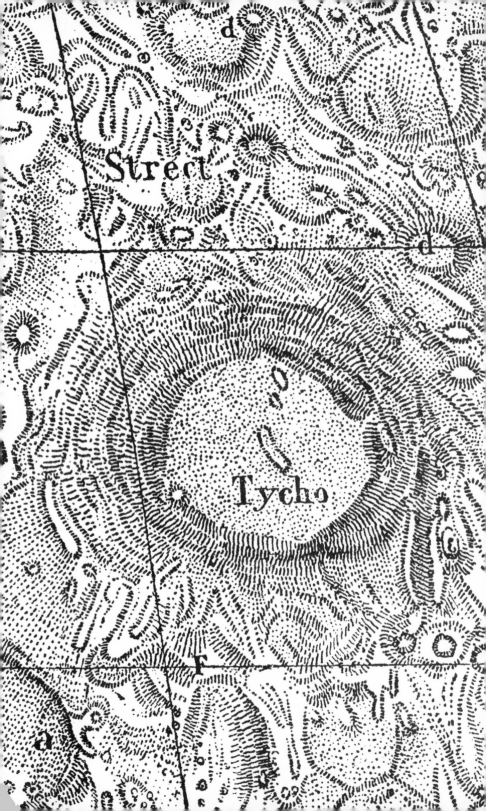

Wilhelm 1

Heinsius

CHAPTER ONE

Wednesday . 03 Nov . 2077
0925 Lunar Standard Time
4.76 km SSW of Slayton Ridge . Luna

The spidertruck's spindly legs shuddered as the astronaut kicked the front wheel for punctuation.

"You. Worthless. Piece. Of. Shit."

He slumped onto the wheel, glaring at the magnificent desolation beyond his battered helmet. Thin silver hair drooped from beneath his communications cap and lines covered a face leathered from a lifetime toiling in the relentless lunar daylight. The name patch that would have identified him as Mil Harrison had long since been torn off his dusty pressure suit. The flag printed on his shoulder was a faded memory.

"Just two more stops . . . dammit." He blew his aggravation into the scratched faceplate.

Overhead, the ten-meter white sphere on the delivery truck loomed like a rock on the back of an insect. Faded decals proclaimed:

Neff Atmospherics, An Amon Neff Company
M. Harrison, Proprietor

Twice a week, he loaded up a sphere with life-sustaining oxygen and headed out to one of the various settlements around the Luna Colony. Most days, he actually got there.

He tapped his wristcomm. "Armstrong Base, this is Harrison, come in." Mil heaved a resigned sigh. "I need a hand."

The video monitor on his cuff blinked to life, revealing the bank of monitors filling the clean white room of the Armstrong Base Command Center communications bay behind Specialist Madison Byers. She raised an eyebrow at the unexpected call. Mil was used to that look. He was sure that just like everyone in the settlements, Maddie knew the legend that was cranky old Mil Harrison, the guy who rarely called in and never asked for anything. She brushed a strand of blonde hair from her cheek.

"Harrison, Armstrong Comms here. What's your issue, Mil?"

Mil pursed his lips and squinted at the far ridge. He hated forced familiarity.

"Byers, right? I've got a blown inductor module on the spider. About twenty klicks southwest of Settlement Two."

"Aww. And you don't have a spare?" She gave the ancient astronaut a perky smirk.

As on every other day of his life, Mil was not in the mood for perky. He started to give a curt reply before remembering he was the one stuck in the middle of nowhere.

"Of course I have a spare. Back at the farm. I just need a quick lift to go get it. Got anybody out here in the boonies?"

Mil watched as Madison scrolled through her holographic display. Her fingers swiped along the image of the lunar surface floating in front of her. A blue triangle moved just along the eastern edge of the orange-tinted exclusion zone. Her finger waved at the triangle and a data point appeared beside it.

"I can reroute Granger. He'd be there around fifteen thirty."

"Fifteen thirty? Hell, I can hike it before then."

"Best I can do. Unless you want to declare an emergency. Do you?"

Mil checked his wristcomm—83 percent on his air tank and six of eight bars on power.

"Shit."

"Say again, the recorders didn't quite register that." A hint of playful sarcasm tinted her reply.

Mil didn't play. "Forget I called. I'll hoof it."

"So logged. Have a fabulous rest of the day. Armstrong out." The wristy, as everyone referred to it, blinked back to show Mil's systems status.

"Yeah. Thanks."

He trudged to the shady side of the spidertruck and opened the dented access panel to the storage compartment. He considered the distance to the far ridge, then dug past the tool kit and pulled out a pair of large aluminum overboots with thin cylinders on the sides. He stepped in and they clamped to his lower legs automatically. He snapped a pair of thin ribbon cables into the power connectors at the knees of his suit, then stomped a small circle to check the boots.

Status indicators on his faceplate flickered yellow, then green. He oriented himself toward his farm, armed the capacitors, and jumped, firing the booster boots.

Mil bounded across the lunar surface, taking sixty meters in a step, kicking up clouds of the ever-present gray dust at each landing. He'd done this often enough to be proficient at it, but boosted hiking across the rock-strewn, cratered terrain required concentration and more than a little co-ordination.

He cursed the unreliable spidertruck. He'd be chewing someone's ass on a vidcall later. This had been a replacement for his old reliable truck—a newer, "better" model. *Sure,* Mil thought between leaps, *better for some bean counter on Earth whose idea of a difficult situation is having to reboot their spreadsheet.*

He angled along the cliffside of the Slayton Ridge Exclusion Zone, cutting the corner into an area deemed off-limits by bureaucrats who would never set foot on the moon. It wasn't the first time he'd bruised the terms of an international treaty.

As expected, his faceplate tinted orange as he crossed the invisible line in the dust. The pleasant feminine voice of his computer system firmly intoned, "This is an exclusion zone notification. You are approaching a posted exclusion zone. This is official notice that any—"

Mil interrupted her. "Bailey, cancel EZ warning."

"Notification canceled. But don't say I didn't warn you." For some reason everyone was sassy today.

He wasn't concerned, just passing through, but then, right as the capacitors fired for another jump, a different warning tone interrupted his concentration. His faceplate tinted red emphasizing the warning. He looked down to the monitor on his wrist but instead saw the power cable snake free from his right leg.

"Alert. Malfunction," Bailey said.

Thrown wildly off his stride by the failure, he flailed over the crater's rim into the blackness beyond the ridgeline, an area forever shaded from the sun. The surface came too quickly, and his right leg buckled on impact, sending him ass over teakettle, pinballing seventy meters down the darkened backslope of the ridge, bouncing off a boulder before skidding to a stop in a dust cloud of profanity.

He blinked his eyes open in near complete blackness and caught his breath while Bailey completed a systems check. He could just make out the top of the ridge looming above him, the fringes of its edge backlit by Earthshine, as the old home planet floated somewhere on the bright side like a blue jewel in the endless void. His suit lights snapped on, creating a pool of light at the base of the inky, shadowed cliff.

"Pressure suit integrity, good. Systems operating nominally." Bailey completed her checks before he did his. The artificial intelligence paused, waiting for a response. "Should I call for medical attention?"

"No on the medical. I'm okay," Mil lied. Arms and legs moved, his back hurt, but only a little more than usual. He'd have a knot where he banged his head on the inside of his helmet. He groaned his way to his feet, reminding himself that at his age, soreness was just a daily reminder that he was still alive.

Mil pulled a small metal canister from a long-forgotten pocket on his thigh. A twist of the top and pressurized air sprayed the dust from the connector for the booster boot and the suit's electrical supply. He snapped the wiring back together and began his ritual stomp test.

The fourth stomp produced a hollow feeling instead of the expected sturdy clomp of the lunar surface. More stomps, and the emptiness below the surface vibrated through his boots. He bent and dusted the ground with his canned air. The fine gray powder skittered away to reveal a man-made metal hatch a good two meters in diameter.

Mil stood up, hands on his hips, studying the hatch and trying to figure out what it would be doing here on the dark side of Slayton Ridge. One didn't often find a man-made trapdoor at the foot of a basalt rock wall on the moon. He plucked a high-powered light from his vest and illuminated the wall of the ridge he'd just tumbled down. It looked like a rockslide had long ago covered whatever the hell this was.

"Okay, Bailey, let's record this."

A small red light on the mounting ring of his helmet blinked on and a network of tiny cameras on his suit began to document the world in 360-degree virtual reality.

"Ready when you are, Mister Spielberg," Bailey confirmed.

The hatch's metal handle required a heave but then snicked up and away from the locking mechanism. Pent-up pressure inside helped push it open. The suit lights revealed an airlock just large enough for two people and not much equipment. Mil looked around again and swept the blackness with his light.

Whatever the hell this was, it was seriously out of place. Mil shook his head. Only one way to find out what it was. He paused a moment and surveyed the empty blackness around the ridge, sweeping the barren moonscape with the lights on his suit.

There was nothing here. A bunch of boulders and the top of the ridge seemed to be the only witnesses.

Satisfied he was alone, Mil climbed down through the hatch and turned to the airlock door covered in the stenciled warnings he recognized as good old American military overprotection.

"Bailey, any idea what this is?"

The AI system scanned the warning notices. "That's a warning to close the overhead hatch before opening the inner airlock."

"You really think I don't know that?"

"You did ask."

Mil rolled his eyes, slightly aggravated at how years of his own smartass responses had influenced his digital assistant.

He pulled the overhead hatch closed, then turned and opened the inner door. It swung through to a vertical passageway with a simple ladder bolted to the wall. Mil looked down into the darkness. This was mysterious. He activated the remainder of the lighting on his suit.

At the base of the ladder, Mil undogged yet another hatch, triggering the clicking of a Geiger counter in his headset.

"Radiation notice," Bailey's more serious voice intoned. "Rem levels are two point six five times ambient background standard."

"Got it." Mil frowned and played his lights around the single room. Two hammock-style bunks hung on the far wall beside another hatch. A full meter overhead, the rounded ceiling blended into another wall of controls, switches, and ancient, dark CRT display screens.

"Radiation notice. Please check personal protective gear. Rem levels are two—"

"Check, let me know if we get close to an evac level."

"Affirmative."

He stepped into the center of the room, slowly turning to take it in. On one wall, a binder hung by a D-ring. He lifted it and the aged navy-blue vinyl cracked and crumbled. Mil recognized the faded logo from the antique aircraft displayed outside the old Johnson Space Center in his hometown. The star-and-bars mark of the twentieth-century US Air Force. Time had not been kind to the pages inside; whatever copy had once been printed was faded and gone. Mil's hand went to the top of his helmet to scratch his head by reflex.

What the hell?

A closer look at the wall showed what appeared to be storage slots, lockers, and a box with a door and handle beside a transparent window labeled Radarange. He flipped switches on the wall and white interior lighting filled the room. A tattered plastic curtain hung from a track around what he'd swear was a relief tube.

Crew quarters?

"Bailey, what is this place?"

The digital assistant muted the steady clicking volume of the Geiger counter.

"There is insufficient data to support a conclusion."

"So pry a little," Mil suggested as he opened and closed empty drawers.

"Inadequate signal strength to access system networks. Locally available data indicates that all records for the Slayton Ridge Exclusion Zone are classified."

"So there's nothing that says why it's an exclusion zone?"

"All records are sealed."

He moved to the hatch on the far side. The room carried a thin coating of fine dust. *No one's been here in years,* he thought. *Maybe decades.*

"How deep in the zone are we?"

"Approximately three point seven kilometers inside the nearest border of the Slayton Ridge Exclusion Zone. Off-limits to all personnel per the Minsk Lunar Accords of 2036."

"So this is different from the EZs around the Apollo sites?"

"The Apollo exclusion zones exist to protect the historically significant areas."

Mil paused at the hatch, a wary feeling creeping up his spine. He vaguely remembered that the old yellow-and-magenta bullseye symbol above the door once meant a radiation hazard of some kind. He really didn't need another rad event in his life.

"And you can't find anything?"

"The seal on the records predates the creation of Internet One. It's even older than you are."

"Funny. So, twentieth-century documentation? It'd be on what? Paper?"

"Or microfilm. Neither is a stable media for long-term storage."

"And it'd be on Earth," he spat. "Possibly just an old exclusion zone somebody forgot about?"

"The zone's status has been reclassified on a consistent basis."

"So somebody is keeping a secret." He took hold of the hatch handle.

"That is a logical assumption."

"Yeah, I'm good at those."

"There is insufficient data to support that conclusion."

He unlatched the hatch, the door swung open, and the world went berserk. His faceplate flashed to bright red. The Geiger counter crackle became a scream, and Bailey's serious voice boomed in his ears.

"Radiation emergency. Evacuate immediately. Radiation emergency. Evacuate immediately."

Mil threw his shoulder against the door and cranked the lever to a lock. The tint on his faceplate toned down to orange. He scrambled for the airlock door.

"Radiation Alert. Extreme potential hazard to human life. Confirm personal protective gear. Evacuation strongly recommended."

He heaved himself up the airlock ladder. "Way ahead of you."

He earned a new pain in his right shoulder as he slammed the upper door behind him, then vaulted through the hatch, huffing and puffing to the dark lunar surface on his hands and knees. He gulped air as he crawled to the hatch and slammed it closed, then scooped great handfuls of lunar soil and piled it back over the hatch. He'd rather not explain that he'd once again trespassed through forbidden territory and ignored the lofty Minsk Accords. That part would just be his little secret. But somebody planted a radioactive EZ on his moon. And he was going to find out who.

He squirted his canned air around the area to cover his tracks and then armed his boosters and jumped away.

Leaving a single boot print in the shadowed dust.

CHAPTER TWO

Wednesday . 03 Nov . 2077
1035 Lunar Standard Time
Command Center . Armstrong Base . Luna

Maddie Byers frowned at the alert that popped up on her holodisplay. "Command. I just got a rad alert in the Slayton EZ."

Commander Desmond Rafferty swiveled his chair from the workstation that served as his command center.

"Confirm, Eli."

Across the room, Specialist Eli Yenko studied his display.

"Confirm, Command. But just a flash. It appeared, then faded. Maybe a glitch?"

Rafferty stroked his gray-fringed goatee. "Meteorite?"

"That could do it." Yenko swiveled in his chair. "There's nothing else out there that'd cause it."

Maddie cleared her throat. "I did get a call from Mil Harrison. But he's well away from the alert."

"Harrison, hmm." Rafferty pursed his lips and gave Byers a long look. "Log it. Granger will be through that sector on patrol next week. Task him with checking it, just to be sure."

Mil bounded across the moon, his boots rhythmically firing as he timed his steps to crest a low hill. On the far horizon, he could just make out Harrison Station, the collection of domes, storage tanks, and gleaming solar panels that made up his oxygen farm. A dozen giant silvery-white spheres, each identical to the one on the back of his faulty spidertruck, seemed to glow in the reflected raw sunlight. Beyond them, arrays of photovoltaic collectors sucked in that sun, while tall orange cylinders stood guard, steadily filling with the life-sustaining oxygen the farm produced.

In two more leaps, the small network of light gray geodesic domes that made up his home appeared, along with the production facilities. He angled his last few leaps toward the largest of the domes—his barn.

Mil clomped through the airlock, pausing for the high-pressure air to wash off dust, then stepped into the forty-meter dome's soft, even light, the translucent geodesic panels above muting the blazing sun. *It isn't much*, he told himself, *but it is home.* He eased down to a bench, supporting himself with one hand while the other involuntarily unlatched his helmet. "Nope. I am not getting too old for this shit. No way."

As the first child of Y2K, just being born had made Millennium Edward Harrison famous. He arrived in the Houston suburb of Clear Lake mere seconds after the stroke of midnight. The crush of the television reporters and the fervor of cameras and microphones crowding in to see the first baby of the new century overwhelmed his parents, a rather nondescript couple of mid-level NASA engineers.

Caught up in the excitement, they gave him a name which set him up for the lifetime of teasing, trouble, and ridicule that had tempered young Millennium's appreciation for the human race.

It wasn't that he genuinely disliked everyone; he'd just rather be here, at home on Luna, than deal with any of those nine billion assholes scrambling for an existence a quarter of a million miles away on Mother Earth. Mil's worst day on the moon was better than any he'd spent on his home planet. And this certainly wasn't near his worst day on the moon.

Mil heaved the helmet over his head and took a deep breath of his crisp, clean air. After all these years, he still took pride in the difference between the recirculated air in the suit and the freshly cracked O2 his farm produced.

His dutiful post-excursion examination of the battered pressure suit noted several new scratches, and he wondered if the dent in the aluminum sleeve was a result of tumbling down the Slayton crater rim or if he was just forgetting something. He mentioned that to his distorted reflection in the scratched faceplate, "Nope, not too old at all."

He weaved his way through the packed workshop along a well-choreographed path through, around, and in some cases over, a variety of projects amid construction. The barn was a crowded compendium of components, tools, production equipment, and vehicles he might eventually get around to repairing. An old Axial Mark III robot leaned on one leg, gathering dust in a corner. It was simply the accumulated junk of a bachelor farmer who had lived in the same place for the last thirty-plus years.

At his workbench on the far side, he shoved pieces and parts aside and uncovered a dusty rebuilt inductor module hiding under a spool of fiber-optic cable he had been searching for last week. He found his diagnostic scanner and checked the test port. The green light said it should work.

Mil ducked into his attached apartment. "Bailey, set for three pain-killers."

"Mediprinter set."

Mil drained a double ration of water and pressed the mediprinter's applicator to his sore shoulder as the device hissed the medication through his skin. He swapped out a full battery pack and air tank, then paused at the workbench to replace the problematic power cable on his booster boot before shrugging back into his suit. Since he'd worked up a sweat on the jog to the farm, the damp suit put up a fight. It didn't smell great either. He made, and promptly forgot, a mental note to refresh the filters.

Stepping back out into the glare of the sun, he plotted his return hike into the wristcomm, making sure to set the way point outside the far corner of the EZ. It added ten minutes to the trip.

The additional time allowed him to ponder his discovery as he bounded across the gray plains, past gray boulders and the odd gray crater. Whatever the facility was—capsule? bunker?—why was it irradiated? And how come no one had ever mentioned it? He'd been on the moon longer than anybody. If he didn't know about it, then it was a secret somebody was working hard to keep. After a quick roadside repair, Mil rebooted the spidertruck and reprogrammed the route along the smooth, graded path to Settlement Two. He sat back, engaged the autopilot, and punched up the holodisplay.

The head and shoulders of Dr. Emma Wilkerson appeared, and she wrinkled her freckled nose in irritation. "You're late."

Mil nodded in agreement. "Yep. I had a mechanical issue."

"Mechanical? Was it your comms?"

Mil's involuntary smartass reflex kicked in. "Why yes. Of course. My comms died and I had to realign the quantum-field generating Johnson rod and completely overhaul the speaker bearings. These things take time."

"For what you charge for O2, you should be here the instant I snap my fingers."

"Finger snap availability is another ten thousand a month. I can add that to your plan if you'd like."

She smirked. "Ha. The new guys have real-time contact for deliveries. They're here when they say they will be."

"Right. If you had me at your beck and call, you'd probably abuse the privilege." Mil winked at the dashcam lens.

"Oh, I'd abuse you all right."

"See, the new guys don't know what they're in for."

"Just get here, will you? I'm bushed and I want to go home." She wiped her brow with the back of her hand.

"Still with the Mars crew physicals?"

"Done for now. One more team when *Humanity* makes orbit."

"So then, you're free for an early dinner?" He toggled the autopilot switch and manually steered the truck back to the center of the road.

"Your treat? I'm in."

"See you in twenty minutes." The holodisplay image blinked off.

Mil spent the remainder of the trip doing network searches about Slayton Ridge while the spidertruck handled navigating across the moonscape. He learned the entire ridge had been classified since around the beginning of lunar exploration, but little more. Every thread he followed ended at a classified firewall.

He also discovered that his rebooted spidertruck still couldn't drive for shit and hit every rock and crater it could find. He'd once again have to reflash the system and update the maps. He added that to his mental to-do list right below "refresh pressure-suit filters."

Settlement Two's network of gray domes dwarfed Mil's farm. Hamster tunnels connected residence domes to the large labs and main work areas. A gigantic hydroponic greenhouse sat next to a formation of newly installed O2 balloons and a half dozen of Mil's weathered gray O2 spheres.

A spidertruck and sphere identical to Mil's but wearing the giant red numeral four on the side took up Mil's reserved parking space in the loading area. He growled.

"Harrison to Unit Four."

A pair of astronauts paused at their examination of the manifolds and piping that made up the receiving area. Their helmets faced each other, then looked to Mil's approaching truck.

"Unit Four, come in. This is Harrison. Move your damn truck. You're in my delivery space." Mil parked a few meters away and hopped down.

Both astronauts swiveled to find the old oxygen farmer headed their way at a deliberate clip. The one closest came to meet him.

"Sir. We'll be done in just a moment. We thought your delivery slot was hours ago."

"You're not to touch any of my equipment and that includes the delivery area. Understand?"

"Sir, we—"

"That was a yes-or-no question."

"Yessir." The astronaut stepped back as Mil got inside the boundaries of social distancing.

"See that it doesn't happen again. Now move."

The other astronaut stepped in. The twin blue stripes on her sleeve identified her as a supervisor. "Cool your jets, Harrison. We're almost finished unloading. Your system is down to almost sixty percent, and I was performing a maintenance check. Calm down."

Mil faced her. "You're not to access my equipment in any situation except an emergency. Three spheres out of four is not an emergency. Is that clear?"

She stepped back and raised both hands. "Never touched it. But hey, these are your toys. I'm not getting in the middle of it."

Mil watched as her partner moved back to the new system and disconnected their truck. "Damn right you're not."

"Besides, this will all be gone in a month." She waved to the wall of manifolds and pressurized piping. "All this archaic piping and old wireline sensors? It's scrap."

"Archaic?" Mil and his late wife held more than a dozen patents on the system. "That was designed before you were, kid."

"Point made." She turned and waved her associate back to their truck. "We're done here. It's all yours."

The two interlopers hopped to the cab and pulled away, throwing a cloud of dust Mil's way.

He pulled to the designated hookup area and performed his long-practiced routine of swapping out hoses and fittings. He ran a quick series of tests on the other spheres and had started for the main facility when the thought hit him. He stopped in his tracks and slowly turned to the web of piping, manifolds, valves, and manual controls.

This was it. The last time he'd deliver to this facility.

It wasn't archaic. It was his life's work.

His, and his late wife's.

Mil had led the mechanical engineering team that brought Settlement Two online, but his late wife, Dr. Olivia Harrison, was the brains behind the system. She'd been on the forefront of applied science, transforming the theories of electrolyzing lunar regolith to release the oxygen locked in the soil into a functioning reality. She'd also designed the delivery systems and the apparatus that made up this first-generation system. Mil's job had been engineering and leading the fabrication teams who'd built this array of piping, pressurization, and production from scratch. Mil stood and marveled at Olivia's elegant genius. Together, their achievements made colonization a possibility.

Their farm and this delivery system provided O2 to the first generation of off-planet humans. The effort also carried a dark edge for Mil—memories tainted by the countless hours of work as a blessed distraction from the grief of losing his wife and research partner. He evaluated the new system towering over theirs. The new crew had completed their beta testing and production ramp-up was underway. From here on out, the Luna Settlements would get their O2 from Amon Neff's new state-of-the-art facility.

He allowed himself a small moment, then slapped the side of the spidertruck and crow-hopped the familiar moonwalking gait to the airlock. He hung his helmet by the secondary entry door and pulled a crumpled orange ball cap from his pocket. He found Dr. Emma working in the greenhouse. "This has really grown."

She looked up from repairing a valve on the aeroponics system that supplied the barest amount of necessary water to the lettuce in this particular row and blew a lock of hair out of her eyes. "New botanist came in last month. Prep for the Mars mission. He really knows his stuff." She sniffed the sour odor that had followed him in. "You okay? You look tired."

He dismissed it with a wave. "You know, if this takes hold you won't need the new guys." He took a deep breath. "Nothing makes O2 like good old horticulture."

"You ever miss it?"

"Miss what? It's right here."

"You know what I mean. Horticulture. Real plants. Freshly mown grass, aspens in the Rockies on a spring morning. Evergreens blanketed in snow on a crisp winter evening."

"You mean Earth? Nah." He snorted. "I get the sniffles just thinking about all that ragweed down there."

"Anyone ever tell you how hopelessly romantic you are?"

"All the time."

"Anyone but me?" She smirked.

"Well, there's this guy over at Settlement Four . . ." He snapped off a tiny lettuce leaf and ate it.

She threw a glove at him. "Did you hear? About the rad spike this afternoon?"

Mil raised an eyebrow. "Really?"

"You weren't out in it, about ten thirty, were you?"

"I was hiking back to the farm."

"We should take a look at you, hon. You could have caught a dose. Your lifetime numbers are high enough." She studied her plants, avoiding eye contact.

"My numbers are so far off the charts, I oughta glow in the dark."

"Still, it might be a good time to check you out. You should swing by the office."

Mil feigned an annoyed look. "It doesn't take you long to go to full doctor mode, does it?"

She smirked. "You fix tractors, farm boy. I fix people." With that she tapped her wrist and set the appointment. His wristy buzzed acceptance. "When we get done, you can buy me another dinner."

Mil gave an evil half grin. "How about we make it breakfast? It can be a really thorough physical."

She threw the other glove.

CHAPTER THREE

Wednesday . 03 Nov . 2077
1755 Lunar Standard Time
Harrison Station . Luna

Mil's apartment testified to his existence as a man too long single. He'd lived by himself since what people around him cryptically referred to as the "Accident," the transport incident that had taken his wife, Olivia, over thirty years before. The fallout from that changed his life, destroyed his relationship with his only daughter, and cemented his desire to live "off-planet," as his business partners on Earth referred to it.

He spent the entire day in the barn with his dataslate tethered to the spidertruck. He tapped at the screen and queried the onboard systems to diagnose the inductor issue, then having determined he'd be ordering new components from Earth, he reprogrammed the mapping systems and tried to sort out the problem with the vehicle's synthetic vision system. The networked dataslate gave him access to all the technical manuals, virtual reality assembly content, and a direct connection to the manufacturer's tech support team. It still took hours to uncover what the manufacturer now said was a design flaw that was overstressing the inductor.

Much like his overall mood, Mil's stomach growled as he entered the apartment, his diagnostic scanner in one hand, the scorched inductor module in the other. He dumped the equipment on the dining bar and punched up the menu controls for the meal printer on his wristy.

For a bachelor farmer, dinnertime meant an opportunity to fix the inductor while the meal printer chugged some nameless protein into the shape of chicken cordon bleu. He pulled the steaming plate from the printer and sampled it. It tasted an awful lot like last night's Salisbury steak. Where were the meal tablets they were always promised?

Neither the institutional supper nor the fried inductor held Mil's interest. His mind hadn't been on the mundane repair tasks all day; instead it traversed the foot of Slayton Ridge. While the spidertruck engineering AI plotted ways to fix his truck, bigger questions kept turning over in his mind: Why would there be an EZ in the middle of nowhere and why bury an entire facility? What kind of facility was it, and why would it be generating radiation? Not to mention, why would the entire mess be continuously classified?

Before he knew it, he'd finished his meal, replaced the blackened circuit chip in the module, and ginned up far more questions than answers. As Mil wiped down his spork and tossed the bactericide towelette in the composter, he glanced at the faded crayon drawing of a stick figure in a space helmet that had been stuck to his composter door for years. A rare smile cracked his face. He knew someone who might be able to get an answer for him. It was just a matter of a little salesmanship.

Mil buckled on his weight belt and settled into a comfortable pace on the treadmill just across the dining bar. As the oldest citizen of the moon, he knew more than anyone the requirement for near-constant enhanced-weight exercise to fight off bone degradation in the lower gravity of Luna. After all these years, it was as much a part of him as breathing. He toggled the holodisplay and made a few quick taps to log on to the secure vidcall link. Only a handful of people could access his private encrypted network. The security tones chimed in and the vidcall window opened. He straightened his ever-present baseball cap as if that made him more presentable and keyed the contact listing. The young woman who answered the vidcall looked concerned. She had large brown eyes and dusky golden skin, and her hair fell in brown, almost black, ringlets. Behind her, a party was in full swing.

"Grandad?" Nique Rivera asked. "Is everything okay?"

"Hey, there. Got a question I need some help with."

Nique frowned, looked over her shoulder at the room full of people celebrating behind her. "Right now? I'm kind of in the middle of a thing."

"Well, you answered the call."

"Because you only call for emergencies or when you need something. I was pretty sure it wasn't for the big event." Nique waved her hand and the camera panned around the party. Random people nodded, raised a glass, or waved.

"Oh. Yeah. Congratulations—didn't I send some money?" Mil's mind tried to shift gears.

"That was graduation. Why bother to show up when you can click a button and put money in my account? I sent you a note. This is Mars! I made it. I'm on the team. It's just comms crew, but still . . ." Her face brightened and the note of pride rang in her voice.

"Mars? Really? Hey, that's great. I guess it does run in the family. Look, Nique, I need some help on something. I've found a—" He paused a moment at the thought of self-incrimination. "Can we talk in private? Can you go somewhere?" He leaned into the camera.

Nique waved her camera across another shot of the party. "You mean, can I drop everything I'm doing and immediately make your problem my top priority? Instead of celebrating the greatest thing I've ever done? With my friends and family? I might add that Mom will be here any minute. Maybe you'd like to wait and talk to her?"

"Not particularly."

"I didn't think so."

"Look, I just wanted to ask you to look at some—"

"You wanted. You. Wanted. Come on, Grandad. It doesn't always have to be about Mr. Moon. Even though he's oh sooooo special. Everyone drop everything and do what Millennium Harrison wants because he's the guy who's breaking new frontiers and living on the moon. Big damn deal. What about everyone else? What about your family? What about us, Grandad?" She folded her arms and threw out a defiant hip.

Mil raised an eyebrow. "You better now? Get all of that out of your system?"

"Really?"

"You said it yourself, I wouldn't call if it wasn't important. This qualifies. I need some help. From Earth."

"And I happen to be on Earth." Her face grew large on his dataslate tablet computer as she leaned into the camera to emphasize the imposition.

"You happen to be the only person on Earth I trust."

She paused. That was an unusual admission for her grandfather. "It's that important?"

"Something tells me it is. But if you don't have the time, I can find someone else . . ."

She growled at the old man. "Give me a second." The call screen went dark.

Mil waited. It took longer than he wanted, but he was the one asking the favor. Finally, a tone chimed and the window reopened. He recognized the background as the stark confines of his granddaughter's Space Force quarters.

"Okay," she asked, "what's going on?"

"I need to know why there's an exclusion zone on Slayton Ridge."

"There's always been an EZ on Slayton Ridge."

"I know that. But why is it an EZ? What's there?" Mil explained slowly.

"I have no clue."

Mil rolled his eyes. "I know you have no clue. I need you to find out. There's nothing on the net, or it's all firewalled."

"What's this about?" She canted her head.

"It's better if you don't know. That way if someone asks, you don't have to play dumb. Call it a research project."

Nique pursed her lips. "You want my help, but you don't want to tell me why."

"I don't know why, but I've got a gut feeling about this. There's something there." Mil shot a glance to his screen showing the exclusion zone in bright orange.

"You went into the EZ, didn't you?" It was a flat accusation and the old man blinked.

"Why would you say that?" He pushed his ball cap back on his head.

"Because it's off-limits and you never feel like anything on the moon should be off-limits to you. So you go where you please. And now you found something."

"Now just a minute, young lady." He raised his hands in an attempt at protest.

"Grandad, I minored in undergrad psych and you were the source of most of my papers. A man who chooses to live alone on the moon? Away from all of humanity? Good stuff. Even my professor wanted to publish papers on you."

"Another reason I like living on Luna. Fewer shrinks."

"You know going in an EZ is punishable. They could . . ."

"Exile me to the moon?" He gave a half smile.

"Worse—they could send you to Earth." She smirked back. Two could be coy.

"Trust me, that's the last thing they want to do."

"You're changing the subject."

"I am. Just see what you can find on the EZ, will you? See what a classified-files search turns up."

"I just got my clearance! Now you want me to risk it?"

"Of course. It's what I do. I make my priorities your problem."

"I think I had that the other way around."

"Love you, kiddo."

"You too, Grandad. Want me to tell Mom hi—"

Mil tapped off. He didn't think he'd intentionally cut her off, but if she was about to start the "you and Mom need to repair your relationship" lecture, he had better things to do.

A baseball game replaced the vidcall projection. The London Monarchs led his Houston Astros by three runs in the seventh. Mil swiped a finger to bring up the old-school box score. The Astros had a power-hitting lineup and had won the 2065 and 2066 Series. He felt they could come back to their former glory. Mil swiped the air again, and a 3-D rendering of Luna's sun side appeared, shrinking the display of the ball game. Another few swipes and several orange dots floated above the surface of the moon. He tapped one at random.

"Bailey, what do you have on this?"

The display zoomed into the surface and the orange-tinted area filled the screen. In the center were footprints, random hardware, and the lower segment of a century-old NASA lunar module.

"The indicated area is the Ocean of Storms Exclusion Zone. Set aside per the Minsk Lunar Accords of 2036 to protect the historical significance of the Apollo 12 landing site. On November 19, 1969, Astronauts Charles "Pete" Conrad, Alan L. Bean, and—"

"Thanks, Bailey, I know about Apollo 12." He'd visited the site and the visitor center several times over the years. It was one of the better spots to see the footprints and the remaining descent stage of the lunar lander. Plus, it had the advantage of not being as crowded as the Tranquility Base site. That place was typically packed with tourists ogling the history of Buzz and Neil and giant leaps for all mankind.

A question crossed his face. "So, what's the penalty for entering an exclusion zone?"

"Per the Minsk Accords, trespassing in an exclusion zone is punishable by fines, incarceration, and/or extradition to Earth. There is no record of anyone having been charged with violating the boundaries of an exclusion zone."

"Nobody?"

"There appears to be great respect for the sanctity of the exclusion zones."

"That figures."

Harrison checked the ball game once more. His Astros weren't coming back. Bottom of the eighth in London, and the Americans hadn't scored yet. He shut down his treadmill program, grabbed the repaired inductor, and crow-hopped toward the barn.

At the airlock door he donned his lightweight coverall and a slimline helmet. He'd be working in the outer barn and didn't need what he considered the overprotection of the full level-two extravehicular EVA suit. He checked the thin pressure bladder on the backpack and confirmed it had enough O2 so he could work on his equipment. The power cell still had enough juice to power his suit for more than three days.

He opened the airlock into the barn. Along one wall sat a worktable with a variety of hand tools, chargers, and parts. Harrison pulled open one of the drawers below the tabletop and rummaged for the right wrench. Mil pointed the wrench to the trusty old Axial robot slumped against the wall. One battered, disembodied leg sat atop a container of parts that needed to be replaced.

"All right, Axe, old buddy. Let's dig in and see if we can get you going. Bailey, bring up Axial schematics."

"Displaying lower motor controls section. Reminder. Abnormality report due to corporate."

"Nah. We don't need to bother corporate just yet. I don't know enough to report."

"Section six, paragraph five, subsection three of the Luna operations protocol requires a contact report on—"

Mil scowled. "All right, all right. But this isn't going through normal channels. Prep this as CONFIDENTIAL—AMON'S EYES ONLY. Include the VR file."

CHAPTER FOUR

Thursday . 04 Nov . 2077
0840 Pacific Standard Time
Space Force Crew Launch Center . Vandenberg Space Force Base . Earth

N ique pressed her thumb to the fingerprint reader, then looked into the camera as the blue beam of the retina scanner played across her eye. She blinked and recited, "Rivera, Monique A. 7734261105-E."

The red light on the old tablet-style computer turned green and the snow on the screen unscrambled to reveal a page of files. She selected the one marked LUNA and worked her way through the data nodes until she came to a section marked with coded numerals and the heading EXCLUSION ZONES. A few taps and she found the directory for Slayton Ridge.

It was empty. She frowned just as a chime vibrated the tablet and the tablet screen froze. A sudden chill went through her. A security subroutine had been activated by her inquiry. An official notice popped up, ordering her to contact the Records Security Office immediately. This was bad. She slumped back in the chair. What had her grandfather gotten her into this time?

She shut down the search and toggled the viewer, which filled the screen with the stern visage of the contract security officer. Neff Security. This was not good. He had bright red hair and looked like he'd crush the next person who mentioned it. From the size of the biceps straining at his blue Neff Aerospace coverall, he might be able to do it.

"Lieutenant Rivera, I need to log a reason why you accessed the exclusion zone records."

"Um . . . personal research. I'm being deployed to Armstrong Base as prep for the Mars program and I was looking for information."

"Information on what?"

"Nothing specific . . . I saw the EZ directory and was curious. The first directory I hit was empty. I assume there are no records on the EZs?" She gave him her most earnest, friendly smile.

The officer wasn't fazed at all. "Says here, you've only had a clearance for a few months, so I'm going to give you the benefit of the doubt and assume you aren't familiar with the seriousness of the rules. You don't go snooping through the Q section. Ever."

"I didn't know—"

"You do now. Never. Ever. If this happens again, you will lose the clearance and"—he paused for dramatic effect—"maybe more. Confirm?"

He tapped keys and the iris security scanner notification appeared on her screen. She dutifully stared into the camera above the screen and was documented with a red light scan. An ominous chime and text note informed her that her identity had been recorded and the incident would become a matter of her permanent record. *Damn.*

"Got it. Q section is off-limits." Nique tried to hide the curiosity this had now sparked.

The officer gave another glare for good measure, then punched the screen to black.

Nique pushed herself back from the display and frowned. It certainly didn't take long to bring Security down on Grandad's science project. She stood up and unfolded the exercise bike from the wall of her cabin.

She thought better when she worked out. She started pedaling, and the holodisplay appeared with a long road that curved up toward a mountain range. She swiped the air, not wanting a full bike program, then keyed in the number for her grandfather. He answered more quickly than she'd expected.

"What'd you find?" He looked a little ridiculous. His faded orange ball cap carried a grimy Houston Astros logo hidden by a homemade contraption of articulating arms with a magnifying lens attached to the bill. An intensely bright light that flashed into the camera when he looked up. She blinked against the glare.

"Find? Nothing. They threatened to take my clearance for this. I hope you appreciate it." Nique pumped the bike harder as the realization of what playing spy for her grandfather could cost her began to dawn. Her head and shoulders bobbed up and down on Mil's view screen as she pedaled the skeletal elliptic bike.

"You didn't find a damn thing?"

"I found out how easy it is to have your clearance yanked."

"You're too worried about that. They almost never do it." On her screen, Mil fiddled with another inductor module. At least he didn't look concerned about it.

"They took yours."

"One of the reasons they put up with me—I'm an excellent bad example. Shows the kids what can happen if you don't follow the rules."

"So now what? I've only got a few days." Nique frowned.

"When do you lift off?"

"Thursday. We get to Luna at fourteen forty-five on Sunday. The full team assembles there at Armstrong Base for final medicals and checkouts, then—assuming you've made enough fuel—it's off to Mars."

"Last of my O2 goes to orbit before the end of the month. I think they're serious about doing this thing."

Nique screwed her face into a scowl. "You really should call Mom. This is a big deal for her. You should be proud."

"I am proud of her; I've always been proud of her. Just as she's always been ashamed of me."

"She's not ashamed of you. She's mad at you." Nique had been in the middle of this feud her entire life. It got old.

"She's been mad since she was twelve. You know, she never even called me when she married your dad. I bet there are people she's known for years who have no idea I exist."

"Grandad, please." Her eyes rolled. "You're famous. Everyone knows you exist."

"Maybe, but they don't know the connection between the head of the agency and the Man on the Moon."

"Sure they do. They even brought it up in the Mars program interview she did."

"You mean the one where she told the world that we'd been estranged for years and it was a relationship she didn't want to comment on? That little gem?" He switched off the bright light.

Nique bit her lip. "Yeah. I didn't know you heard about that."

Mil waved a hand through the air, brushing off the slight. "We do get the news here on the moon. If your mother wanted to talk to me, it's easier than reaching four hundred million Americans on a magazine vidlog. Look, I called to congratulate her when she got appointed and she didn't have time to talk to me. Sent me to some PR flunky and then never called back. It's not like I've changed addresses in the last thirty-five years. Ball's in her court."

"Ohhh-kay then. Good to know this little family squabble isn't ending anytime soon."

"Is it that big a deal? I mean your mother is just one of thousands of people who don't want to talk to me and one of billions I don't care to talk to. It's only a problem if you let it be. So don't. I don't, she doesn't, you shouldn't."

"Right. So to change the subject—anything I can bring you?"

"From Earth? Yes. I need a new ball cap." Mill tapped his hat. "Astros. Size a hundred and eighty-seven millimeters."

"I'll pick one up."

"Thanks, kiddo. See you Sunday."

Nique slowed her pedaling, darkened the bike program, and sighed. She had a good glow going and was just starting to get winded. A tap on the wrist computer told her that her BP and heart rate were okay, but for some strange reason her stress indicators were all elevated. Her grandfather wouldn't let the security team stop him. Her mother wouldn't either. She needed to be creative and a little bolder in her approach. And she knew just who to talk to about it.

She keyed the videophone and waited. The panel brightened and her mother's face broke into a smile. "Hey! What's up?"

Nique smiled back. "I wanted to come see you before we lift off. Are you around between now and Thursday?"

The director of the Space Agency didn't even consult the calendar. "I'm here until the last of the crew goes to stage at Luna, but I'll be pretty busy— maybe dinner Tuesday? That might have to be quick."

"Oh, I know, I'll have to get a pass to be there before we launch, but I think I can make that happen. I could use a few more flight hours in my training log."

"You're not trading on your family ties, are you?" The director tapped through her dataslate as she spoke. Multitasking was a way of life.

"Nah. Almost nobody knows we're related."

"Just the ones who can get you a pass, right?"

"Well, yeah." Nique nodded.

"Do it. Just this once—it'll be the last time I see you for a long, long time."

"See you Tuesday night. Barbecue?"

"You're coming to Houston, we're having barbecue."

"Just like the old days. See you then."

CHAPTER FIVE

Tuesday . 09 Nov . 2077
1320 Central Standard Time
Ellington Field . Houston . TX . USA . Earth

The canopy of the ancient T-7 Redhawk trainer jet creaked open into the morning light, and the dank coastal fume that passed for air in Houston greeted Nique. Home. She'd been born and raised here, growing up as it transitioned from a seaport to a spaceport. It still had the ever-present odor of oil refineries with slight overtones of rotting seaweed that the chamber of commerce attempted to sell as exotic. Nique had been away for a few years, and though the atmosphere was the same, it struck her as different. Texas hadn't changed, she realized. She had.

She caught a transport pod to the transient crew facilities. As a little girl, coming to the Space Agency on Bring Your Kid To Work Day, she'd giggled at the sterile autonomous buses. To her younger self the transports looked like a fleet of giant white jellybeans zipping quietly between the dozens of buildings that made up the campus. She stepped aboard and nodded to the two other passengers in the near empty twenty-seat pod. She tapped her wristy to let the yeoman manning the incoming personnel processing center know she'd be there in minutes.

Moments later the pod announced its stop under the entrance awning of the concrete tower, confirming the generic governmental sign that declared that Nique had successfully found the visiting officers quarters. She steered her wheeled duffel through the sliding entrance and her wristy vibrated as it connected to the VOQ's systems and acknowledged her arrival.

Her fourth-floor room had a simple bunk, a desk, and a window overlooking the rooftops of miles of suburbs that she'd seen flying in. She thought they seemed to be even more dense than when she'd last visited, and wondered if they stretched all the way to Galveston.

She stowed her flight gear and freshened up. Another appliance vehicle then whisked her off to her morning appointment.

The autonomous pod moved her silently past historic buildings that had stood for most of the hundred-plus-year history of the space center, contrasting with newer glass office towers and blocky institutional engineering facilities. Ribbons of green spaces wound through the campus as if the agency was trying to remind those who worked in the airless desolation of space that their home planet was indeed a very special place.

She counted off the static displays of rockets, jets, and capsules marking history on manicured lawns. She'd grown up around these relics, and the fact that she'd be taking a craft to Mars that might very well come back here to join the time line hadn't really sunk in. The silent electric vehicle whizzed past yet another anonymous ten-story building and the large administration complex. Nique knew that somewhere deep inside, her mother was engaged in a daily battle against the forces of bureaucracy, in her lifelong effort to get humans to the surface of Mars.

The pod turned out into the surrounding residential area. Nique considered this long shot meeting her best chance to see what her grandfather had stumbled onto. She didn't have all the time in the world to help him, but he was the closest thing she had to a father. They didn't talk as often as they used to, but he'd been the one who'd reached out to her as a child. Years later, her psych classes told her that he was making up for the issues between himself and her mother—transferring that belated parental effort to her to atone for his failings as a father. Though he'd never admit that. It also didn't hurt that his fame and a small portion of his fortune paid for most of her PhD. She felt she owed him at least a small degree of debt.

The robotic voice of the autonomous microvan announced their arrival at the all-too-ordinary strip shopping center. "We have arrived at your destination. Archive Services Corporation."

Nique tapped her wristy to make the payment for the transport and stepped to the glass storefront. Inside, a simple desk and receptionist waited.

"Monique Rivera, here to see Adrian Evanston."

The receptionist swiped through her holodisplay. "Do you know the way?"

"I do. I interned here a long time ago."

A small light on the receptionist's console glowed green. Nique knew the system had just queried her wristy, run a biomedical ID scan, approved her clearance and given the receptionist the admittance approval through her hidden earpiece. The process didn't appear to have changed since her summer job in college.

A door disguised as an innocent wall panel buzzed open, and Nique passed through it, smiling at the Amazonian MP standing guard at the elevator doors. She didn't return the smile. Nique activated the hidden menu of subterranean facilities waiting beneath the unassuming facade of the strip center. She tapped the menu prompt for the secure archives and waited while the elevator dropped a dozen floors.

Adrian Evanston broke into an enormous grin, her brilliant white teeth contrasting with her wrinkled brown skin. A contemporary of Nique's grandfather, she'd been the chief archivist for the Space Agency since back when six months on a space station was a big deal. The old woman heaved herself from behind the desk and waddled over to greet her visitor.

"Monique. It is so good to see you." After the expected hug and air kisses, Adrian grabbed her firmly by the shoulders and cocked her head.

"So, what do you want?"

Nique tried evasion. "Want? I can't come see my old mentor, before I leave for Mars?"

"Horseshit. Mentor. You worked here three summers." Adrian crossed her arms. "I almost never see you online anymore and I haven't heard from you in a month of Sundays."

"I have been a little busy, Adrian." She tapped the Mars crew patch on her Space Agency shirt. "I was in town to see Mom before the flight and thought I'd run by and see you before I left.

"Well, not that I'm not honored by a visit from a Mars-bound astronaut, but I am good at telling when someone is trying to pump sunshine up my skirt. What do you want?"

Nique considered her options and decided on the direct approach. "It's for my grandfather."

"Ha! He's got you doing his dirty work? The old bastard."

"He asked me to look into some things for him. He's retiring and is trying to figure out what to do next."

Adrian smirked. "Mil Harrison retiring? More like people finally had enough of him and kicked his ass out. What does he want to know?"

"Why the Slayton Ridge Exclusion Zone is classified. He says the records aren't accessible from Luna, and when I went to check it out, I got a security lockout."

"Slayton Ridge? You don't have the clearance for that, do you? And what in the world does that have to do with him retiring?"

"When I got the Mars assignment, they told me I was cleared for everything." Nique moved past the real question.

The aged librarian parked her ample frame back into her desk chair.

"Nobody's cleared for everything." Adrian smiled. "Except me."

"So you could log me on to see why it's secured?" Nique failed at her attempted naiveté.

"Nope."

"No? Because of Granddad?"

"No, because it's not online. That's old-school material. Very old school. Been secured since before the end of the twentieth century. Most of that highly sensitive material was never even digitized. It's not even a part of the blockchain. It's a pain to catalog, but it's so much more secure."

"You mean it can't be hacked?"

"Better than that, it's on paper. Boxes and boxes of dusty, old, fading paper. Takes a shitload of rooms and secure storage space. A remnant of the good old days." Adrian got a touch wistful. "Except they weren't all that good, those days."

"But secure?"

"It takes more than a genius kid with a supercomputer who can fake a secure comm link, or a curious Indonesian mafioso to hack into those. Gotta have a cat burglar with smarts and access. Those are rare nowadays."

"So how does a non-cat burglar with clearance get in to see them?"

"For that? Well, you'd need agency director-level clearance or higher. Presidential or Q-clearance, congressional authority. Those would work. Got any of that?"

"Ummm. I haven't asked Mom."

"And I'm sure your grandfather hasn't either."

"Yeah, they're not exactly big on communication."

Adrian picked the dataslate off her desk. "Kid, admit it. Your grandfather is an asshole. That's why none of us talk to him."

"So you're not inclined to do him a favor?"

"I am not."

"How about me?"

"Do you a favor? I'm afraid it's too late for that."

Behind them, the elevator door slid open and Nique's new friend, the hulking redheaded officer from Neff Security stepped out.

CHAPTER SIX

Monday . 15 Nov . 2077
0955 Lunar Standard Time
Main Receiving Portal Lobby . Armstrong Base . Luna

"You greet every one of 'em? That must suck." Mil ran a hand through his thin hair as he and Des Rafferty watched through a wall of windows looking out from Armstrong Base to the landing pad in the distance. The institutional light gray walls and the few charcoal-colored seating areas of the receiving lounge/lobby gave the Luna transport's arriving passengers their first taste of the stark conditions they were entering.

Rafferty nodded. "There's almost too many arrivals now, but I figure if you're going to make the duty choice to serve on Luna, the base commander ought to at least acknowledge your arrival."

Rafferty was five centimeters taller than Mil and more solidly built. He wore his afro cropped high and tight and it added a menacing touch to his presence. The Brit had once been a middleweight mixed martial arts fighter for the Royal Space Service, and twenty years later he still had the stance of an athlete. Beyond the building a bulky transport ship eased down on the pad, its braking rockets stirring a thin dust cloud. It was instantly surrounded by a herd of robotic craft opening access panels and removing cargo compartments from the interior. Personal luggage, supplies from Earth, mail parcels, and the accumulated refuse from the thirty-six-hour trip from the subspace station orbiting Earth.

"Make 'em think you care, huh?" Mil grinned.

"I do care." Rafferty habitually stroked his goatee.

"Really? I mean if they're dumb enough to come here . . ."

An enclosed bridge snaked out to the main hatch and attached itself to the craft, then pressurized. The two interested parties in the overlook area watched through the transparent walls as the passengers disembarked.

"You'd want the commander to greet your granddaughter, wouldn't you?"

"If that's what you want to do. It doesn't matter to me. I've been working with Amon Neff for thirty years and I've never met him in the flesh. Personal contact is overrated."

"You and Neff aren't exactly the poster kids for interpersonal relationships. He doesn't leave his compound and you don't leave the moon. I can see how you two would get along very well."

"Nothing wrong with Amon. Most folks don't trust him any farther than they could throw him, but he's always done right by me."

"Made you both rich." Rafferty pointed to the bridge. "Is that Nique? She's grown."

"Tell me about it. My baby granddaughter—Lieutenant Monique Rivera, PhD." There was more than a hint of pride in Mil's voice.

"Top of her class. We'll be glad to have her."

Mil frowned. "You'll have her? I thought she was on the Mars program? She's just here to get through to Mars."

"Maybe she was, but I got an assignment notice, yesterday. She's re-assigned to Armstrong to support the Mars mission from here as a comms specialist. It appears someone high up pulled her ticket to Mars and set her down here. I'm going to have to find quarters for her; we're full up."

"She's not going to Mars? That won't go over—"

A bright orange ball cap smacked him in the chest, startling him. The brand-new Astros cap hit the ground and the person who had thrown it marched straight toward him.

"You did this!" Nique had her slimline helmet under one arm and the other hand balled into a fist that shot out an accusing index finger. "I was going to Mars!"

"What the hell is this?" Mil's confusion showed in his frown.

"I got the reassignment notice yesterday. On the way up! I'm not on the Mars mission now. First, I was assigned to quarters until launch and then reassigned here!"

"And you think that was me?" Mil raised both hands in surrender.

"Of course it was you!" There might have been an extra dose of drama as she got as close to a tantrum as a highly trained professional could. "What the hell, Grandad? What the genuine hell did you get me into?"

Mil winced a bit. "Now, before you throw a hissy fit—"

She got in his face. "Oh, we're way past that. I've spent years working my ass off to get into this program, and on the eve of it, you get me assigned to a support role here! Here? On this . . . this . . . fuel dump to the stars—"

"Stop." Mil could still put some steel in a single word. "Before you go too much farther, I'd like to introduce you to an old friend—this is Desmond Rafferty, Commander Desmond Rafferty, he runs this fuel dump to the stars and is apparently your new CO. He comes out to welcome all the eager new recruits who volunteer for a career-enhancing posting here on Luna."

Nique froze. Rafferty gave his new recruit a sly smile. "Welcome to Luna, Lieutenant. Glad to have you."

She came to attention with the expected salute. "Sir, I sincerely apologize. I had no idea." Nique shot a side glance at her grandfather, who shrugged in a feeble attempt at innocence.

Rafferty smiled. "I wasn't thrilled when I got here either. The place grows on you. Maybe you'll be like your grandfather and never leave."

"Yes, Commander."

Rafferty snapped off a crisp salute. "If you'll excuse me, I have some people to greet. Mil, good to see you."

He shook Mil's hand and headed across the room to a gaggle of young astronauts who'd just come down the bridge.

"This trip just gets better and better." Nique slumped against the window and slid slowly to the floor. She wrapped her arms around her knees.

"So what happened?"

"I got an order text yesterday. Report to the CO at oh seven hundred tomorrow for reassignment to Armstrong Base communications. Not Mars mission communications. Luna. I was going to be one of the first explorers on another planet. Now, I'm going to be a glorified police dispatcher on a rock where nobody lives, much less breaks the law. All because of your little hunting expedition."

Her lower lip was trembling and somewhere deep in the recesses of Mil's brain he remembered that this was a clue that a young woman was on the verge of tears.

He figured he should say something comforting. "Look, I had no idea. I mean, not that I wouldn't love having your sunny disposition around, but I could have used your help on Earth. I didn't want this, you're no good to me here or on Mars."

She looked up at him. "What does that even mean?"

Mil struggled. This was light-years out of his comfort zone. "Who signed the transfer orders?"

"I have no idea. Security kept me incommunicado in my quarters. I found out yesterday." She raised her wrist and scrolled through to find the document. "Verbal authorization, agency director."

"So, it's your mother."

"You think?"

Mil gave her a hand and hoisted her to her feet. He took her helmet and led her down the tunnel to the cargo claim area. Nique followed like a sad puppy.

"Yeah. It's just a gut reaction on her part. We'll calm her down and get you back on the crew. She just went off over a little thing and is making an example of you. Her mother was that way too. Sometimes, it's a really handy trait."

"Sometimes?"

"Other times it just pisses you off."

He touched his wrist and noted the time. "North America is a few hours behind us. Depending on where she is, it's either one thirty or four thirty in the morning. We'll get you settled in and see what's going on."

Nique retrieved her luggage pod and Mil watched as she and a yeoman had a slightly heated discussion. She marched back to where he stood.

"And they don't have quarters for me! I'm supposed to hold here and await further instructions."

"Hurry up and wait, isn't that still the Space Force motto?" Mil had served plenty of time in uniform. "Let me see if I can call in a favor." He walked across the luggage bay and tapped Rafferty on the shoulder. It was a brief conversation.

She watched him nod thanks to the commander and then head back.

"They'll have a billet for you eventually, but I'm pretty sure it's a squad room with five or ten bunkmates. If you're up for it, I've got room at the farm. It's a bit of a commute, but it will beat the barracks here."

Eyes rolled. "So I can help solve your mystery? Yeah, I'm going to be all about that."

"Your call. But there's nobody who can help you find your way around here better than me. I helped build most of this."

She scowled and turned to leave.

Mil touched her arm to stop her. His voice softened in a way he didn't fully recognize. "Look, I'm sorry my research got your plans screwed up. Come, stay at the farm—you'll have your own galley, I've got a spare room that never gets used, secure comms to anywhere, and I just finished fixing a spidertruck you can use to get around. We'll see what we can do to get you back on the Mars program." He hadn't felt this contrite in years and his discomfort came through as sincerity.

She rubbed her forehead, but the pained expression remained. "You know, a week ago the world had been right where I wanted it. But now . . ."

Across the bay, the squad of new recruits assembled and turned as one to march off to quarters. She watched them go.

She relented. "Oh . . . all right."

A quick conversation with the yeoman, and ten minutes later they were in the cab of Mil's spidertruck, cruising along the smooth graded road that made up the main thoroughfare from Armstrong Base to the settlements and the less traveled path that would take them to Harrison's oxygen farm.

"Is this new?" Nique ran her glove over the dash panel.

"Came up last year as part of the new O2 program. It's buggy as hell. When you get a lemon on Earth, it's inconvenient. Here, it can kill you. I've asked the company for another one—I think it'll get here about the time I'm done. The Mars push has everyone's schedule screwed up."

"That's what left you stranded in the EZ?"

"Yeah, I keep spare parts, but not enough to replace all of 'em on this piece of shit. And right now I need it to work because I've got to move all of the fuel O2 to the launch platform by next week."

"This is a big deal for you too."

"Fuel a booster to go to Mars? Biggest thing we've ever done. This is the big finish."

"Then you're really retiring?"

"Apparently. They're telling me I'm done after this. Neff has a whole organization on Earth that runs the show. I just work the dirt, repair the bots, and make the deliveries. Now the tech has improved and demand has increased."

"Can you keep up? I mean this seems like a lot of work for—"

"An old man? Yeah, Neff said the same thing. Then he did something about it and didn't tell me."

"But you found out."

"Well, sure. But not until they brought up the crews to start construction and they needed O2. He's built a whole new facility over by the base to support Luna and the Mars program. That much fuel and breathing oxygen is too much for my aging facility, is what he said. They've been doing pilot work for the last month and supplying Settlements One and Three. Slowly taking over the fuel program. In another couple of weeks my whole operation will be decommissioned."

"Wow. And you're okay with that?"

"I said I was. But now the reality is starting to set in and I'm not so sure."

As he said it, they crested the hill and the spheres of the farm lay before them. Mil pointed to the tall orange tanks next to the rows of empty O2 hookups.

"Those are LOX, liquified O2 going over for fuel at Armstrong's launch facility. Last delivery I make."

Nique gestured to the empty slots. "And the others? You used to have a bunch. Where are they?"

"Last batch went to Settlement Two. The rest are staged in orbit. When the good ship *Humanity* gets here, they'll load 'em all aboard and have enough fuel oxidizer and breathing O2 to get to Mars and back with a full reserve. Saves the agency from having to launch bulky commodities from the higher gravity on Earth."

"You've been busy."

"I'm working the robots and cracking processors like circus monkeys. Not to mention the battery systems. Takes a ton of electricity to crack the oxygen from regolith. Now that it's all going to the new plant, I'll be able to sell the extra electricity to Armstrong."

"So you excavate the soil, electrify it, and it releases the trapped oxygen molecules?"

"That's it. Basic chemistry to extract oxygen from lunar dirt. Crack it, capture it, bottle it, sell it to the GOCO. It's been a good business for these last thirty years."

"The GOCO?"

Mil smiled. "Acronyms. Government owned, contractor operated. Luna—hell, the whole space program—is this weird hydra-headed monster. The politicians figure out what they want to do. Then they hire contractors like Amon Neff and yours truly to do the dirty work and make it happen. And then the Space Agency takes all the credit."

"Right. And Space Force? How do we fit in?" asked the lieutenant.

"Training, security, and generally making my life harder than it needs to be." Mil checked the displays and double-checked that the spidertruck was not going to drive into his storage tanks.

"Uh-huh. So you spent a twenty-year Space Force career getting in your own way?"

"Things were a lot different before I retired from the Force. Fewer chair warmers and more engineering. We were doing things. We were explorers. Then they decided to outsource everything to ridiculously expensive contractors."

"So you left the service, hooked up with Amon Neff and became a ridiculously expensive contractor yourself?"

"It's called double-dipping. You get your military retirement and a contractor paycheck. Good gig."

"And now you retire? Again? Just fade away?" She admired the expansive operation that was the Harrison Station oxygen farming operation.

Mil cracked a smile. "Some would hope."

"Or is tracking down what's on Slayton Ridge your next career?"

"I hope to hell it's not that big a deal. At first, I thought it might be just a clerical error. Somebody tagged it and forgot about it. But now that you've been flagged by Security, it tells me that this is not just something somebody put in a drawer and forget about."

"Glad I could help."

"Don't get sarcastic, young lady. This could be something large. You'll see when we get to the farm."

"I'll see? I thought you just stumbled upon the EZ. Grandad? What the hell did you do?"

"Oh, look, here's the farm." Mil toggled the spidertruck to manual control and steered toward the airlock.

"You do have impressive timing when you don't want to talk about something."

Mil ignored the remark and punched a button on the overhead console. Ahead, the outer airlock doors of the barn opened.

The inner doors closed, the airlock pressurized, and Mil drove into the barn.

Nique sized up her new quarters. "You know, if you're looking for something to do, you could start with cleaning out this scrapyard."

"What?" Mil tried to visualize his collected projects and spares through the fresh eyes of his granddaughter. He could see how the unenlightened might view it solely as a recycling opportunity. "Don't let it fool you. Everything here is a curated vital component for a system I'm working on."

Nique nodded. "Uh-huh. What's that?" She pointed a thumb at a first-generation spidertruck sitting in a dusty corner. It leaned on its three remaining wheels; one door and the windshield were missing.

"That . . ." Mil hadn't expected a quiz. "Spares for the spiders—that's got two good inductors left on it. I might need them at any time."

"And the robot? Is that an Axial? A Mark II? Those things are older than I am."

"It's a Mark III, best ones they ever made." He hoisted himself out of the cab. "Let's get you settled in."

When they entered the airlock from the barn to the main apartment dome, Nique's eyes widened. "Hey, this isn't too bad. Why the big difference between housekeeping out there and in here? You have a cleaning bot?"

She ran her finger across a shelf and made a face at the line in the dust. Mil caught it.

"Even the bots can't keep up with the dust. They can vacuum and try, but lunar dust is thin and light and everywhere. That's not just out here. You'll see it everywhere. It's a moon thing."

He showed her to the vacant spare room: a bunk against the far wall of the dome, a small desk, and charger for a dataslate. The bed had newish, clean linen and he showed her how to operate the blackout system.

"We have to have the blackout system 'cause a day lasts two Earth weeks. Then night lasts the next two weeks. But Earthshine gives you about sixty percent of total daylight. It almost never gets completely dark. Like Alaska in the summer. Everybody knows that when they come up, but nobody's ready for it."

Nique toggled the manual override, and the ceiling and wall panels darkened smoothly down to a nearly total darkness.

"Makes it a lot easier to sleep. After a while you forget about it completely."

"This is a pretty good idea." Nique was impressed.

"Thanks."

"Thanks? You came up with this?"

"Well, sure. I've been here longer than anybody. Most of the things we have here are stuff we had to figure out early on. Keeping the battery systems up through two weeks of lunar night. Maximizing the solar for reflected Earthshine. Cracking O2. All of it. The guys on the ground had designs and theory, but we were the ones putting it into practice. It's been a lot of work to the make the moon a place people can come visit on a whim."

"Not exactly a whim, Grandad. It's still an effort to get here."

"Well, it's not a big media circus like it used to be. You're the daughter of the head of the Space Agency. Granddaughter of the longest-term resident of the moon. Fairly high profile passenger. Anybody talk to you about coming up here? Ask what you thought about the risks?"

She thought for a second. "No. Not really. But then, I was in astronaut jail."

"Going to the moon ought to be a bigger deal. People don't appreciate the risks anymore."

"It's a manageable risk."

"Maybe." Mil grew quiet as he couldn't help but flash back to the horrendous death of his wife Olivia decades before.

"I didn't mean that . . . it wasn't dangerous, Granddad . . ." She trailed off.

"I know you didn't, honey." His gruff demeanor softened, and for a moment he felt the years and loss taking their toll. He brushed away any sentimentality. Maybe the doc was right about his radiation numbers. Maybe he had caught more than he thought on the ridge.

"Hey." She brightened and tried to change the mood. "Show me what you found."

"Let's do that. I've got a VR setup out in the barn."

CHAPTER SEVEN

M il never gave a thought to how ridiculous he looked. The virtual reality headset wasn't any more intrusive than a pair of sunglasses, the small earbuds were almost unnoticeable. But an onlooker watching the way he and Nique were moving around the empty VR bay of the barn would have thought they were zombies, dancing silently through their virtual reality world.

Nique lost herself inside the experience as her grandfather led her through what he was now referring to as "the facility."

"How long were you in here?"

"Not even ten minutes. There's something beyond that door that is giving off enough radiation that it spooked me."

Nique walked to the sealed hatch, stepping in place as the sensors on her gloves and headset equated the motion with moving through the digital space of VR. She opened the hatch to blackness as her viewer tinted red and Mil's digital assistant, Bailey, warned, "Radiation emergency. Evacuate immediately. Radiation emergency. Evacuate immediately."

"Mom?" Nique stopped in mid-step, waving her hands. "Whoa, whoa, whoa. What the hell?"

"Bailey, cancel warnings. Exit program." Mil removed his goggles. "Yeah. I use your mom's voice as the interface."

Nique pulled her headset off and put her hands on her hips. "That's just too weird. You haven't spoken to her in ten years? But you talk to her all the time."

"More like fifteen. This way she doesn't talk back and does what I tell her."

"You guys are screwed up."

"Careful—it's hereditary."

"Great, maybe someday I'll have the chance to mess up my kid."

Mil gave his naive granddaughter a knowing look. "Seriously? Your mother is capable of damn near anything to advance her agenda. Never forget that. Can we get back to this?"

He slipped back into his goggles and turned to wait on her. "You coming?" Mil tapped his headset.

"I'm right here," she said, but then muttered under her breath, "Trying to figure out when we get to the fun part of dysfunctional."

She lowered her goggles and stepped back into the virtual world of the bunker.

Mil watched as Nique's avatar entered and looked around the simulation. She went to the far virtual wall and flipped open the binder.

"Blank?"

"Faded away. One of the few things my research turned up. Apparently, there is an acid in old twentieth-century paper that can consume the pigments in the ink. But it takes a long time. This thing has been here for years. I'd say decades."

"Any idea what it said?"

"No, but I have this research assistant on Earth . . ."

"Not funny." She closed the binder and examined the fading silk-screened logo. "USAF? Air Force?"

Mil was examining the wall of shelves and stowage compartments. "Yeah. Odd, huh? I'd understand an old NASA logo, or Space Force, but Air Force? I never knew they mounted a mission to the moon."

"That does narrow it down—NASA put astronauts here in the 1970s, and Space Force didn't get to the moon until the late 2020s."

"So there's about a fifty-year window when the Air Force could have been involved."

"And behind that door?" Nique pointed.

"I have no clue, but it's radioactive as hell. I'll need a full level-four rad suit to even open the door. And it's shielded—some sort of Faraday cage that screws with network access. So even if I build a bot to get in there, it's going to play hell with remote operations."

"Whoever was here, it was an extended stay—more than a few weeks." Nique looked through the array of compartments. "There's enough rations storage here for a crew of five or six for a month."

"But only two sleeping berths. Unless they hot bunked for some reason."

"So a crew of two for three months, or four for forty-five days?"

"Feels like it."

"What would you do here for three months?"

"What would the military do here for three months, you mean." Mil studied the binder and the sleeping racks. The virtual reality recording didn't have any answers. He pulled off the goggles and ran a hand over the gray stubble on his face.

"We've got a secret facility, put on the moon by the military some time after the original Apollo missions and before the mid-nineties, when Internet One came online." Nique pursed her puzzled lips.

"This is why I asked you to look into it. There's something to this that no one wants found. No records. No history. And all swept under a rug decades ago."

"I don't think it's on the shadowed side of Slayton Ridge by accident either." Nique nodded her agreement. "You don't land in the dark unless it's on purpose."

"Yeah, in moonspeak we call it a PDA—permanently dark area. It never sees sunlight. Good point."

"But there were no lunar expeditions for over sixty years. Between the end of Apollo and the first colonization efforts, the agency spent their whole efforts in low Earth orbit, building the core of the ISS/Alpha Station."

"Took history at the academy, did you?"

"I was the class celebrity—my grandad was on the curriculum."

"I bet—how to win friends and influence administrators."

"You're a legend," she said as she watched Mil turn to stow the VR gear and noticed his jumpsuit had a tear in the rear that revealed he wasn't wearing any underwear. "At least in the textbooks."

CHAPTER EIGHT

Tuesday . 16 Nov . 2077
0920 Lunar Standard Time
Neff Fueling Dock . Armstrong Base . Luna

M il maneuvered the giant tank into position, guiding it into the only remaining empty slot. The last of dozens of other identical white balloons that stood in a row, waiting for the trip to orbit where they'd be fitted to *Humanity*, the enormous Russian-built craft that would carry the first humans to Mars. This had been Mil's business for the last twenty-five years, and he was good at it. The years had made him far too used to the hum of conversation in his helmet as transportation vans were cleared in and out of the giant motor pool garage. The enormous airlock doors slid open, strobe lights blinked, alert tones sounded in his earpiece as warning notifications scrolled across his faceplate. All so he could watch for traffic coming through.

He unhooked the spidertruck, checked both ways by habit and walked to the huddle of astronauts working the fuel depot. Mil had little use for them. They stayed a respectful distance away from any actual work, in their safety-yellow pressure suits and their mirrored faceplates.

Not that it mattered to Mil. The safest suit in the world wouldn't save your butt if something went wrong here. A minor amount of danger lingered over this simple delivery because a wayward spark, unforeseen static electricity, or just plain bad luck could ignite the volatile O2 and incinerate the entire facility. Mil had done the mental math, wondering if an explosion in Neff's fuel storage area might even nudge the moon out of orbit.

"That's it for me. You guys have enough gas to get to Mars."

The tallest of the group stepped closer to acknowledge the delivery. He tapped his wristy and Mil felt the buzz on his own arm. He tapped back his response, and the transaction was complete.

A shorter astronaut came forward, his mirrored faceplate looking up to Mil. "Mr. Harrison? Can I just say that it's been an honor to work with you?"

Mil turned. "Work with me? Have we even met? I mean you've been standing there watching me work for months, but I don't know you, never even seen your face. What's more, if I ever see you again, I won't know you then either."

"Um . . . well, I mean . . ."

"You mean, now you've got a story to tell at the rec center? Yes, you do. Tell 'em you met Mil Harrison and he's an asshole, just like everybody says."

And with that Mil crow-hopped to the spider and drove off to his next appointment.

"Armstrong Base, Harrison. Delivery complete. You can send people to Mars now."

Nique's voice came through his headset. "Harrison, Armstrong Base. Affirmative. Delivery time logged. Oh nine twenty-five. Any other traffic?"

Harrison smiled. She performed like a complete professional, just as she should. "Nothing further, Armstrong. Other than you sound like you're learning the ropes. Harrison out."

———•◦•— ⚙ —•◦•———

The consoles of the Armstrong Base communications bay sat just in front of the base commander's console. Rafferty could see everything they did and they in turn ran the large display wall at the front of the room that could show video feeds from the multitudes of video, VR, and holo-cameras networked across the moon. Rows of other workstations—monitoring base operations, launch and landing control, and facilities—sat in three tiers stepping down to the large main screen.

Nique looked at Maddie Byers beside her as she punched off the call. The holodisplay in front of her showed a marker moving away from the fuel depot adjacent to the launch and landing complex. At the front of the semicircular room, the wall of screens clicked through the major traffic areas of the base. Screens on the room's left and right walls showed banks of telemetry for everything from garbage pickup status to the countdown clock for the upcoming Mars mission.

Byers nodded with a smile. "Ninety-nine percent of the job is just like that. Routine in and out."

"That's what I figured." Nique was still ticked off about her reassignment to this menial babysitting job. "And the other one percent?"

"That's when you call the deck officer for instructions. Our job is to handle basic requests and relay information to those who need it. We don't decide anything. We don't filter anything."

"Sounds dull as toast."

The morning's deck officer, Specialist Eli Yenko, sat at his console on the other side of the command center. He tapped a series of gestures across the flat screen of his dataslate. "It is. But it's a stop on the duty roster that you have to punch if you want to move up."

Yenko was dark-skinned but with clear blue eyes and a thick beard that just skirted the regulations.

Maddie smiled and whispered to Nique, "And nobody wants to move up and go to Mars like Eli."

"And I will. One day." He nodded to Maddie across the currently empty stations where technicians would control launches, landings, or the exceedingly rare emergency drill. "So when do you head home?"

"Not this next transport, but the one after." Maddie checked her wristy. "One hundred and fifty-seven hours and thirty-two minutes. Not that I'm counting."

Nique grinned.

"Armstrong Base, Granger."

Nique adjusted her headset. "Granger, Armstrong Base, go ahead."

Thirty-five kilometers away, a beefier, utility vehicle version of Mil's spidertruck moved deliberately across the surface. The comms bay screens showed the inside of the transvan just as Specialist Micah Granger craned his neck to see up to the high wall of the crater that made up the crest of Slaton Ridge. He turned to the camera and registered surprise.

"Hey! It's the new girl. Are you really Millennium Harrison's granddaughter?" Granger grinned.

"The one and only." Nique was used to being just a few degrees from celebrity.

Maddie leaned into the screen. "Specialist Micah Granger, meet Lieutenant Monique Rivera."

"Nique. Just Nique. Only Mom calls me Monique."

"Everybody calls me Granger. I'm a big fan of your gramps."

"Oh yeah?"

"Yeah, I drop in on him every now and then. I like to make sure he's okay. He's not real social." Granger leaned in as if he were telling her a secret.

"Don't I know it. How come he talks to you?"

"We talk sports. He's a big baseball fan."

"That makes sense. So what can we do for you today, Specialist?"

"I'm here in the Slayton EZ. What the heck am I supposed to be looking for?"

Nique perked up at the mention of the EZ. Then caught herself. She looked to Maddie with a question and hoped she looked innocent. The trainer keyed her own mic. "Micah, we had a mystery rad spike out there last week. Command said check it out."

She tapped her headset and whispered to Nique, "He's sweet and damned cute but not real sharp."

Maddie's hands flew through the air scrolling the holodisplay and bringing up information, finally landing on the 3-D map that showed Granger's utility vehicle as a blue triangle and the rad spike as an orange dot. Between the two was the vast crater's high rim that made up Slayton Ridge. Nique was impressed with her speed and knowledge of the system.

"The point of interest is in the PDA on the other side of the ridge."

Nique nodded. "Permanently dark area, right."

Eli had walked over from his post in the open room of the command center. He leaned in. "That's it. Spooky." He waggled his fingers.

Granger's voice crackled through the speaker. "Roger, POI on the shadow side. How the hell do I get there, Maddie? You want me to climb the ridge?"

The door opened and Desmond Rafferty stepped in, stopping behind the two communicators at their console and taking in the situation. "So he's there? Slayton Ridge?"

"Yes, sir," the three said at once.

Rafferty leaned in and swiped his fingertips along the holodisplay, scrolling the map this way and that.

"Granger, Armstrong Command. I want to know what's on that back side. If you'll backtrack about half a klick east, there's a low pass through the ridge. You should be able to cross there."

Rafferty positioned the map and tapped the thin air of the display. A green dot appeared on the pass, then traced a dashed line that connected the blue marker of Granger's transvan and the orange marker of the rad spike. He swiped again. "Sending you routing."

Beside him, Eli confirmed the position with a nod.

Nique watched her screen as Granger nodded to the holodisplay on his dash and a blinking green dot illuminated the location of the pass.

"Got it, Command. Five hundred meters east. I'll report when I know more. Talk to you later, new girl. Granger out."

Maddie nodded again to Nique, who keyed her headset mic. "Armstrong out."

"And that," Maddie said, "is how you handle the other one percent."

CHAPTER NINE

Tuesday . 16 Nov . 2077
0950 Lunar Standard Time
Slayton Ridge . North Mare Crisium . Luna

At the far northern edge of Luna's Sea of Crisis, the edge of a gigantic crater made up the wall of Slayton Ridge. Eons before, a meteor impacted the surface with such force that the concussion shoved the rim a hundred meters above the basin below.

Pure blackness shadowed behind the high ridge, an area where neither sunlight nor Earthshine ever reached as the Earth and her moon danced around the universe.

What little illumination there happened to be was reflected from distant rock formations jutting into the sunlight. The blaze of the dozens of lights positioned all over the transvan gave Specialist Micah Granger an incredible view of a boulder field.

He studied it a moment, trying to determine the best means to crawl over a rock half the size of his truck. He angled the truck left, putting one wheel on the edge of the boulder, tipping the transvan almost to the point of dumping it on its side as alerts beeped into his helmet.

Maddie's voice giggled over the communications loop. "Careful, if you flip the transvan it comes out of your pay."

"Armstrong. Mark this position. I wish this rock to be forever known as Granger Boulder."

Past that, he stopped, reaching the indicated point on his map display. Granger zoomed in his display as tight as possible and then did a perimeter exterior radiation check. Nothing. Whatever had been glowing was long gone. *Weird.* He took his academy ball cap off and ran a hand down his face. He knew exactly what Rafferty would tell him to do.

"Nique, I'm on station. I got nothing. No readings, no disturbances." He looked to the screen and found it showing Armstrong's commander. The boss was watching.

"Roger that, patrol. Let's do an EVA, Specialist. If there's nothing there, we'll have to do a complete diagnostic teardown of the sensor network. No one wants that. Take a walk, go find out what it was."

"Yessir." Granger shook his weary head. EVAs, extravehicular activities —the Space Agency did love its acronyms, this one left over from old NASA's very first space walks on the Gemini programs—were a genuine pain in the ass. It meant he had to suit up, depressurize the truck, go wander around in the dirt. Which meant he'd have to vacuum the truck again when he got back to the motor pool, decon the suit, write up the reports . . . a long list of post-EVA protocols just because you went outside and got dirty.

When he was a kid, the mere dream of walking on the moon was amazing. He remembered his spaceman Halloween costume and hopping around the neighborhood with his friends, the joy when they'd lowered him into the microgravity tank at the academy training center for the first time, and the incredible feeling of walking on the moon on his first assignment on Luna. Getting to hang out and watch ball games with the likes of Mil Harrison? He'd never even dreamed of that.

Now, the excitement level was just above brushing his teeth.

He grabbed the handholds on the ceiling, hoisted himself off the floor of the cargo compartment and lowered his legs into the bottom half of the EVA pressure suit. His hands found the sleeves and the rack release in the same motion as his head popped into the helmet.

Granger leaned back into the life-support backpack. The familiar metallic snick of the magnetic metal rings connecting told him the alignment was correct. A series of green indicators on his faceplate confirmed it.

A slight breeze of crisp, clean air brushed his face as the O2 system kicked in and the suit ran through its systems check. A readout of his electrical and O2 status flickered onto his helmet's faceplate. Granger snapped his gloves into the locked position and fully pressurized the suit. From nowhere a computerized voice announced, "All systems green for EVA."

"Yeah. Yeah. Yeah." He had heard this a thousand times. "Armstrong, Granger. Comms check. Depressurizing for EVA."

"Granger, Armstrong. Good comms. Reading you five by five." Nique's voice was quiet in his ear, and he tapped the wristy on his suit to increase the volume.

"Good read here, Armstrong." Granger rotated a wall switch 90 degrees and a compressor kicked in, sucking the atmosphere out of the patrol vehicle and saving it for his return. A light flashed green and he rotated the switch another 90 degrees to exit. The upper portion of the rear doors swung up, and the lower section dropped to the surface as an exit ramp.

Granger clomped out onto the moon and the harsh shadows from the transvan's blue-white artificial light. He toggled on the tiny spotting lights on his gloves. He waved a hand around and saw nothing but the bare, desolate gray that made up Luna. It wasn't romantic. It wasn't sexy. It was gray dust.

He played the lights around and up the side of the ridge. A rockslide or something had covered the area in gray dirt. That was a little odd. Maybe a micrometeorite had hit out here and left a trail of radiation. He filed that away in his brain as a possible reason.

Granger shuffled away from the transvan and toward the wall of the ridge, waving his lights around, looking for anything else.

He almost missed it. Something at the corner of his eye in the dirt. It almost looked like a . . . boot print? Here? He stepped toward it—

And promptly tripped and fell to his knees. Granger scrambled up. Everything was being recorded. He'd catch hell for that. The squad room was merciless on the slightest screwup. He looked for the rock he'd stumbled over and saw instead a handle sticking out through the dust.

"Um . . . Armstrong, Granger. You getting this?"

"Every step." At the command center, Maddie grinned. Nique smiled to mask her concern that her grandfather's discovery was about to be unveiled to the world. The fleeting image of the red-haired Security sergeant back home sent a chill down her back. She keyed a panel on the console and a video window opened. It relayed the feed from Granger's helmet camera.

"Put that on main view." Rafferty leaned forward in his command chair to study the image as it appeared on the wall display.

Nique keyed her mic. "Roger that, Granger. We see it."

"What is it?" Granger asked.

Rafferty's puzzled look said he had no clue. "Can you dig it out? Let's see some more of it."

On the command center's large wallscreen, Granger dropped to a knee and swept away the loose soil. "It's a hatch."

"It seems to be. Does it open?" Rafferty was seriously curious now. Nique and Maddie watched intently as Granger hefted the handle up and out, then pulled open the hatch.

They saw Granger flinch before the warning flashed across their screens. The computerized warning crackled through the speakers. "Radiation advisory. Rem levels are point five two times ambient background standard. Personal protective measures should be considered. Radiation advisory."

Behind Nique, Maddie pointed to the display and clapped. "That's it! That's like the rad spike I got!"

Nique furrowed her brow; the old man had mentioned radiation behind a door, but not that he'd gotten a rad warning when he'd gone down inside.

"It's an airlock." Granger was playing his light around the inside of the hatchway. "Rads don't look too bad. I'm showing point five above ambient here."

Nique checked her display. "Confirmed. Point five. Elevated, but only enough to generate a notification, not an alert." Maybe it wasn't worth mentioning.

Maddie slumped back in her chair. "Yeah. Right location but not as strong."

Rafferty stepped behind her, double-checking the levels the specialist had reported. He checked his dataslate and flicked through protocols and established procedures. There was a routine for investigating this type of event, buried somewhere in the depths of the file structure.

On the big wallscreen, Granger was stepping through the hatch. "I'll check it out."

He pulled the hatch closed over him just as Rafferty said, "Let's wait on that, Specialist."

But he was already inside.

"Granger, Armstrong Base. Come in." Rafferty frowned. "Granger. Come in."

Silence.

"Get him back, Lieutenant." Rafferty was irked. Nique tapped switches. Maddie moved to her own console and duplicated her efforts. The screen showed snow and then a blue screen and the legend *SIGNAL INTER-RUPTED*.

"No signal, sir. Wherever he went, the signal isn't getting through." Nique frowned at her display.

"Can he hear us?"

Nique and Maddie shared a look. Maddie spoke for them. "No way to tell, sir."

Rafferty's brow furrowed. "Get me a view from his transvan. Show me outside."

Nique tapped, then moved the cameras remotely. The scene was black. "That's not helping, Lieutenant."

She nodded. "Working on it, sir." She tapped the console display, swiped through menus, and then brought up the control panel of the transvan on the holodisplay. She threw a switch and moved a small virtual joystick. On the main screen, a spotlight blinked on, then swiveled the light across the gray moonscape to the hatch.

"Better. Thank you." Rafferty nodded. Then he frowned and waited for something to happen. "We'll give him a minute before I call out the cavalry."

Granger knew protocol dictated that he simply mark the location and send for a survey team, but this was the first interesting thing that had happened to him in the fourteen months he'd been on Luna. He opened the inner door of the airlock and saw the ladder to the crew quarters, despite the unrelenting warnings. "Radiation alert. Rem levels now two point six five times ambient background standard. Personal protective gear recommended. Radiation alert."

"I got it, now shut up. Warnings to set point three. Just give me the really important stuff." Training always said his EVA suit could handle a good load of radiation. He climbed down the ladder.

"Warnings depreciated."

He stepped through the door at the base of the ladder and did a slow scan around the room. "Armstrong, any idea what the hell this is?" He waited a long moment for no response.

"Armstrong?" Probably the hull of whatever this was blocked his comms. He'd only be a moment. He played his light around the room. *What the hell was this? An abandoned outpost? For what? And why here in the PDA? Who would do that?*

He opened and closed a variety of drawers and doors. Empty. Whoever had been here had cleaned house and taken everything with them. A blue binder hung from the D-ring on the wall, but the pages were blank. Weird. There had been humans here at some point, but what were they doing in an EZ?

Then he noticed the floor. The fine layer of dust had been disturbed. From the looks of the thin coating on everything else, his gut feeling told him it was recent. Boot prints led across the room to the hatch on the far side. He crossed the room, and as he did the radiation warning came again.

"Radiation alert. Rem levels are three point six five times ambient background standard. Personal protective gear recommended. Radiation alert."

Granger tapped his wrist. "Enough of that."

Granger cranked the handle on the inner hatch and swung open the door. His faceplate tinted red and he ignored it. He had full trust in his protective gear. He'd be fine.

Granger stepped through the portal and into a small room with a half dozen orange columns holding up the ceiling, each wearing a large stenciled number, the two nearest labeled 1 and 2. He guessed they were each two meters in diameter. Big. He played his light around the room. An old-school radiation symbol adorned the side wall and he noticed that at the back column corrosion appeared to be leaking from the bottom. The wall looked bent. He leaned closer and the crack widened at the base of the column. He could feel the warmth even through the EVA suit.

"Depreciation override. This is a radiation emergency. Evacuate immediately. Radiation emergency. Evacuate immediately. Significant hazard to human life."

That can't be good, Granger thought. He turned to the open door, but for some reason his feet didn't want to move.

He stumbled, but he hadn't tripped over anything. The temperature in his suit was rising. A flash of terror went through him. He fought it back and told himself to think and concentrate on getting out of here.

There seemed to be a disconnect between his brain and his body. Granger blinked hard as his vision fogged. Sweat popped on his forehead and a wave of panic ran through him. He wiped at the faceplate of the helmet and forced his legs to move, stumbling to the open hatch in a frantic effort to get away from the invisible threat.

"Command? Do you read? I've got a prob—" he stood and fell again, pulling the door closed behind him. He collapsed and grabbed the door lever for support, hoisting himself to his feet and turning to the far door. The room spun around him. "Command . . ."

A wave of heat washed over him and the young astronaut crumpled to the floor of the mysterious facility, the unseen rays penetrating his suit at a much more advanced rate than he'd bargained for. He crawled, the heat rising in his suit as he put his hand to the frame of the lower airlock and his arm failed. His helmet crashed to the floor and his forehead to the faceplate. He sucked in air, pulling himself to the ladder to escape the hidden terror.

Each rung of the ladder was more difficult than the one before. He buckled over the threshold of the upper airlock hatch, his breath coming in great heaving gasps. Above him, the door handle of the outer airlock seemed an eternity away.

Determination kicked in and Granger crawled, dragging his rapidly deteriorating body across the airlock to the entry hatch. It took three tries to move the handle and finally, the door swung up and open. He screamed in pain as the flesh of his hand peeled away on the inside of his glove. Then he vomited into his helmet.

The wallscreens in the command center turned red as one. The warning alarm shrieked, startling Nique as her holodisplay rotated instantly to the position of the hatch. The graphic display showed a representation of a plume of amber pixels streaming out of the area of the hatch.

"Rad alert!" she said far too excitedly for the professional she was supposed to be. "It's the EZ!"

"Get me the transvan camera back on main screen," Rafferty snapped.

Nique's hands flew over the console. The silent, colorless, still image of the open hatch replaced the emergency alert notice on the screen.

"Is that live?"

Nique panned the camera. The picture waggled back and forth. "Yes, sir." Her fingers danced through the air and triggered a second display window showing the view from Granger's suit camera. A gloved hand reached for the open hatch. It wavered and fell back.

Rafferty slapped his hand on the command console. "Granger! Come in!"

On the wallscreen, the dying astronaut flailed at the open hatch. "Command . . ."

His voice cracked and with his last breath he threw himself up the airlock step, falling forward through the open exterior hatch. On the secondary screens in the command center, the now red pixel stream representing the radiation leak gushed around his body and into the lunar darkness.

The unblinking camera on the patrol ute transmitted one last movement as Granger lurched half his body through the hatch, landing face down in the gray dust, half in and half out of the opening.

Nique looked at the screens. What she saw seemed surreal. "Granger? This is Armstrong. Come in."

The EVA suit cams were still transmitting, and the display was a deathly still tilted image of the patrol ute.

"Granger? Come in?"

"Granger?"

CHAPTER TEN

Tuesday . 16 Nov . 2077
1020 Lunar Standard Time
Exam Room Two . Sickbay . Armstrong Base . Luna

The scanner beeped as the doctor switched it on and held it to the wristy. She handed the device back to Mil with a frown.

"You just got a mild dose."

Dr. Emma read the scanner's screen as Mil refastened it to his arm and rolled down the sleeve of his jumpsuit.

"Really? Like I told you, I'm surprised I don't glow—"

The room lights blinked, then switched over to red emergency lamps.

"—in the dark."

In the eerie glow of the exam room, Emma raised an eyebrow at her patient. "How did you—"

The settlement-wide public address system cut her off. "This is a radiation emergency. Proceed immediately to designated shelter areas." The announcement and red alert lamps were a practiced drill.

"That's odd." Mil looked to the ceiling with a question, then grabbed his new ballcap and held the door for the doctor. "We're in Solar Min, there shouldn't be a flare big enough to trigger an alarm."

They exited the medical bay and joined the stream of people headed for the shielded habitat dome.

"Just because it should be a low-flare period doesn't mean it can't happen." Emma took his arm as they hustled along the crowded passageway.

"I'm out in it more than you are, Doc. I get it. Just feels weird. Solar Min is one of the reasons the higher-ups are humping it to get to Mars. They've got an extremely rare window of orbits, solar flares, and funding."

They entered the large dome. A dozen meters across, it was the junction for several of the hallways to the various modules. Pressure doors guarded each hallway ready to seal the intersection, or any of the other modules, in an emergency. The entire dome was shielded against radiation from solar flare activity, and the procedure was a practiced routine.

A growing crowd of technicians and crew members took shelter. The red emergency lamps blinked to reassure the growing crowd that an invisible force was trying to penetrate the shielding and kill them all. The large room felt warm.

"You think this will cost them the launch?"

Mil thought a beat. "If it's a predicted solar weather event, it'll pass, they'll be good to go, but I haven't seen any kind of watch or warning in the forecasts. If the weather wienies can't tell what's happening on the sun, if they don't have absolute confidence that a rogue flare won't cook the crew, they'll have to consider it."

"You think she'd call it off? Or would she put the crew at risk and not abort the mission?"

Mil got a distant look in his eye.

His daughter, Bailey Harrison Rivera, was the high-profile chief administrator of the Space Agency and her name was even being bandied about as a potential vice presidential candidate. She'd staked her entire legacy on getting mankind to Mars. She had moved up through the ranks of the agency with her pet project, shepherding it through three presidential administrations, countless congressional hearings, budget cycle after budget cycle as the program administrator. Now as the chief, she'd have her name on the plaque that the crew would leave on the Red Planet. Dr. Bailey Rivera was a driven woman. It had cost her a marriage and was one reason her relationship with Mil had never been repaired. Once she had devoted her life to populating Mars, any distraction was ignored.

"She might."

"Wow." Emma took in the weight of those two words. "She'd risk an incident?"

"If they don't go now, the window closes, orbits don't align for another two years. Her clock's ticking. I bet it's killing her."

"How so?"

"The lack of control. She can't fight solar weather. It's the one thing that can shut down her life's work."

"So who ultimately makes the call?"

"She'll have primary input. The president could overrule her, but she's being considered for the ticket for this very reason. It'd be a stupid move to go against your hand-picked expert on putting humans on Mars. And, of course, Neff. They'll have to bring him in."

"Neff? This isn't totally the Space Agency's call?"

"Most people never even think about how much sway Amon Neff has in operations. All the hardware, the infrastructure."

"I know Neff Medical Systems makes most of our gear in sickbay."

"Hell, Neff companies make all the fuel, all the air, the water. Most of the vehicles, the engines, the subsystems. None of this happens without that long tail of industrial contractor backup." Mil waved an arm at the room and people around them. "And Amon has made a fortune building that and running it for the last half century."

Just as suddenly as they had turned the world red, the emergency lights faded out and the soft yellow-white glow of the filtered daylight kicked back on.

Mil frowned. "That's not right." He checked his wristy. "Even the smallest flare takes longer than that to pass. We should be here for at least twenty minutes."

The wristy buzzed and Rafferty's face appeared on the small screen.

"Mil, I need the Emergency Response Team. Report to the command center immediately."

Mil almost collided with Rafferty as he turned the corner into the command center.

The dark-skinned Brit was direct. "Follow me. We've got a level-one emergency. A man down and Yamamoto is the only response from your team."

"My team? What team? Hanratty is on leave on Earth. Bohannan is in quarantine after a strep test. No response from Granger?"

"Granger's the problem."

Rafferty led them to the communications holodisplay where Maddie and Nique waited. His granddaughter shot him a concerned look.

"It's not a flare?" Mil scratched his chin.

"It's a surface event, not a flare. We had a radiation spike in the Slayton Ridge Exclusion Zone."

"No kidding. Any ideas?" Mil feigned innocence.

Rafferty keyed the holodisplay. It centered on Slayton Ridge.

An orange triangle appeared on the surface map at the location of Mil's breakdown. Then a red spike at the position of the rad alert. A dotted line connected the two and continued straight to a blue circle on the other side of the EZ. Mil recognized the location as his farm.

"Tell me what you know." Rafferty looked straight into his eyes.

Mil scowled at Maddie. "You did log it. Dammit."

Rafferty growled. "She doesn't have any say. It's all recorded. You want to tell me what's there?"

"I don't have any idea what it is. I thought you'd send a patrol, check it out."

"I did. Granger's there now." He flicked the air and the screen showed the fallen astronaut half in and half out of the hatch. "And whatever it is, it's taken him down. The rad alert is coming from that location. Granger found it and can't—couldn't get out. It shows no signs of spreading, but we have to clear it and get him out of there. And find out what's causing the issue."

"Granger's a good kid. How long has he been there?"

"It's been fifteen minutes. Telemetry on his life signs are spotty. But he hasn't moved. I've been online with Earth. They want you to go get him."

"Well sure, but with an incomplete response team? That's not protocol. Who on Earth authorized that?"

Rafferty folded his hands and looked at the table. "I just got off the call. You can guess who on Earth. This is a significant issue. It calls for a high level of expertise and problem solving. They want you to go get Granger and see if you can contain the leak."

Mil frowned. This was completely outside of protocol. "And not wait for Yammy? I could use her help."

"Earth doesn't want to risk the rest of the team."

"Earth doesn't." Mil looked to Granger's unmoving form on the screen. He turned to face Rafferty.

"And since I just happen to be at the end of my contract, Earth can just let me go get a max dose? I'm expendable now that the new O2 system is in place?" His fists went to his hips.

Rafferty met his eyes with a glare. "While that's not exactly how it was stated, it is a basic truth. But may I remind you that if you'd reported this in the first place, this young officer would most likely not be in jeopardy right now."

Mil swallowed hard at the rebuke. He owed it to the kid.

"Doesn't sound like I have much choice."

"You can choose not to. I will personally arrest you for failure to act as the Emergency Response Team leader. We'd send Yamamoto. She'd do what you refuse to—"

"You know I'll go." Mil looked to the far wall in disgust. "I'll need a vehicle and a robot."

"There's a rad rigged transvan and an exposure suit waiting for you in the motor pool. Deal with the leak and bring Granger"—Rafferty paused and swallowed hard—"or his body back here. We'll have a full decon system in place."

"And what are you going to do, while I prepare to die?"

"I'm going to call Granger's mother, the admiral, and inform her that her oldest son, her pride and joy, the academy's all-conference running back, is more than likely coming home from the moon in a body bag."

Mil paused. "I guess I might have the better end of this deal."

"You might."

Nique stepped out of the command center and leaned against the wall. The nausea rising in her stomach and the welling tears caught her off guard. She sniffed and took a deep breath, then turned away as the bay door slid open.

"Hey, you okay?" It was Eli. He approached her and reached out a hand, pausing it in midair as she drew back.

"I'm okay," she lied.

"It's all right. That was tough." He dropped his hand to his side. "I've never seen someone die before."

"You think he's really dead?"

"I mean there's always a chance he's okay. There hasn't been a fatality on Luna in years. It's a bit of a shock for everyone." He nodded toward the command center.

"But you're all so calm. And I'm out here, just barely keeping it to-gether." She hung her head.

"Why do you think I came out here?" he admitted.

There was an awkward moment as they both tried to think of some-thing to say.

"Did you know him? Granger?" Nique had a catch in her throat.

"Everyone knows . . . knew . . . Micah. And everyone liked him. He's the big goofy guy that always has a joke." Eli paused. "Or he was." He swallowed the lump in his throat.

"What do we do now?"

"We've got a few minutes while they get prepped. With your grandfather taking over for the ERT, that's the Emergency Response Team, our all-purpose problem-solving group. They'll get him geared up to shut down whatever is causing the radiation." He swallowed again. "And bring back Micah."

"By himself?" Nique forgot her nausea and looked to the doors. "He's a civilian contractor; why does he have to go? Why not a Space Force team or even the agency staffers? Why Grandad?"

"Well, he designed the ERT—it was his idea. Like an old-school volunteer fire department where everyone pitches in whether they're military, contractors, even admins. If you've got a specialty, you can be asked to join the team." There was more than a little admiration in Eli's voice. "Besides, if anyone can do it, it's your grandad. I wouldn't be surprised if he told them he'd do it alone just to keep someone else from being put in danger."

"I don't think he's that gallant, but I do know he'd almost always rather do it himself."

Eli checked his wristy.

"I'm sorry," Nique said. "I'm holding you up."

"Oh no. They're getting ready for the recovery, and I was going to the galley and get a cup of coffee before this starts. Kind of clear my head. Can I bring you something?"

"Mind if I walk with you?" She met his eyes for a moment.

"Not at all. A little company might keep me from thinking about it."

"Yeah. And, sorry, I was a little emotional there. I didn't mean to be."

"I think this qualifies as extenuating circumstances."

Nique nodded as they entered the main galley.

Eli paused at the beverage center and then gave her a long look. "I'm guessing a tall, half-caf, skinny mocha latte."

Nique grinned. "So close. Double-shot tall Americano. No room."

Eli's fingers danced across the control pad and the machine hissed out two coffees. "You run on full caffeine, huh?"

"Well, the world's been spinning pretty fast lately."

"The rumor mill has been spinning pretty fast too. You're quite the topic around here."

"I am?" She took the cup he offered.

"Priority reassignment. Verbal orders of the agency director. Transferred off the Mars mission." He took a hot sip and met her eyes over the cup. "Word is that you hacked into the agency server and snarked some secret docs."

"I wish it was that dramatic. Grandad asked if I could find a file. I didn't try to break into anything. I didn't hack anything. I just asked. Politely. And my own mother has me locked in the tower and throws away the key."

"Harsh. I'd kill to be on a Mars mission."

"Let me just say that the agency can be very serious when they want to be. Apparently, to avoid a scandal, I've been banished to the far side of the moon." She put air quotes around the word *agency*.

"And that was for your granddad?"

"Yes. That manipulative old goat. He can—"

"Hey now. He's the reason I'm here. Don't go knocking on him."

"What do you mean?"

"Well, it's a little embarrassing, but my master's thesis was on his work here. I did everything I could to get this assignment. So that maybe I could . . . meet him? Someday?"

He looked at her hopefully.

"You're kidding." Nique shook her head.

"He's a great man! He—and your grandmother—did so much to make Luna a reality." He winked. "I'll not allow another word against Millennium Harrison."

His smile told Nique he was slightly kidding but she could see a hint of serious idol worship behind his eyes.

He checked his wristy. "We better get back. They'll be launching the op."

CHAPTER ELEVEN

Tuesday . 16 Nov . 2077
1235 Lunar Standard Time
Motor pool . Armstrong Base . Luna

T he level-4 radiation protective EVA suit was several kilos heavier than his old reliable pressure suit, and while it was in much better shape, it was newer and stiffer. Mil trudged through the airlock.

He occasionally had to make deliveries or repairs during a solar event and these suits offered considerable protection, but while he'd never admit it, the limitations on his movement and the extra weight made it a tough kit for a man of his age to drag around.

The large six-wheeled box that served as the outpost's radiation-resistant transvan sat in the center of the motor-pool garage dome. He struggled through the door, situated himself at the driver's console, and keyed in the start sequence. The screens blinked on, and the vehicle's systems registered normal. Another set of key taps raised the interior airlock door, and he pulled the cumbersome vehicle into the hold. The door lowered and the depressurization pump emptied the atmosphere from the chamber, saving the precious O2 and equalizing the airlock with the outside environment.

"Armstrong, Harrison. Leaving the airlock."

Inside the communications bay, Maddie Byers looked at Nique in the main comms seat. "If you want, I'll stay and do this. It could be pretty tough."

Nique nodded. "It will be. But it's what we signed up to do." She shot a look over her shoulder and Eli gave her a thumbs-up.

Mil navigated to the dark side of the ridge and then made a sweeping turn, picking up the tracks of Granger's patrol vehicle in the array of lights mounted to the fender, roof, and bumper guard of the transvan. The lights were brighter in Mil's transvan so he saw the rock that had nearly tipped Granger's patrol unit and steered wide around the tracks that led right to it. On the far side, he found himself blocked by a crater somewhat deeper than he expected. He put the van in reverse and the lights caught a glimmer in the distance.

"Armstrong Base, Harrison. Approaching POI."

"How are your readings, Harrison?" Nique's voice was a surprise, but he nodded, knowing at least he wouldn't die alone.

"Rad numbers are nominal, Armstrong. Whatever it is, it isn't registering just yet. Do you have good visuals? Camera check?"

"Good visuals," Nique confirmed.

Mil squinted at the reflection across the distance. He couldn't make it out, but there shouldn't be anything among the rocks and boulders that would sparkle. "Reference contact at one hundred eighty-seven degrees my position? Range shows as two hundred twenty-six meters."

"Nothing on the charts." If Nique was looking hard at the monitors, he was sure she'd pick up the glint ahead as well.

Mil backtracked behind Granger's boulder and then swung the other direction and got his first big look at the dark side of the ridge. The array of lights on the transvan revealed much more than the tiny spotlights of his suit had been able to show on his original visit. The entire face of the ridge had crumbled to the base in what must have been a giant landslide. Near the foot of the rubble, Granger's patrol vehicle sat with its lights still blazing.

"Armstrong. Tally ho. I got it. Eyes on the patrol vehicle."

He swung to the side of the patrol unit, and immediately saw Granger's lifeless EVA suit half in and half out of the hatch. Mil frowned. Extracting the young astronaut was not going to be easy. He backed the shielded transvan close.

"Bailey, give me a rad check."

"Interior radiation levels are one point eight five percent above ambient norms," his computer assistant responded. "Fifteen percent below evac warning threshold."

"First good news I've had all week." He began flipping switches on the overhead console to illuminate the area and transfer controls to his wristcomm.

"Would you like a news report?" Bailey asked.

"No, thanks. I think we're about to make our own." He tapped the comms switch on the console. "Granger, this is Mil Harrison. Do you read?"

Nothing.

"Granger, Harrison. Do you read?"

Not even static.

"Harrison. Armstrong. We read five by five. He should be able to hear you."

"Well, shit." Mil took a deep breath and looked to the video feed of Granger's body lying half in and half out of the hatch. He double-checked his suit connections, depressurized the transvan, and tapped the comms switch once again.

"Armstrong, I'm deploying the robot."

He keyed the rear hatch and the upper half clam-shelled up and out of the way as the lower half dropped to the dust as a ramp. The instant it cracked open his faceplate turned red.

Bailey's unexcited voice came through his headset.

"This is a radiation emergency. Evacuate immediately. Radiation emergency. Evacuate immediately. Significant hazard to human life."

"Yeah, that's why they sent me. Override the warning. Let me know if there's a significant change, say, ten percent either way."

He pulled up the control panel for the robot and manipulated it down the ramp. The six small wheels dug into the fine dust of the surface and headed toward the specialist's lifeless form. The doors of the transvan closed behind the robot.

Years of operating remote robots made the system second nature to Mil. He traced the route to the unmoving astronaut on the screen of his wristcomm and then activated the control application that slaved the robot's mechanical claws to his suit gloves.

Forty-five meters away, the six-wheeled robot mimicked his every move. The cameras on the bot projected the stereoscopic view onto the faceplate of his helmet and gave Mil a remote presence at the scene from the relative safety of the transvan.

Mil navigated the robot to a spot directly in front of Granger's helmet and articulated the arms of the robot, latching onto the epaulets molded into the shoulders of every space suit for just such an emergency.

He toggled the switchgear to back the robot out and drag the young astronaut's dead weight from the hatch, applying all the torque the robot's powerful electric motors possessed.

The robot dug in, applying its force, and then the traction broke and all six wheels spun in the regolith dust.

"Shit."

Mil rocked the robot back and forth, trying to gain traction; instead, the tires dug deeper into the dust. He paused. If he kept this up, the robot would high-center and spin uselessly atop the mound of soil piled between the wheels.

He bit his lip. There was only one option left, and it wasn't a good one. A deep breath steeled him. He thumbed the controls and the robot backed away from the lifeless astronaut.

"Armstrong. I'm going to have to get him." He transferred his controls from the van to his suit and the status indicators for his internal systems flickered to green. Mil unstrapped and swiveled the driver's seat to the cargo compartment.

Rafferty appeared on his wristy. "Concur. His readouts are weak, but I think he's alive. I don't see any alternative, Mil. Be as quick as you can."

"Wilco." He heaved himself from the seat and double-checked the O2 system. The gauge display on the wall of the van glowed red, showing the atmosphere had been removed, equalizing to the vacuum of the lunar surface.

He twisted the ramp controller and the rear doors cracked open again. Bailey's voice crackled in his headset. "This is a radiation emergency. Evacuate immediately. Radiation emergency. Evacuate immediately. Significant hazard to human life."

"Depreciate warnings for ten minutes."

He moved as quickly as he could, throwing a leg over the still opening ramp, and crow-hopped directly to Granger's body.

He grabbed the handholds on the specialist's suit and heaved. The lunar gravity helped, but the deadweight of a football-playing human male and EVA suit was a considerable challenge for Mil. He heaved. The young astronaut didn't budge. Mil took a knee and analyzed the situation. The lower half of Granger's suit was jammed against the sealing rim of the airlock. Mil straddled the opening and grabbed the handholds from above, lifting the unconscious form away from the lip and supporting him with his own body. He let go of the handholds and grabbed the specialist by the torso, lifting him up and out of the airlock. It was the most weight Mil had attempted to lift in years, and his grunt became a yell into his faceplate as he strained under the weight.

He threw himself to the ground, bringing Granger's lifeless form on top of him, crashing to the surface in a cloud of dust. Mil's helmet smacked into the back of Granger's. He rolled them both away from the opening, then slumped to catch his breath.

Bailey's radiation warning returned. Had that taken ten minutes?

He crawled through the dirt to the hatch, slammed it shut then collapsed to his side.

"Bailey cancel warnings," he rasped. They weren't doing him much good at this point.

The shadowy world fell to a disturbing silence, broken only by his own heavy, exhausted breathing. The excited voice of his granddaughter broke through.

"You did it, Grandad! Rad alerts depreciating. Ambient levels returning to nominal."

"Affirmative, Armstrong." His voice cracked and sweat broke on his forehead. He blew an exhausted breath into his helmet and struggled to one knee. He shoved himself upright and fought off a wave of dizzying nausea. His hands went to his knees and brought his breathing under control. The task was only half complete.

He grabbed the handholds on Granger's EVA suit and heaved the deadweight into a fireman's carry, hoisting him up across his shoulders, staggering under the weight. His first deliberate step oriented him to the transvan ramp. He grunted with each step, the guttural sounds echoing through his own headset. His breathing grew sharper and deeper and quicker as he shuffled heavily to the ramp.

Mil went to one knee on the ramp, rolling the fallen astronaut into the cargo area and slamming his fist to a large button on the wall. The rear of the transvan folded closed. He collapsed next to the specialist's prone form, face down on the floor.

Mil was spent. Exhausted like he'd never been in his life.

He rolled to his side and nudged Granger. "Don't be dead, kid. This is a shitty way to die."

There was no response.

He struggled to his knees and rolled the stricken astronaut over. Through the bile-coated faceplate, Mil could see the lifeless staring eyes. The blistered burns of a major exposure covered the young man's face, bulging and broken. Mil looked away and found his helmet's hydration tube, swallowing his own gag reflex.

"Armstrong. Harrison. I've got Granger. He's dead." The matter-of-fact tone hid the defeat Mil felt.

Rafferty's voice was calm in his ear. "Roger that. We register rad levels dropping."

"That's just peachy, Armstrong." With all his strength Mil raised his body from the floor. He made it to one knee.

"I'm headed back. You might call the doc and have her there at decon."

"Everything okay?" It was the concern of a granddaughter, not the dispassionate professional communicator.

"Never had a dose like that before. I could feel that one." He paused and blinked the rapidly forming sweat out of his eyes. "Harrison out."

Mil crawled past Granger's body to the driver's compartment of the transport, catching a glimpse of the red light of the camera above the windshield staring at him. Watching his every move. He reached up and shut off the offending eyeball, then slowly moved one trembling hand to the steering yoke and eased the transvan into the darkness. The headlight array played across the boulders, giving a ghostly feel to the dark moonscape— and then—the glint he'd seen earlier, a shape Mil had only seen in ancient videos and exclusion zones.

A hundred meters in front of him stood the empty, lower descent stage of an Apollo-era lunar excursion module landing craft. The upper ascent stage of the LEM had long since blasted back to Earth carrying whoever and whatever secret might have visited this black area of the moon a very long time ago.

An hour later, Des Rafferty paced in the command center. There'd been no communications with the transvan. Telemetry showed it leaving Slayton Ridge and heading directly back to the Base. But Mil was incommunicado.

Rafferty watched the holodisplay as the motor-pool garage airlock opened and the transvan glided through—and then didn't stop. It rolled deliberately into another vehicle, pushing it into yet another.

Rafferty sprinted to the garage.

Four yellow-suited technicians ran to the wreckage and threw open the driver's door. Mil was slumped, unconscious, at the controls. They carried him from the vehicle to a waiting gurney, wheeling his unmoving body into the hastily prepped radiation washdown facility.

Inside, Emma and Nique waited, each wearing a radiation suit. The gurney burst through the doors, still dripping from the pressure wash designed to remove contaminated particles.

The decon lab's task lights blazed down as the team went to work. Wall screens synced with Mil's wrist computer and his vital signs appeared before the doctor. Nique could read the concern in Emma's eyes through the faceplate of her rad suit. A technician unlatched the helmet and Mil's head rocked back.

Immediately Emma slapped an oxygen mask on him.

The rush of the cold air brought him around and his first reaction threw a solid right cross to the helmet of the nearest technician. Two others grabbed his arms as he struggled on the table.

"Grandad!"

"Mil!" Nique and Emma shouted at the same time. Harrison's response was wild-eyed half terror and half rage. He wasn't about to go quietly.

Emma leaned in close. "Mil! Settle down! Let us get you out of this suit!"

Mil collapsed back and his voice cracked. The hoarse whisper was almost indecipherable. "I do love it when you say that."

Emma smiled. "Well, you're not dead yet."

His eyes grew wide, and he swallowed hard, then again. The doctor hopped back and yelled, "Bucket!" knowing the vomit was coming. Mil swatted the oxygen mask away and didn't disappoint. But he did miss the bucket.

She held his gloved hand as his stomach wretched inside out. He crumpled back on the gurney, exhausted. Slowly his eyes closed and his head fell back against the surface. Emma looked at his ashen face and felt her eyes begin to water.

Twenty minutes later, Rafferty was still pacing. He turned at the sound of the opening doors. "Bad?"

The doctor looked weary. "It's not good. He's sedated. I've got him in the bariatric chamber to give his cells a fighting chance, but he caught a major dose. His wristy dosimeter registers four point two grays. On top of his lifetime numbers, I don't know. It's touch and go. It'll take hours, maybe days in the chamber."

"Granger?"

She looked at Rafferty and shook her head. "But he did shut it down, right?"

"He did. Now we have to find out what 'it' was."

She looked at him with an accusation. "Yes. Yes, we do."

CHAPTER TWELVE

Friday . 19 Nov . 2077
1235 Lunar Standard Time
Mess Hall . Armstrong Base . Luna

66 I don't even know if I can get in." Nique looked over her protein plate at Emma. "I haven't gotten an entry code from him yet."

The doctor leaned across her breakfast and whispered, "I can. I need to talk to you, and the comms room at the farm is the only place I trust."

All around the galley, techs and workers were rushing through meals. *Humanity*, the Russian-built spacecraft that would carry the settlement team to Mars, was due on station later that day, and the Armstrong base meal printers had been working almost around the clock.

Nique watched as the techs at the table next to them ran through checklists between bites. "Why the farm? Have you been there? It's an old, dusty place that he only cleans when it gets so bad he can't find things."

"Yes, it's . . . rustic, but it's the one place I'm certain no one has ever put recorders. He'd kill them if they tried."

"This is that important?"

"He seems to think so."

Ten minutes later, the two were gliding across the groomed lunar road to Mil's farm in his spidertruck.

"How often do you go to the farm?" Nique asked as she turned the spider over to the autopilot for the trip across the barren gray moonscape.

"Your grandfather and I are . . . close."

"Close? As in . . . ?" The doctor gave a confirming look and Nique stammered at the realization. "Oh . . . oh, I see."

"Well, it's not something either of us publicize."

Nique felt the flush of embarrassment. Followed by a thought she could only categorize as "icky."

"So, how are you liking the moon so far?" Emma changed the subject, to their mutual relief.

"It's different. I thought it'd be long hours of nothing, like doing police dispatch in a small town. But things have been crazy since I got here."

"Different than training to go to Mars, huh?"

"We had a detailed schedule, simulator training, classwork, even crew rest was all lined out and prepped for us. I knew what I'd be doing two weeks ahead of time. Here it feels like anything can happen, anytime."

"And it seems to." Emma smiled. She'd had similar thoughts when taking her position five years ago. Now she didn't even think about returning to Earth.

"So it's not just Grandad?"

"Oh, he helps. You never know what kind of mess he'll dig up next."

Nique watched the moonscape pass by. "You can say that again."

The farm was as silent as a tomb as the airlock repressurized and the green light switched on. Emma led the way into the main house with a familiarity that made Nique pause a beat.

"Can I ask a personal question?"

Emma placed her helmet on the designated shelf and began the ritual of suit removal. One eyebrow arched. "Sure."

"Is me staying here going to get in the way? I mean between you two? I don't want to cause a problem."

"Mil and I have a very comfortable arrangement. If you were in the way, he'd tell you."

That brought a chuckle. "I guess he would. But I've been here less than a week and we haven't really seen much of each other. His schedule and mine don't really sync up."

Nique followed as Emma entered the apartment and went directly to the media control panel, where she inserted a small data chip and toggled the media player. "He and I have the same problem. Don't worry about us, we've made this work for a while now. You're not in the way." She turned to the younger woman and slipped into doctor mode. "He's going to need some on-site care, though. I know him well enough to see what's coming. He's not going to stay in sickbay. Unless I sedate him, restrain him, and lock him up, he'll come here."

Nique pursed her lips. "I'm not exactly a nurse."

"Oh, he'd never let us bring in a nurse. God forbid. But I would appreciate it if you could keep an eye on him. Lend a hand. He doesn't know how weak he'll be. Or how sick he's going to be. 'Rest and recovery' is not a phrase in his vocabulary."

"So, make sure he eats and rests? I can do that."

"Keep his medpatches on schedule and get him well enough to travel." She met Nique's eyes.

"Travel?"

"That's my next major challenge." Emma touched a key and stepped back from the video display. The screen flicked on to a security screen for the chip and registered that the system was decoding the data.

Emma pointed to the system. "He gave me this when we wheeled him in from decon. I have no idea what it is, but he pressed it hard into my hand, and the look in his eye said it was important."

The system asked for an identity; Emma looked into the small camera port, and the network recognized her.

The security tones chimed and the system blinked on.

"You're on his pass list? You guys really are close."

The screen filled with the camera view of the lunar landscape rolling past. It continued for several minutes. Emma shuttled it forward and then the rolling terrain on video slowed and stopped. The camera jolted around and then went black.

"Well, that was pretty worthless." Nique wrinkled her nose.

"There's a VR file on here too."

She tapped a few prompts, then stood and opened a storage compartment on the wall. She turned and handed Nique a VR headset.

Nique recognized the scene they were in. "This is Granger's EVA suit cam. This is agency property! How'd he get this?"

"Have you met your grandad? He's quite capable of bending the rules to fit his preconceived idea of what needs to be done."

"He took the video surveillance chip off a dead guy? What's he going to do with it?" Nique looked around, taking in the lunar landscape and the patrol ute they were now leaving behind as Granger's virtual presence carried them to the hatch. Then descended the ladder to the inside of the mystery facility.

Two bunks hung on one wall with a variety of storage bins, and the remnants of a vinyl curtain drooped from another. Then the screens tinted orange and the emergency voice came through the background with the now-familiar radiation advisory.

"What is this place?" Emma had yet to understand that this was anything out of the ordinary.

"Grandad showed me his version of this VR. He said it's a twentieth-century US Air Force installation."

"Twentieth century? They had a facility like this on Luna? I never knew that."

"I don't think anyone knew."

"A secret base on the moon? Leave it to Mil to stumble upon something nobody ever wanted uncovered."

The orange tint on the screen faded as Granger depreciated the radiation alert. Nique paused the VR and they looked all around the room, examining the antique technology and trying to find clues as to what the facility might have been.

"I don't get it," she said.

Nique forwarded the clip, and Granger moved them toward the far hatch. Opening the door illuminated a small red radiation symbol on the wall but behind the virtual representation of the young astronaut. With the 360-degree view afforded them by the suit cameras, Emma spotted it instantly.

"That's an old-time radiation alert. Still works after all this time, but he can't see it." Emma was slowly turning, her VR rig allowing her to see behind the young astronaut.

"He's too focused on what's behind the door."

Granger entered the room and his lights played across the interior. A half dozen orange columns supported the roof. They were evenly spaced in two rows with white numerals one through six painted as to be easily seen from a standing desk on the near wall. The desktop featured six identical control panels, each with a darkened digital readout and a numeric keypad.

Two separate stations appeared to house identical main controls set a few feet apart. Each featured dials and gauges around a dark CRT monitor and keyboard beside a covered red toggle switch and an old-fashioned mechanical key. Emma hadn't seen one of those since she was a child.

"What the heck is this?" Emma looked around and then stepped through the door and attempted to pass beyond the first cylinder, but she was met by a black wall and a checkerboard image indicating the absence of any VR imagery beyond that point.

"I guess he didn't go much farther inside," Nique said.

"I don't think he could. With the level of radiation this place is giving off, he was as good as dead the minute he stepped into this room."

"Did you see that?" Nique pointed to a stain on the floor at the base of the number-five column. "Corrosion."

"I wonder if these are nuclear fuel cells?" Emma squatted to look at the corrosion. "That would make sense—twentieth-century technology to power a base of operations on the moon."

"They only had primitive solar. Almost no electrical storage—nuclear would have been their only option for long-term power back then."

"And if they had a leak, it makes sense that they would have buried this and not wanted anyone to find it."

"They never counted on Granddad."

"So if this is nuclear fuel, I wonder what they were doing? I don't remember any plans for a moon settlement prior to Armstrong base. That didn't happen until—"

"The year 2037," Nique interjected. "I did my master's thesis on lessons learned that could be applied to colonizing Mars. A big one was solar power. After the disaster that obliterated the launch facilities in China back in 2041, no one really wanted to launch nuclear packages."

"I wonder what happened that they would abandon this kind of investment?"

"It was unbelievably dangerous. They lost fourteen crew members and half of their shuttle fleet just trying to work in low Earth orbit. With that kind of cost, I'm certain they weren't able to sustain a settlement independent from Earth with the tech back then."

Emma pulled her goggles off and ended the program. "So why would you try and transport nuclear fuel on a launch vehicle you knew to be that unreliable? That seems foolhardy."

"Grandad said this was from before Internet One. There might not have been a choice in those days. Before the Space Force and private contracting went big-time, the US went years with no ability to put crews in space. They had to buy seats from the Russians."

Emma plopped down in the lounger and checked her wrist. "One more thing we need to talk about when he's ready to get out of the chamber."

Nique placed her headset in its charging cradle.

"How bad is this? I mean, he'll recover, right?"

Emma nodded. "He's a tough old bird. That will figure into it, but he's not had an easy go of it here. He works all the time and never gets enough rest. I don't think he's taken a real vacation in years—maybe decades. Top that with the fact this isn't his first brush with radiation—he's been out in solar flares. He spends all that time out in the elements making deliveries."

"And this isn't his first trip to this site."

Emma's eyes rolled. "Right. That's how this whole mess started."

"But he's protected, right? I mean he's got a level-four suit and all the gear."

Emma chuckled despite herself. "When he actually decides to wear the level four. And have you seen his everyday work suit? It's twenty years old. I'm amazed it doesn't just fall apart. It might offer some rad protection, but still, when you try to get him to do something for his own good, for his own safety, he mostly just ignores it."

"He thinks he's invincible."

"This might change his mind."

CHAPTER THIRTEEN

Monday . 22 Nov . 2077
1235 Lunar Standard Time
Mess Hall . Armstrong Base . Luna

Nique toyed with her food with one hand and flicked through her dataslate with the other, absently scanning the news. She'd thought the activity in the mess hall might take her mind off her grandfather's condition, but even with the dozens of crew members queued at the meal printers and the din of conversations at the other tables, his situation and her own predicament gnawed at her.

She returned to the message she was crafting to her mother. She kept putting it off. It was a mashup of contrition for violating the security protocols, hope for a return to the Mars crew, and a slight dose of familial guilt trip for not inquiring about her grandfather.

There had to be a balance to make her case, but she needed one more rewrite to find it.

"Hey, want some company?"

She looked up to see Eli and Maddie making their way toward her, each with their own tray.

Nique brightened. "Sure."

"How's your granddad?" Maddie parked across the table.

"Dr. Wilkerson says he's stable and that's good. They're going to slowly bring him back to consciousness. I can tell she's worried, though."

"Yeah, they're pretty tight. But that's good—he'll get an extra level of care from her." Eli took the seat next to Nique and stabbed a straw into his drink box. "Have they said what the prognosis is for him? Can they even tell you that?"

"I'm on his to-be-informed-list, so yes, they can tell me stuff, but they don't know much right now, beyond he's lucky to be alive at all."

The table grew silent. Nique looked up to her friends as they shared a concerned look. "Let's talk about something less depressing. How is it that your food actually looks like dinner?"

She pointed her spork to his salad with blackened chicken-looking protein. He followed her eyes and gave a veteran's smile. "One of the advantages of being in the command center and seeing the traffic logs. You know when fresh food moves from the greenhouse to the mess hall." He stabbed a leaf of lettuce and admired it.

"And the chicken?" She considered her own plate of sadness.

Maddie waved a spork at her own. "That one you learn from experience. The meal printers aren't great with chicken-style protein, so you season it with all the Cajun spice you can and it sorta tastes like food."

Eli politely offered her his plate and Nique declined with a smile. "Thanks, no. I'm chalking this up to a lesson learned."

A trio of med techs hurried by, carrying their meals back to their workstations.

"Medical seems pretty busy right now." Maddie's gaze flitted from the passing group back to Eli, then Nique. Then back. She raised an eyebrow and Nique caught the look. She glanced at Eli and tilted her head to indicate she'd consider the eligible bachelor.

For his part, Eli was munching his lettuce, clueless, and nodded.

"And the whole place is crowded right now with everyone ramping up for *Humanity* to arrive. I see the duty logs for every department. Medical has it the worst: they're doing physicals for everyone who has any contact with the crew. I got called in for mine the day before yesterday and I don't think I'll even see anyone on the mission crew."

"Ouch." Nique grimaced.

"Oh, sorry. Touchy subject." Eli flinched as Maddie elbowed him and followed with a dirty look for Nique's benefit.

"Yeah. I'm not envious of the workload in the med lab right now," Maddie deftly changed the subject.

"You're not envious of anyone. Short-timer." Eli grinned.

"This won't affect your leave, will it?" Nique sprinkled an extra dose of seasoning on her protein.

It didn't help much.

Maddie thought a second. "I'm not sure. We haven't had an event out of the ordinary in so long I'm not sure what the procedure is." She looked to Eli.

"It could slow things down. When I first got here, we had an injury. A guy fell off a scaffold working on the renovations over in the main landing area. They pushed back two cycles of launch and landing to rework operations checklists. Totally unrelated to a guy breaking his arm, but the agency is tough on their procedures."

"You can break your arm in one-sixth G?" Nique pushed her plate back.

Maddie shook her head. "Long-timers can. I'm surprised your Grandad hasn't given you the lowdown on that. Bone density is an issue here. Do the stress workouts and keep up your mineral intake."

"Duly noted." Nique made a mental note.

"Yeah," Eli nodded. "I need to be better at that."

"Or you can just rotate back to Earth." Maddie gave them both a smug smile.

———— ❀ ————

Thursday . 25 Nov . 2077
0630 Lunar Standard Time
Hyperbaric Pressure Chamber . Med Lab . Armstrong Base . Luna

Mil woke feeling like shit. The tiny room was swimming and his head pounded. Slowly, through the fog, the memory cleared. He raised his head and looked around. He was on a military-issue cot. Next to the cot sat a chair and small table. At the foot of the cot, a toilet and a washbasin. His eyes found the wall with the pressure door and the reinforced housing holding the porthole.

A brain cell fired off the memory of a pressure-chamber test in his pilot training days a million years ago. That was beyond the worst hangover he'd ever had, and he didn't recall it being quite this tough.

He sat up and the nausea tsunami hit. He rolled from the cot and lurched to the toilet, stumbling on two weak legs with one hand on the floor in a half-crawling, stooped, animalistic move to get to the bowl before he filled it in a series of bone-racking heaves that left him gasping.

A tinny voice came from somewhere. "Believe it or not, that's a good thing."

Mil looked to the porthole and saw the smiling face of his doctor. "How long am I in for, warden?"

Emma grinned. "A little while yet. Couple of hours. We'll get you out once you eliminate the bulk radioactive particulates."

"Eliminate?"

"What you just did. Also urinate and defecate."

"So all I have to do to get out of here is take a radioactive shit?"

The doctor shook off her smile. "Essentially, yes. You do have a way with words."

He started to get up from the floor. Instead, he sank back down to one knee and steadied himself on the sink.

"Been there, done that."

"You have?"

"Yeah, remember that taco place in Houston? Across from the main gate? The habanero combo plate would wreck you for two days."

She smiled. "Ah yes, Gamma Ray Jose's salsa. This is a little different kind of radioactivity."

Mil filled a glass with water from the tap.

"Don't—"

He swallowed and the liquid triggered another violent reflex and he twisted from his knees and wretched over the toilet again.

"You might wait on drinking."

"Thanks for the tip. You have great timing."

"Your gastrointestinal tract is in full revolt. You took over four grays. Most of your internal organs have been cooked. Think of it as an internal sunburn that people die from."

"I know. I met that guy." His hand unconsciously went to his gut. He could feel it.

On the other side of the porthole, Emma consulted her chart. "Right now, we're working to clear the contamination from your body. Stop the damage. The binding agents and the hyperbarics will aid in that. There will be some residual bone issues but we'll deal with that with supplements down the line."

"As long as I don't break my back throwing up." He staggered to his feet and supported himself on the sink as he shuffled to the cot and collapsed.

"I don't think that will happen."

"You don't know how tough it is to barf uranium."

"After the particles are cleared, you'll still have some serious scarring. We can treat that with some LPA therapies and put you on some DNA repair protocols."

"Any of them pleasant?"

"No. Sorry."

"Just wondered if my luck had changed."

She bit her lip, searching for the right words.

The result was an uncomfortable pause.

Mil sensed the delay. He raised the heavy weight of his head and looked to the porthole. "What is it?"

"Mil. We don't really have the facilities to care for you here."

"What does that mean?"

"The agency wants to transport you. There's a recovery facility in Japan that knows more about treating radiation sickness than anyplace on—"

"Earth." Mil spat the word.

"Yes. I'm sorry. The container on the table has a packet with a transderm patch you need to put on your arm. That'll help with the nausea and maybe get you to where you can drink and keep some food down."

"I can't wait." Mil's brain had begun the clear a bit. "Did you get the information I sent?"

"I did. Very interesting. Nique and I looked through it. She told me some interesting things about your discovery. We should talk when you feel better." She gave him a knowing look. Comms weren't secure here. He nodded his understanding.

"So you expect me to feel better."

"You will." She smiled. "But, I have to tell you the truth—it'll be worse before you get better."

"I just vomited my toenails up, how much worse can it be?"

"A lot. Trust me."

Forty-five minutes later the convulsions started and Mil decided his girlfriend, the doctor, really did know what she was talking about.

CHAPTER FOURTEEN

Friday . 26 Nov . 2077
0455 Lunar Standard Time
Portside fueling pylon . *Humanity* . Orbiting Luna

———— ❁ ————

*W*orking in orbit is not supposed to be this big of a pain in the ass. Jack Chow blindly felt with his left boot for the aluminum eyelet that was supposed to be his anchor point. By reflex he let go of the giant sphere and grabbed for the spar that he was floating against. His bulky gloves and the extra mass of the pressure suit made the grab even more cumbersome. Below him, the gray surface of the moon sped by as he hovered just off the outer fuel ring of *Humanity*.

At least Jack was pretty sure that the moon was down there. The reality was that he couldn't see shit. This was ridiculously more difficult than it had been in the sims. Or the water tank. Or the practice session in Earth orbit before they left. It seemed no one had accounted for the fact that the unfiltered sun would be lighting up the floating array of brilliant white oxygen spheres. That little unforeseen detail produced a hundred miniature suns that blinded the one guy who was trying to attach the spheres of life sustaining oxygen to the spacecraft that would get them to Mars.

That spacecraft, *Humanity*, was not an elegant piece of aerodynamic sculpture. It had been designed to travel between two planets across the empty vacuum of space, where aesthetics and aerodynamics meant nothing. The linked globes of soft-sided habitats were surrounded by a webbed titanium superstructure bristling with solar arrays and antenna dishes. At odd intervals, nozzles of rockets sprouted from spars and girders. *Humanity* was the purest expression of form following function that mankind had ever created.

Floating just twenty meters away, dozens of Mil Harrison's white spheres had been waiting for months to fuel the ship. They hovered motionless in orbit, a stalk that seemed to sprout giant glowing gas-filled balloons.

Now with *Humanity* parked this close, the first vehicle to carry human beings to another planet looked more like a colony of mating insects than the majestic starships of movie universes.

Fuel system specialist Jack Chow's job was to simply detach the O2 sphere from its orbital hitching post and secure it to the ring of attachment manifolds that circled the girth of the good ship *Humanity*.

"Watch it, Jack, you're drifting off the port stay." The never pleasant voice of Captain Ethan "Pete" Peterson crackled in his earpiece.

No shit, Jack thought as he secured himself against the spar and pulled the ungainly globe back to him. "Got it now. Sir, we're going to have to rethink this entire procedure. It's blinding out here. Can't see a thing."

"We will realign the ship to the fuel tree for the next EVA." This voice belonged to the ship's commander, Dimitri Litinov. Jack knew the two guys in charge were watching his every move and second-guessing his decisions. He'd been at this almost twice as long as he should have. The worst-case scenarios in the simulation tank never took this long.

"Jack, when you lock that one down, come on back inside. We'll figure this out."

Inside the officers' control room, Peterson zoomed the holodisplay to see the connector moving slowly away from the alignment holes on the structure. The astronaut attending the giant sphere released a jet of compressed gas from his backpack, nudging himself and the sphere to float toward the attachment point, and the locking mechanism engaged.

Litinov, a compact man, with a quick smile, leaned forward and nodded. "Better."

The Russian's ice-blue eyes conveyed a confidence that made him an easy man for his crew to follow. Sitting across the table from him, his executive officer was almost his polar opposite. Peterson was tall for an astronaut, and his stature, crew cut, and bearing told most people he was a proud member of the Space Force long before he mentioned it. But he always mentioned it.

The large white spheres filled with breathing oxygen and fuel for the trip to Mars were the key to the entire voyage. Chemical rockets were old, outdated technology, but they were still more powerful than ion drive and ten times faster than a solar sail.

For all the wonders promised by science fiction, physics were a bitch to overcome. Two years of Mil Harrison's production had been filling these great spheres with the oxygen he steadily farmed. The giant balloons had been lifted into lunar orbit, where they waited to be attached to *Humanity*.

Chow's voice came through the speaker. "Sirs, you should take a look from my helmet feed, you'll see what we're dealing with here."

Peterson swiped and tapped air, and the holodisplay image resolved to a brilliant glow that obscured everything.

"That's with all the polarization filters and glare reduction engaged. It just overwhelms the sensors."

"We will get to work on it. It may be as simple as putting *Humanity* on the sun side and working in the shadow." Litinov studied the image, unable to see any more than his fuel expert floating outside the ship. "Let's set a meeting to get on this."

He turned away, leaving Chow to his task. Peterson frowned and studied his dataslate. This was a significant issue, but they would solve it with time, study, and patience. Unfortunately, none of those were in good supply right now.

"If we reposition, it'll take longer to move the fuel cells to the portside. We'll need a new procedure if we're going to launch on time." His eyes met Litinov's. This was the last major milestone before heading to Mars.

Litinov sipped his pouch of tea, waiting for his XO to deliver the anticipated gloom.

The American tapped his dataslate impatiently. "This is scheduled for a three-hour EVA. Chow's been out there four and a half. If they don't get faster, we won't just miss the launch window, we won't be able to carry enough oxidizer to make it home."

Litinov smiled. "This is why you're here, XO. To worry about the things that might happen. Let's deal with the reality of the things that we can make happen. Get Jack and the rest of the team together and do a debrief. Discover a means to do this. Borrow manpower from Armstrong Base if necessary. This system was tested in the tank and at the station; it's been done flawlessly in Earth orbit. Our team can do this."

Peterson stood, clasped his hands behind him, and began to pace a small circle. "Well, if they were Space Force, perhaps, but most of the Luna colony fuel guys are civilians. Jack Chow is a contractor. Military crews know their systems and their training."

Litinov smiled again. "And civilians design the equipment. Chow has been on this project since that fuel system was just a twinkle in an engineer's imagination. He knows it better than any noncom ever will. What else?"

"Any possibility it's still communications issues? Maybe the English-as-a-second-language guys are having trouble."

"Like me?" Litinov grinned. He'd been speaking English since grade school. It was the language of flight and space, and he occasionally worried that he'd lose his native Russian. "You worry too much, Pete. This is just the first sphere. If it were number sixteen or number twenty, I might worry. The team will get better, and I would wager we'll be fueled and ready to go long before the optimum window."

"Well, I'm not going to bet against you, but there's a lot of room for improvement."

"I have seen it before. The first runs uncover problems you never know you have. Reality requires adjusting to the fact that it's not the sim. They'll get it."

"Right. *Semper supra*. It's the Space Force way. I'll go prep the debrief. And then we'll do it again." Peterson logged off the holodisplay and stood. His hand went to his chest reflexively and he stopped short.

"What is it?" Litinov arched an eyebrow.

Peterson shook his head. "Nothing. Probably the chili mac from lunch." He winked at his Russian commander. "Or that battery acid you call tea." He nodded and closed the hatch as he floated through it.

Litinov sat back and looked through the window to the surface of the moon sixty miles below with a knowing smile. He had served two tours at Armstrong Base, one in operations and the second as facility commander. His time there showed the selection staff for this mission that his inventiveness, temperament, and judgment were the perfect combination for the extended trip. He would be gone from Earth for the bulk of the next decade and would be almost seventy years old when he returned. But oh, when he landed, Mother Russia would have a toehold on Mars and the pride of having constructed the great ship *Humanity* itself, and he would have a legacy that would match Gagarin's.

But before they fired the rockets and set off, he would spend a week at his old home, among friends. He had turned the base over to Desmond Rafferty almost four years before and by all accounts, his old command was in good shape. They were to dine this evening and he was looking forward to seeing old compatriots and his former chess nemesis Mil Harrison. Perhaps they'd have time for one last game. A wry smile revealed his anticipation. Mil had never dealt with anything like his new modified Karkov's opening.

CHAPTER FIFTEEN

Tuesday . 14 Dec . 2077
0945 Lunar Standard Time
Exam Room One . Sickbay . Armstrong Base . Luna

———⊛———

"**D**amned wobbly." Mil reached for the exam table as soon as he stood up. Emma grabbed his elbow to lend support.

"Is it strength or equilibrium?"

"Both. And it sucks." He lowered himself back to sit on the edge of the table. "The damned room is moving, and I feel like my knees are going to buckle any second."

"It takes the body a while to reorient. You'll get there. Right now, we need to get you strong enough for evac."

"About that. What are they going to do on Earth that can't be done here?"

"We don't have any type of convalescent facilities here. You need monitoring until you get your strength back. Assistance, routine care. Hyperbarics. Nutrition and strength training."

He shook his head. "Horseshit."

"Mil, don't fight me on this. I'm the only doctor for a quarter of a million miles—as much as I'd like to play nursemaid to you, I don't have the time. There are other patients, I have a full time slot here. You need to shuttle to Osaka and the treatment center there."

"What about the doc on *Humanity*? He's not doing anything for the next few weeks. Have him come down and fill in."

"Do you hear yourself? It's a lousy trip to Earth, you're making way too big a deal out of this. Go R and R and get better. A couple of weeks from now you'll be back to your old cantankerous self."

Mil hung his head and confided his worst fear. "They won't let me come back."

"Why wouldn't they? It's your home."

"They don't care. They don't need me here anymore. The new O2 plant makes my farm obsolete. Neff won't cover the cost of the return flight. He's already said I need to retire and return to Earth."

"And Amon Neff controls your future?"

"Well, yeah." Mil shrugged. "He's my boss, so he kinda does. We had a frank discussion about it back when the new plant was under construction."

"Do you ever not have frank discussions?"

He gave her the side-eye. "Neff's point is there's no system in place for people dying here. No one dies of natural causes on the moon."

"Right. They never thought about it. Nobody considered that when they established permanent settlements on the moon, the people living there would eventually die." Her eyes rolled.

"We've had very few people die in the last thirty years—three accidents that killed somebody. Four, counting whatever they'll call this recent fuckup. There's not a lot of protocol for hospices and funerals or cemeteries. And as you know, the agency doesn't do anything without a protocol."

"So . . .?"

"So they'll fly my ass back to Earth and make me die there."

He pushed off the table and tried to take a defiant step as the room wobbled around him. She took his arm.

"You're free to travel back if you want. It's not like you don't have the money squirreled away. Buy out your contract from Neff and come back on your own."

"It's not like buying a bus ticket to Cleveland."

"How would you know? You've never been to Cleveland. You haven't been off this rock in what—fifteen, twenty years? Everyone is crazy for Mars right now, coming to the moon is like going to the store for milk. Quit feeling sorry for yourself: go home and get well." She guided him back to the stability of the table.

"This is home."

"Maybe it's time to reconsider that."

Mil eyed his girlfriend. "When do they want to do this?"

She bit her lip and hesitated. Mil cocked his head, waiting for the prognosis.

"Soon. Now. Consider this your preflight physical. You're on Flight 2705. Transport launches at sixteen hundred."

Anger flashed across his face. He looked like shit and felt worse, but his future was at stake here. He crossed his arms and shook his head.

"No can do. I can't just drop everything and go to Earth."

"It's not up to you. Rafferty's orders. He told me to write it up as a medical evacuation."

"That son of a bitch."

"I didn't argue with him." She took his face in her hands and looked into his gray eyes. "It's the right thing to do, Mil."

He looked away, glaring at the far wall. This was almost as bad as getting irradiated in the first place.

"You can't just yank me out. Production is still running. I have loose ends at the farm that have to get tied down."

Emma crossed her arms. "I'm not clearing you to drive or operate equipment. Hell, you can barely stand up."

"So have somebody run me out there, I'll take care of shutting the place down for the duration. Really, we can't leave the production system on automatic. If there's a malfunction—well, you don't want that. It's a safety issue."

"Nique's there." She closed down her computers and logged off the files. Mil could see this conversation was coming to an unsatisfactory end.

"She doesn't know the systems. Look, she's a smart girl, but she doesn't know the sequencing, the emergency procedures. I know how to shut everything down so there won't be an issue."

"How long will this take?" Emma wavered.

"An hour, maybe two. I'll be back in plenty of time to make the launch."

Emma looked deep into his eyes. "You better, mister." She keyed her wrist computer.

"Cross my heart," he said, crossing his fingers behind his back like a schoolboy lying to his mom.

She looked to the door of the exam room. "Well, it's not that I don't trust you, farm boy, but—"

The door opened and Med Tech First Class Isaak Rodriguez filled it with his hulking frame. Mil swallowed hard as he looked up at the giant bodybuilder, who towered fifteen centimeters over him.

"Ike, would you take Mr. Harrison out to his farm and bring him back in time for his launch? Ideally you should be back before Granger's memorial service. By thirteen thirty?"

Rodriguez smiled. "I would be honored, Doc."

Mil shot a questioning look to the doctor. "Memorial service?"

Emma looked to his eyes. "They are sending Micah home with full honors before he's taken aboard."

An hour later, Rodriguez and Mil were on the trail to his farm. The driver fidgeted and Mil tried to think, but the big guy's eyes kept flicking toward him and then away. "What?" Mil shook the exasperation out.

"Sorry."

They rode in silence for a half a klick.

"It's just that . . ." Rodriguez's voice trailed off.

"What?"

"I mean, it's just that . . . everybody knows you, but nobody ever sees you and, I dunno, here you are. Nobody will believe me."

"Here I am." Mil sighed back in his seat and watched the moon go by beyond the plexiglass window.

The big man half turned in his seat to face Mil. "Here's the deal. I am a big fan. I mean, none of us would be here if it wasn't for what you do. You're a pioneer. A legend."

"Kid, all that takes is getting old. That's it. I do my job, stay out of the way, and am currently just trying not to die." Mil shifted in his suit. The legend's new adult diaper was riding up.

"But you went and got Granger. That's serious hero shit. Nobody does that."

"For good reason."

"I mean, yeah, it looks like it wiped you out. And if they're sending you to Osaka, that's heavy, but still what you did. Damn, man."

"Um, yeah. Thanks."

They crested the hill and the farm filled the windshield. Rodriguez waved a hand ahead. "And all this? Exceptional, man."

Mil tapped on his wristy and Emma's face filled the screen. "Everything okay?"

"Checking in. Just wanted to let you know we're approaching the farm." He toggled the audio to his comms earpiece.

She smiled. "He asked specifically if he could help."

"And I really appreciate it. I do." Mil nodded to Rodriguez.

"Hurry back." She grinned and the screen went dark.

"Oh yes." Mil watched the familiar craters and boulders roll by. Perhaps for the last time?

Rodriguez trailed behind like a puppy as Mil gingerly made his way through the farm, holding the tech's arm for support and pausing to sit and catch a breath as they went through the facility, shutting off lights, powering down equipment, and unplugging chargers on various vehicles and remotes. The winded old man nodded agreeably as the big man chattered away about his own career in the medical division and the challenges of being a med tech first class and how he'd once saved the life of a trainee who had failed a simulation in the water tank in Russia.

"That must have been a scary situation," Mil said as he grasped the door frame to steady himself and stepped through the airlock from the barn to the main house.

"It was! We had less than four minutes—that's how long the brain can survive without oxygen."

"Say, son, would you mind grabbing that scanner on the workbench over there?" Mil was weary. He paused at the entrance and pointed back into the barn.

"The scanner? Yeah, sure. So, he had failed to secure one glove and when he got to the bottom of the tank, the seal blew and it filled his suit with wat—Mr. Harrison?"

Rodriguez paused and cocked his head as Mil secured the airlock from the house side of the chamber.

"Mr. Harrison. We have to get you back for the launch."

Through the porthole Mil put his hand to his ear and mimed not being able to hear. Rodriguez frowned. Then he angrily tapped his wrist computer.

"Really, Mr. Harrison? You're doing this?"

Mil tapped his own communicator and pointed to the controls on his side of the door. "Sorry, son, I need to rest a minute. Looks like there's a malfunction on the door circuit. It doesn't want to open. If I had that diagnostic scanner, I could test the circuit and see what the issue might be."

Rodriguez slumped to a seat at the workbench. "How long do we wait?"

"Launch window for the Earth shuttle closes in about three hours. If we get there about, oh, seventeen twenty, they'll have had to either launch without me or scrub it."

"They'll just put you on the next flight."

"I'll cross that crater when I get to it."

CHAPTER SIXTEEN

Tuesday . 14 Dec . 2077
1335 Lunar Standard Time
Loading Platform Alpha . Launch Pad 2 . Armstrong Base . Luna

———⚙——

The fading strains of bagpipes echoed through the cavernous loading facility as the last notes of "Amazing Grace" closed the memorial service. Vehicles had been moved out and instead of rows of incoming and outgoing cargo containers, Armstrong Base personnel filled two columns on either side of the vacated warehouse floor.

In the center aisle, a loading dolly hidden under a black drape supported Specialist Micah Granger's flag-covered coffin. Three meters behind it, a black lectern emblazoned with the Space Force logo was flanked by an arrangement of flags of the countries represented in the Luna Settlements.

The chaplain closed her book of scripture and nodded to the honor guard. At the rear left of the six pallbearers, Maddie Byers sniffed and stiffened her lip as she fought to stare straight ahead and not let the emotion of the moment crack her facade. Space Force officers did not show emotion in moments like this. Like the others on the honors detail, Maddie's class-A pressure suit gleamed in the bright lights of the cargo facility. She'd put in an extra level of polish out of respect for Micah.

The detail stood waiting, their faceplates raised, ready to be lowered before they escorted the cortege to the airlock and the waiting transvan that was serving as the hearse that would take Micah to his final flight.

Commander Desmond Rafferty stepped from the rows of formal Space Force uniforms and took his place beside his fallen officer. His dress blues contrasted with the workday environment of the receiving area. The gleaming panel of medals on his chest, the gold insignia on his collar, and the detail on the cuffs showed that this formal turnout was the highest respect a Space Force commander could show to a fallen comrade.

"At-ten hut!" Rafferty's voice was crisp, loud, and clear.

Maddie, the escort detail, and the entire congregation came instantly to attention. Maddie waited a heartbeat and then she and the five other pallbearers stepped to their assigned positions alongside the casket. The sterile box didn't connect with her memory of Micah laughing in the rec center, or Micah showing off in the gym, or Micah giving her a hard time during a lonely patrol. She was going to really miss the big lug. Tears began to well.

"Sah-lute!" Rafferty's voice broke.

A lone bugler in the rear of the facility brought his instrument to his lips and taps honored the fallen young man. Maddie blinked back the sorrow. On the other side of the coffin, a sniff escaped from one of her fellow pallbearers and the subtle sound cost Maddie her stoicism. A lone tear slipped down her cheek.

She sniffed again. Why Micah? Of all the people in Luna? The one genuinely good guy everyone liked.

As the mournful tune ended, Maddie turned to the casket and locked reddened eyes with her counterpart. They removed the flag, snapped it tight and folded it in perfect unison. The lead astronaut presented the flag to Rafferty with a salute.

"Detail. Secure for departure."

Maddie and her colleagues' gloved hands went to their helmets. Visors were lowered and secured into place. Green systems status readouts flickered across her faceplate.

The inner airlock door rose, and the six astronauts guided the dolly through and paused as the inner door closed behind them.

Rafferty swallowed hard and executed a perfect turn to the assembled congregation.

"Company. Dismissed."

Two rows from the back of the congregation, Nique relaxed and whispered to Eli standing beside her: "Did you see Yamamoto? I thought she and Micah were tight?"

Eli scanned the assembled personnel as knots of people began to drift away from the service.

He and Nique shuffled along with the crowd. "She's pretty torn up. Feels it should have been her out there to get him. They were same class at the academy. I think she's working."

Nique frowned. "When I asked Rafferty if I could readjust my schedule to see my grandfather off, he said it was taken care of. You think she took my shift?"

"That's Yammy. Trying to be tough, not show emotion, because that's weakness and she never wants to be seen as weak."

"So you miss your friend's funeral?"

"Rather than show tears in public? Yeah, she'd sign up to work the command center instead of that." He paused a moment, still looking around. "I don't see your grandfather anywhere either."

"I'm sure Dr. Wilkerson has him on hold as part of prepping for the flight. Besides, I can't see him doing anything like this—too many people. Too much emotion."

They followed the thinning crowd to the arch-topped hallway leading back to the main dome. Large windows punctuated the white walls of the corridor offering a view of the launch and landing pads.

Nique paused to watch the hearse creep toward the waiting Earthbound rocket. "You're the ops guy—what happens next? Is there a set schedule for things like this? Help a newbie out."

"I hate to say it, but they'll handle Micah like cargo. That loads first, then they start fueling and load passengers and pilots. Once they start, that takes about a half hour, and then they're off."

"So to see Grandad and Maddie off, when should we be at the departure area?"

"We've got a couple of hours. But then I've got duty."

Nique watched the hearse pull out of sight. "So we've got a little time. You want to go get a cup of coffee? Or something?"

Eli studied her profile as she watched the window. "Or something?"

Tuesday . 14 Dec . 2077
1500 Lunar Standard Time
Departure Prep Area . Armstrong Base . Luna

"You two be good." Maddie pulled her helmet out of her carry bag and began to polish the inside of the faceplate. She looked up at her friends gathered in the departure ready room.

"I think we will," Eli said as he and Nique shared a look.

"He means, of course we'll make sure to maintain the level of professional excellence Armstrong comms has reached during your tenure."

"Sure he does." Maddie winked. "Speaking of comms—let's see how Yammy's doing, minding the store." She toggled the switch on the comms cap she'd been wearing since early that morning. "Byers on comms. Radio check."

"Byers, Armstrong control. Radio check, loud and clear." Yamamoto's reply boomed through the room speakers and Maddie dialed down the volume.

"Tell her thanks for covering my shift." Nique appreciated getting to see Maddie off. And her grandfather. She'd miss them both.

"Sounds like you've got it handled, Yammy. Nique says thanks!"

"Affirmative. Armstrong out."

"She's taking this really hard. You guys look in on her, okay?"

Maddie pulled her gloves tight and connected them to her flight suit sleeves.

"Of course," Eli said.

A launch crew specialist stuck his head in the ready room door. "Lieutenant Byers, we're ready for boarding."

"Finally." Maddie stowed her helmet cover in its pocket on her auxiliary oxygen pack and connected the hose. She donned her shining helmet and snicked the locking ring in place.

"Well guys, it's been fun." Maddie gave hugs and then stepped to the door. "Give me a call next time we're all on the same planet."

She turned and nearly bumped into Commander Rafferty coming through the door. He pointed an accusing finger at Nique. "Rivera. Come with me."

Tuesday . 14 Dec . 2077
1755 Lunar Standard Time
Departure and Receiving Lounge . Armstrong Base . Luna

Rafferty paced in front of the wide view window overlooking the distant main landing pad that served Armstrong Base. The waiting rocket was off-gassing steam as the O2 continued to vent, marking the time it waited for launch. He glared into the window and checked the large countdown clock on the far wall. The clock had been holding a T-minus ten minutes for most of the last hour.

Nique stepped to him. "Sir, he's not answering my calls, and Dr. Wilkerson can't reach her tech. I'm starting to worry, sir."

Rafferty stroked his goatee. "I'm sure he's fine, Lieutenant. This isn't the first time he's pulled a stunt like this." He turned to the wall of windows, focusing his anger on the crew compartment atop the launch vehicle and said to no one in particular, "I'll kill the sunuvabitch."

"Do you want me to go and get him, sir?"

"If he won't take your call, he's not going to be walking through our airlock."

"Yes, sir."

Fifteen minutes later, Nique's wristy buzzed and Maddie's smiling face appeared. "Did they find him? We're about to lose our launch window."

Nique stepped to the room's farthest window and whispered. "I think you're going without him. I heard launch control call off the hold. Rafferty's pissed."

"He's still in departure? He's usually there when a transport leaves. But not this long."

"He's still in full class-A uniform. Honors for Micah. It's so sad. Somber."

They were interrupted by the intercom. "Fuel load complete. Sixty seconds on mark. Mark. All nonessential comms closing. Vehicle to autonomous control."

"We better sign off. Have a great trip! Thanks for everything!" Nique smiled into her wristy.

Maddie waved a gloved hand from the screen. "You'll do great. See ya!"

Nique punched off the call and stepped to the window to watch the liftoff. Rafferty joined her.

"This is the first Luna launch I've seen in person," she said.

It took Rafferty out of his anger for a moment. He remembered his own early fascination with launches. "It's not like Earth. No big billowing clouds of steam. No bone-rattling roar. A few sparks from the ignitors and then it's up and out."

"Launch commit. Thirty seconds . . ." the anonymous public address voice stated.

Behind him, Mil and his giant babysitter approached slowly. The old man couldn't help the wry smile he wore. "You really do come out for every launch."

Rafferty turned slowly, trying hard not to let his anger drive the response. "You're a real asshole, you know that?"

On the far wall, the countdown clock ticked down the final few digits.

Rodriguez examined the floor. "I'm really very sorry, sir."

"I'm more than certain it's not your fault, Rodriguez. I should have seen this coming." Rafferty locked his eyes on Mil's smug expression. "I feel a great need to kick your ass."

Mil chuckled. "I'm a very sick old man, you should show some respect."

"Right. When the doc finds out you're not on that shuttle, you'll think sick is just a minor inconvenience."

Mil nodded to the shuttle venting gasses into the black lunar sky as the PA system counted down the final numbers. "Who got my seat?"

"Nobody." Rafferty glared. "We're deadheading an empty seat worth millions back to Earth because of your little stunt. Maddie Byers is going home for R and R since Nique's here." He nodded at the lieutenant watching at the window.

She turned at the mention of her name.

"And you're here to say bye?" Mil asked.

"I'm here to see you off, old friend. And because Specialist Granger's body is being transported to Houston for an autopsy prior to internment with full honors. That's more than enough to warrant my attention," he explained to the small child in the old-man suit.

Mil winced. "Granger's on this trip? I didn't realize . . ."

Nique crossed her arms. "Grandad, this is not the smartest thing you've ever done."

"Well, I certainly didn't intend to hold up his return. I didn't know." Mil's hand went to his chest in a failed attempt at pleading ignorance.

Nique glared at him. "You didn't ask either. Stop me if you've heard this before, but everything is not always about you."

The moment of rebuke was broken only by the beep of the last countdown tone. By reflex, everyone turned to watch the thrusters ignite. The shuttle paused a heartbeat, then slowly began to rise from the pad. Nique leaned toward the window. Rafferty had been right. There was no smoke or flame; the craft seemed lifted by some invisible hand, the colorless plume from the engine bell pushing it away from the gantry, past the top of the tower, and into the blackness of space.

Suddenly the rocket shuddered, and an incredible silent fireball engulfed the craft and, a blink later, scattered it across the heavens.

CHAPTER SEVENTEEN

Tuesday . 14 Dec . 2077
1902 Lunar Standard Time
Departure and Receiving Lounge . Armstrong Base . Luna

he spectators froze in a stunned moment as realization of the horrific event shook them.

"Oh shit!" four voices said as one.

Rodriguez spun on his heel and sprinted, remarkably fast for a big man, toward the medical bay. Rafferty immediately keyed his wrist computer and began issuing orders as he charged to the command center, hot on the heels of Nique, who bolted ahead of him.

A shiver rocked Mil to his weakened core. The explosion ticked something deep in his memory. Something he'd locked away thirty-odd years before and vowed to never revisit. But now, the memory escaped its box.

The PA voice in the background of scrambling emergency crews brought Mil back to the worst moment of his life.

"We have lost contact with the vehicle."

He'd been in charge at the command center that day. It was to have been a simple course-correction burn on a typical Constellation crew transport flight. The type of flight from the moon back to Earth that had become so routine that no one even thought twice about it. This flight was taking his wife, Olivia, back to Earth for the final relocation arrangements. She'd be home on Earth for four weeks and then return to the newly christened Armstrong Base with their daughter. At that point, the Harrisons would set up house as Earth's first extraplanetary family.

But then the telemetry just stopped. One moment, the rocket had fired to realign the spacecraft to intersect Earth, the standard trans-Earth injection burn. There had been dozens of these trips, well over a hundred, as ships had gone back and forth between Earth and her moon and humans colonized Luna. There had never been a problem. But fifty-four seconds into a sixty-two-second burn, the flame of the rocket somehow reached the fuel tank on Mil Harrison's entire world.

"Repeat. We have lost contact with the vehicle."

The same words from that long-ago memory stunned Mil. He sank to a chair, one hand hunting for the arm for support. Beyond the protective bubble of the departure-area window, the cloud of debris and gases and humanity slowly drifted down from the blackness, the last rays of the late week's lunar sunset giving a mystical sparkle to the remains of the shuttle and the people on it. Flight 2705 had become a memory. It was now an Incident.

In his mind's eye, Mil remembered the smiling face of Maddie Byers sassing him about his broken spidertruck. She had a bright smile and had become a friend and mentor to his granddaughter. He wondered if Maddie had someone somewhere watching. Waiting. And Granger's family? Mil knew the heart-wrenching pain of never having the closure of a loved one to bury. A massive heaviness came over his exhausted frame.

"Emergency Response Team to stations. ERT to stations."

The relentless PA had been calling out instructions, but years of training made Mil hear this above the rest. He struggled to rise from the chair, put one foot in front of the other to go and do his duty. His most personal disaster had created the Emergency Response Team, and he had vowed it would be able to find answers in these situations. Because, more than anyone, he knew the need for those answers. And the emptiness of questions that lingered still.

The command center crew was working through emergency procedures when the door opened and Mil shuffled into the room, wheezing, one hand on the wall for support.

Rafferty glared. "I can't wait for you, old man. If you can't help, stay the hell out of the way."

Mil was huffing. "You need an Emergency Response Team right this instant and . . ."

He gripped the door frame as he struggled through, his breath deserting him. At the consoles working their way through the protocols were Kieran Yamamoto and Jaden Bohannan, two members of Mil's team. Yamamoto bluntly spoke their minds. "We got it, Harrison."

Behind him the doors opened, and Eli stepped to his workstation. He gave a concerned look. "Mr. Harrison, you should be in sickbay."

Bohannan didn't even give him that much thought as he ran through the checklists of procedures to secure the accident site and keep all personnel in place during the investigation that they had just launched. Rafferty looked at his command crew. Years of Mil's diligent training was overtaking emotions as the Emergency Response Team put their personal feelings aside and concentrated on their respective jobs, taking over the processes they'd prepared for in so many drills.

Mil wilted into an empty chair at the back of the room, watching as Nique handled the communications with Earth while the "kids" of his response team ran through action items like clockwork. His thought was not that of a mentor's pride at the efforts of his trainees; it wasn't mourning for the lost, or concern over the disaster, but rather the conceited wash of realization that he was no longer necessary to their efforts. He hung his head. Maybe it would have been better if he'd been onboard.

As the messages flew between Luna and Earth, and the situation transitioned from a disaster to an event to be managed by professionals who had prepared for this exact possibility, Mil heaved himself from the chair and slipped out of the command center. He shuffled his way back to the medical facility, using the corridor walls all too frequently for support.

The shock that faced him when he walked through that door was one he hadn't anticipated. Emma stared at him through wide teary-eyed amazement.

"You missed the shuttle."

She threw her arms around him in a hug that very nearly knocked them both to the floor.

She choked back the emotion. "Oh my God. I thought you were . . . I just knew I'd put you on . . . dammit, Mil, how are you not . . .?"

"I'm a hard guy to kill," he wheezed, not as certain about the statement as it sounded.

"Jesus."

"Doubt he had much to do with it."

"Are they doing emergency response? Why aren't you there?" It was reflexive. She caught herself as soon as she said it and stepped back.

Mil sank to the side chair and looked up like a pitiful pup. "Yeah. It seems they don't need any help from the sick, lame, or lazy. Those kids are pros, they know what they're doing."

"That wasn't what I meant."

"Yes, it was. Needed to be said. I'm not worth a damn here and I should have been on that shuttle. Might have been better for all involved."

The doctor pointed an angry finger. "You need to decide if you're going to suffer from survivor's remorse or just a good old-fashioned pity party. You can't do both."

"Sorry."

"Are you really? That might be a first." She held an angry stare.

Her comms console beeped an interruption. She turned back as the Command Center videoed in with the news and the standby for the medical teams. It didn't appear there were any injuries to deal with, but protocol dictated they be on alert.

He watched distantly as the doctor and command center discussed what the medical services staff could do in this emergency. He knew the procedures. He knew they'd be tied up for hours. He knew that he was not needed. Mil quietly rose and trudged unnoticed out the door and into the deserted hallway.

CHAPTER EIGHTEEN

Thursday . 23 Dec . 2077
1915 Lunar Standard Time
Harrison Station . Luna

L iquor wasn't a part of life on the moon. It was a luxury item and particularly expensive to transport, but the Russian contingent that came to Luna believed that life without vodka was just survival. Mil had learned this firsthand from Dimitri Litinov during the Russian's time in command of Armstrong Base. Dimitri was also a widower and they'd bonded over their shared broken pasts, their commitment to duty, and a passion for the game of chess. They were also both engineers who liked to tinker and had long ago built a still in the corner of the barn. When Dimitri was tapped to command the Mars mission and rotated back to Earth, Mil promised to grow a few potatoes and keep it going for the occasional Russians who would visit.

Truthfully, Dimitri was the only Russian who ever visited, and his last trip through had been several years prior. But like Mil's oxygen systems, as long as he occasionally supplied feedstock, the distillery worked its magic day and night. Mil had liters of the worst vodka ever distilled aging in his barn. His Russian friend would appreciate that for all their hard work building the still, it wasn't going to waste; he mostly used the end result to clean the hydraulics filters on the spidertruck. Dimitri stood to attention and held the shot glass ceremonially in front of him.

"To lost comrades."

Mil didn't stand but gave as respectful a salute as his condition allowed.

Dimitri knocked back the liquor and clapped the empty shot glass to the breakfast bar in Mil's small galley. He pronounced, "That is a fine spirit!"

"And you are as bad a liar as ever."

"Is true. It tastes like parts cleaner." The Russian broke into a broad grin. "So tell me, how does one get four grays of radiation and live to tell the tale?"

He slid a rook across the chessboard between them on the small bar that doubled as Mil's desk, kitchen table, and game room.

"I'm not so sure about the last part just yet. Emma has me so doped up I don't know Mars from Venus." He studied the board through somewhat foggy vision.

"Honestly my friend, you should go to Earth. Take the treatment. Get yourself well."

"You know, the last time this happened, they wouldn't let me go to Earth and I fought them tooth and nail."

Dimitri puzzled over his next move, then paused. "The last time? I didn't know there had been another incident. When was that?"

"The Constellation explosion. The one that took . . . Olivia." His throat got a little tight. "Bailey was just a kid on Earth and she needed her dad. But they wouldn't let me go. Wouldn't let anything get out of here. Bastards stopped every flight out—I couldn't get home. God, I cussed them. Yelling and pushing to get back there to her."

His jaw took a set, remembering the battles over the secure communications network. He'd tried everything—cajoling, threatening, yelling, commanding, resigning. Nothing worked. "Bunch of chair warmers on Earth deciding what's best for people out here on the edge. Sons of bitches."

Dimitri watched Mil go back there. He left a bishop exposed, and the Russian shook his head, taking the piece with his rook. "Your mind is elsewhere, my friend."

Mil searched the board and grimaced. "Yeah, that wasn't brilliant."

"So, is there an ETA on lifting the launch embargo yet?" Dimitri's hand hovered over the board.

"They'll do a full-up board of inquiry. Once they have a clue and can rule out something that affects the entire class of launch vehicles, they'll resume. It's deep, but nowadays the AI can do those sims in hours and days—back then it took weeks and months."

Mil paused a second, collecting his thoughts, and his gaze went to his VR goggles on the shelf across the room. "You ever have any interest in the EZs when you were here, Dim?"

Mil took the rook with a bishop and sprung the trap.

"The EZs? Of course—who doesn't. We went to the Apollo 11 zone back when they did the big centennial celebration. I got close enough to see the footprints. It was a very emotional visit. Those men had *myachi*."

"*Myachi*?"

"Balls. Landing a rickety craft like that old Grumman LEM, manually. With less than fifteen seconds of fuel left? That took *myachi*."

"Agreed. But what about the other zones? The ones that aren't Apollo or historical?" Mil eyed his empty shot glass and paused while he considered his old friend, before crossing a line. "Like, say, Slayton Ridge."

Dimitri was focused on the board. "No clue. It wasn't something I was briefed on or ever thought about."

"That seems to be the prevalent thinking."

Dimitri shuffled a pawn across to take the other bishop and Mil cursed under his breath.

"You have found something. Is that what got you irradiated?"

"In a way. There's something classified in the zone and whatever it is cooked the guy who went to investigate. His body was on the shuttle."

"Not good."

"I was supposed to be on it too."

Dimitri refilled their glasses. "It is good luck."

Mil shook his head. "I better hold off on that. Too many meds."

Dimitri shot his glass back and slid a knight a few squares. "More for me. So you think there is something hidden on Slayton Ridge?"

"Oh, I know there's something hidden. I just don't know what it is. Or why it's hidden and classified." Mil moved a knight out and across. "Or why someone might sabotage a return vehicle to make all the clues disappear."

Dimitri raised his eyes from the board. "Sabotage. That is a bold accusation."

"Yeah. And I don't have anything other than a hunch and set of convenient circumstances that add up to a neat coincidence. But it feels a lot like there is something on Slayton Ridge that someone, somewhere, wants to stay hidden."

Dimitri nodded his understanding. "I could check. I carry enough clearance to get into some places where others would be questioned."

"I don't think you should risk it. Nique poked around and got her wrist slapped." Mil moved the knight again, but he didn't know if he was chasing or baiting.

"She is young and doesn't know how far she can push the rules. Tell me that's not what got her pulled from the *Humanity* crew compliment? She trained well. Surely her mother would have intervened on her behalf."

The Russian moved a knight of his own. Mil frowned.

"I think her mother is the most likely candidate to pull her off the crew. I thought she was going to Mars. She thought she was going to Mars. Then all of a sudden she's not, and believe me, she's pissed off about it." Mil stood with care and shuffled to his coffee machine and prepped a pod.

"Her mother? To avoid nepotism?"

Dimitri considered another shot of parts cleaner, watching his old friend creep through the house. A sad frown crept across his face, but still, he took Mil's remaining knight.

"Possibly. She's in a position to do it, but I don't know why she would pull that at such a late stage."

"She has been mentioned several times for the vice presidency. She wouldn't play politics with her own daughter?"

"Beats me. She hasn't spoken to me in almost fifteen years. I don't know if I'd even recognize her."

Dimitri shot back his drink and nodded to the board.

Mil was checkmated.

Thursday . 23 Dec . 2077
2105 Lunar Standard Time
Mess Hall . Armstrong Base . Luna

"To Maddie Byers." Eli stood at the head of the table, his glass aloft.

"To Maddie." A half dozen toasters raised their salute. Nique looked to their small clique. They'd taken over a corner of the commissary lounge for an impromptu memorial.

"And Micah." Kieran Yamamoto held her toast a moment longer.

"And Micah," Eli repeated. "Of course."

"Captain Townsend and First Officer Devuney as well," Jaden Bohannan reminded the group.

They tossed back their espressos and sat back down in somber silence. It lasted less than a minute.

"I can't do this." Kieran stood up. "I'm not sitting around waiting to see who dies next. This is a part of what we do. This is a dangerous job in a dangerous place, and we all know it. We face it. We handle it. We move on." She walked to the door.

Nique watched her go. "Wow." She looked to the table where her colleagues nodded.

"She's a tough nut," Eli said, and there were more nods. But then it seemed that she'd touched a nerve with the others at the table.

"She's harsh. But she's not wrong. I have to get going." Jaden rose and made his way to the exit. The others around the table followed the lead, one by one they each made a brief excuse and drifted away. Then it was just Eli and Nique.

"You staying? Want another?" He looked to her eyes.

She nodded. "Yeah, I'm off duty. Grandad is home and he's been a bear since all this happened. I'm good sticking around here for a while."

He brought back two cups.

"Did you ever talk to your mom?"

"She won't even take my calls. Ignores messages." Nique took a sip of her coffee. "Sorry. I'm whining. We're not here for the poor pitiful me show. I'll stop."

"I don't blame you. I'd be pissed." He looked through the oversize window that made up the wall of the lounge area and waved his coffee at the moonscape beyond. "I mean, forget the fact that she's the administrator, that she can even make a call on who's on the crew. She's your effing mom."

"I know, right? If your kid had left the planet, even just to go to the moon, you'd want to hear from her to know she'd made it okay. That she didn't need anything out there on a completely different celestial body." Side-eye glances from others in the lounge told Nique she was getting a little loud. She ducked her head.

Eli nodded. "To be fair, she'd have a pretty good idea if something had happened. She has access to all types of data on who is where and when."

"Yeah. But still, it'd be nice to think she was interested." She stared out at the barren gray dust and the ink-black sky. "Why is my entire family so screwed up?" She broke the stare and looked at him. "What's your family like? Tell me they're normal."

His eyebrows went up. "Pretty normal. My folks are growers. Farmers. The family business is brussels sprouts. Acres and acres of 'em."

"Yech."

"That's a pretty typical reaction. But it is a great incentive to leave home."

"That's why you became an astronaut?"

"Sorta. My uncle was a crop duster. Taught me to fly way before I was legal. When I got my private license at sixteen, the instructor signed my ticket, and I went out and did barrel rolls. But it was always going to be Space Force." He took a sip of his coffee. "You're not the only one disappointed about not going to Mars."

Her gaze wandered around the room. Most of the people there were settling for Luna assignments when they all wanted to be posted for a position going to Mars. She'd been closer than anyone. And her family—her grandfather and her mother—screwed that up.

"Hey." He touched her arm. "You want to get out of here? I've got a new VR game that I haven't installed yet. I could sneak you into my quarters and we could try it out."

She considered the proposition for less than a heartbeat. "Let's do that. I'm already on double-secret probation. Might as well give Mom something to really get a bug up her butt about."

CHAPTER NINETEEN

Sunday . 26 Dec . 2077
0650 Mountain Standard Time
White Sands Spaceport . New Mexico . USA . Earth

Bailey Rivera's fair complexion contrasted with the shock of coal-black hair that tended to drop into her blue-gray eyes. She grunted as the G-forces pressed her back into the seat of the lumbering Boeing Lockheed lifting craft as it accelerated down the New Mexico runway. The robotic mothership would get them to forty thousand feet before the jarring release of their transorbital craft. That would trigger another giant kick in the butt as the six vacuum-rated boosters fired to push the cargo and passenger vehicle quickly through Max-Q, out of the Earth's gravity and onto a rendezvous orbit with the space station.

Post-release, the heavy lifter would circle back to the White Sands Spaceport. Later that same afternoon it would repeat the process to carry more cargo, passengers, and fuel to staging at the orbiting space station. Some of that cargo and a few of the passengers would travel on to the moon.

And one day soon, if Bailey had her way, Mars.

Bailey's craft carried little cargo, mostly luggage for her ten-person Tiger Team of accident investigators. She was taking personal charge of this accident investigation, and she'd act as spokesperson to the press, having long been one of the most visible members of the Space Agency outside of the astronauts, cosmonauts, and taikonauts that made up the crews.

Her dataslate chimed. She frowned and tapped the screen. "Good evening, Sophia."

"Good evening. I'm checking in to make sure you don't want me to try and push this interview." Sophia Loggia had been the Space Agency's public information officer for most of Bailey's time there. They were colleagues but not friends.

"Want you to? Hell, yes. Can you? No. We need to be out in front of this. Transparency is paramount right now."

"Just checking. Stand by for the show producer."

"Obviously, when we scheduled this interview, Mrs. Rivera, we had no idea you'd be on your way to Armstrong Base to lead the investigation into the Disaster of Flight 2705." On her screen, Ian Fellowes folded his hands. He canted his head slightly to reveal the BBC/Sky logo behind him.

He left a pause for her to jump into the conversation, but Bailey didn't comply. She was going to give this interview, but she'd make Ian earn his money.

"This event carries a higher profile than the incidents that most of your teams investigate," he continued. "Is that why you're so visible on this?"

"We lost three crew members. Ian. That's more than enough reason for me to be there. The safety of our people and the vehicles they crew is of paramount importance to everyone in the agency."

"That's a big hit to your safety record."

"The agency has an almost perfect safety record. And when you compare us to virtually any other form of transportation, we're as safe as you can get from one place to another on a per passenger mile basis."

"Yet three people died onboard your craft this week."

"And our thoughts and prayers are with their family and friends. This investigative team will determine what caused the event and form the basis for any corrective actions that need to be taken." She gave a proper nod to show her condolences.

"Your own mother died in a space flight explosion." Ian smiled as she flinched ever so slightly.

You bastard. Bailey smiled a mask. "Is that a question?"

"You were twelve years old when your mother was tragically killed in a malfunctioning spacecraft. Does that give you any special insight into the emotional tragedies those families are experiencing?"

"You mean, Was it hard for me as a girl to lose my mom? Yes, Ian. Yes, it was. It was also the genesis of the protocols we established with grief counseling and survivor support services. I know the personal impact these families are feeling."

"Is that what drove you into space flight as a career? The loss of your mother? Your father is the longest-serving resident of the Luna Colony, and yet I see very little about your relationship with him in either the press or the background materials your office provided in advance of this interview."

"My father lives on the moon and I live on Earth. It's difficult for us to get together for dinner." She knew this was going to be a topic and knew how she'd deal with it.

"Some people say you're almost completely estranged. That you never speak."

"We are on completely different schedules, timetables, and we have all-consuming work situations. He does his work and I do mine, and we interact when possible."

"A source told us that's been over ten years. Is that estrangement a by-product of the loss of your mother?"

"Ian, I thought we were here to talk about background information on mankind's first steps on the planet Mars."

"Touché. But this has been your life's work. Our viewers want to know more about the life behind that work." He smiled and she wanted to smack him through the screen.

"It's not just my life. Generations of Space Agency personnel have been planning this mission since back in the days of old NASA. It's going to open the gateway to exploration of this solar system and the stars beyond. This is the realization of humanity becoming a multi-planet species."

"Your daughter, Dr. Monique Rivera, was scheduled to be on the *Humanity* crew, but she's been reassigned. Can you tell us about that?"

"It's a standard crew evaluation. Lieutenant Riviera is an outstanding astronaut but had a slight protocol issue. We're assessing her for assignment to a later flight."

"That sounds very much like a well-crafted PR line. Is it because she's your daughter and you're concerned about rumors of nepotism?"

"Lieutenant Riviera is an exceptional pilot with a PhD in astrophysics to go with her electrical engineering degree. She's among the most-qualified candidates to ever enter the astronaut office."

"Spoken like a proud mother."

"I am."

"Where were you when you lost your mother?"

Bailey flinched again. He'd caught her off guard and gotten the response he'd wanted. She paused a moment. "I'm sorry Ian, we had a little comms drop out there. Could you repeat that?" Beyond her viewport the sky darkened as they approached the boundary between Earth's atmosphere and the harsh reality of space.

"Yes, I'm sure." He tapped the dataslate he hid behind, a signal his viewers knew he'd found a nerve on one of his hundreds of interview victims. "Where were you when your mother passed?"

Bailey stared into the camera. *Okay, fine.* That morning was etched on her soul. "Economics class at Eisenhower High. Mr. Stapleton's class. The principal and two other people came and pulled me out of class. They told me my mother had been killed and my grandparents were on their way to get me."

Her words were cold and detached. An emotionless recounting of a moment she'd relived ever since. She stared into space. Remembering.

"High school? You were twelve years old. Is that typical in America?"

"I was a smart kid."

"So, you and your father, then. He remained on the moon."

"He couldn't come home. Well, to Earth. Launches from Luna were embargoed. He was the facility commander at Luna then. He couldn't have left to come home if he'd wanted." She bit the last words off.

"Did he want to?"

"You'll have to ask him."

The pilot's voice interrupted his next question. "Folks, howdy from the flight deck. Everything is proceeding nominally. Wanted to give you a heads-up we're about two minutes from the drop. We'll count you down at T-minus ten." The autonomous craft's recorded pilot's message was intentionally homespun meant to be reassuring. For Bailey, the casual attitude implied a lack of professionalism that irked her. She made a note to have that changed when they returned to Earth.

"Ian, we may have to pick this up another time. We're on final for orbit insertion. There may be a significant amount of interference. If you'll coordinate with Sophia, I'm sure we can finish this up."

Ian smiled as a wave of distortion rippled across the screen. "I'll do that. Have a good flight." Then the transmission dropped out.

Around the cabin, various members of the Tiger Team buckled back into the helmets they'd removed after takeoff and tightened their belts. A minute later, following the expected countdown, the vehicle's frame transmitted a series of mechanical clunks, followed by the weightlessness of the drop as the ship fell away from the carrier. The anticipated pause—it always seemed too long to Bailey—then the head-snapping jolt as the thrusters kicked in. The rocket angled up through the edge of the atmosphere and blue sky faded to the black of space. She laid her head back and closed her eyes, and from nowhere the image of her father waiting there on the moon came to her: the Millennium Harrison of her childhood, laughing. The father she wished might have stayed. The father he was before the accident left him bitter and distant. Before he'd chosen to work alone, away from all humanity. Before he'd kept her on Earth to grow up and apart. Before he had sent her away because . . . well, she really didn't know why.

They were supposed to be the great experiment. The Harrisons: the first family living off Earth. Could there be permanent settlements on the moon? Could you raise a family and live a semi-normal existence a quarter of a million miles away from all forms of human contact?

Bailey smirked. *Yeah. That experiment had failed miserably. Publicly. Personally. Hideously.* "Catastrophic engine failure," the accident report read. Bailey knew every line of that report by heart. They'd even studied the disaster in her classes when she got to college at Rice. What a treat that had been. Sitting in the lecture hall through the detached repetition of forensic facts—the damaged seal on the fuel line, the resulting explosion fifty-six seconds into the one-minute trans-earth injection burn, the flaming pieces of the vehicle scattered across space between the earth and its moon. If the booster had stayed together for a mere four seconds longer, her entire life would have been different.

Instead, what she remembered were the seven raw days for a tweenage girl, alone with her grandparents, as the wreckage traversed the emptiness. Then finally, on a Sunday evening, the entire world watched in morbid fascination as the remains of the craft and crew returned to Earth, turning into dozens of dramatic fireballs entering the atmosphere and incinerating over ten thousand square miles of the Indian Ocean.

Mom.

Launches from the moon were embargoed until they could discover what had gone so horribly wrong. Eleven months later they knew. A metal fatigue issue. No one's fault. Unpredictable. But her father vowed to predict such issues in the future At first they talked a few times a week, but that stuttered into a weekly call and then at odd times during a month. His job was too important. He was the leader of the lunar community. He made the breathable air, and without him, the entire settlement might die. He had to stay on the moon, he told her. He was heading the lunar side of the investigation to make sure nothing like this ever happened again. And it hadn't. Until now.

She looked to her viewport and out into the blackness of space.

The moon, even space, her father had said back then, was not yet safe enough for a little girl and that she'd be better cared for on Earth. He loved her, and someday she'd understand.

But that day never came. She understood only that for some reason her father had decided that his work and the moon were more important than she was.

CHAPTER TWENTY

Tuesday . 28 Dec . 2077
0805 Lunar Standard Time
Harrison Station . Luna

Sitting on the edge of his bunk, Mil thought he felt better. He didn't hurt all over like he had for the last few days. And there seemed to be a little more strength. He peeled the medpatch from his arm and replaced it with a fresh one. He rose and walked, rather than shuffled, to the galley and poured his ritual morning cup of coffee.

"Nique?" he called to the empty apartment. "You here?" Nothing.

The blinking light on his dataslate charger told him messages had arrived while he slept. A note from his granddaughter that she had left early for a duty shift. He tapped the dataslate surface again, and Rafferty's stern face filled the screen. He was still angry.

"The Tiger Team arrives at eleven hundred. Pad One. They've requested you be there." The screen blanked out, but the message light remained.

He was popular this morning. He tapped once again.

It was Emma. "Hey farmboy. Checking on you. I need the blood-sample data you didn't send yesterday. If you see this before you eat, shoot me a fasting sample, will you? Love you, bye."

At least she wasn't pissed at him. Her smiling face faded to a blank screen and his calendar of appointments and things to do appeared. It was empty. Final deliveries made. Equipment powered down. Production suspended for the foreseeable future.

The last note was from Nique. She was on a date with Eli and would be back "later." A date? When did that happen? Where the hell did kids go for a date on the moon?

He stepped to the personal hygiene area of his quarters. He stripped, and a quick tap on the wall converted the tiny closet into a space for what his bunkmates at the academy sixty years earlier had called the "Triple S:" shit, shower, and shave. He pulled a small kit from a wall compartment and inserted his finger. He grimaced annoyance as the lancing device stabbed, then set off a series of beeps that transmitted his blood data to the powers that be for analysis. Another tap and the shower jets wet him down with recycled water at precisely 40.55 degrees Celsius. He was halfway through rubbing down his face with the battery-powered razor when Emma's call came through. He tapped the shaving mirror and the vidcall transferred there.

"Hey." He contorted his face into the mirror to shave.

"I can call back."

"Nah, I'm about done." He ground away the last of the whiskers. "What'd I do now?"

"Good news. Your white count has stabilized."

"Hey, that is good news."

"Do you even know what that means?"

"Nope, but I have developed complete faith in the medical profession. You say it's good news, so I'm not going to argue." He ran a hand across his face and stowed the razor.

"Not going to argue? I may have a wrong number; I was trying to reach Mil Harrison."

"You said to stay down and get well. You said you didn't have time to mess with taking care of me, so I've been doing it myself."

"That's not exactly what I said—"

"It's pretty damn close." He swished cleanser around his mouth and spat into the drain.

"I said you should go to Osaka because they have the best facilities and could care for you better than we can here. That's a little different."

"That's not what I heard."

"Why are we fighting about this?"

"This isn't fighting. This is disagreeing. Fighting involves fists and biting and head butting. You want fighting? Come out to the intake area at Pad One at eleven hundred."

"Bailey Rivera's Tiger Team. You're going?"

"According to Rafferty, my presence is required."

"Why?"

"He did not elaborate."

Mil had three hours before the Tiger Team arrived. He spent it the way he had spent the last several days: immersed in the research behind the virtual reality of Granger's VR recording of the mystery facility. He had paced the area and examined every centimeter of the interior. He had enabled the image of Granger's holographic body to walk him around the facility as Mil followed, investigating everything the young, doomed astronaut had focused on. He examined the orange columns and the corrosion on the floor. He scoured the walls, doors, and containment areas, went through the bunks and the desk. But the recording gave up little information.

He'd found precious few clues. One binder had the ghosted image of a circular mission patch on it. Old NASA was famous for commemorating every event with a logo, a patch or some form of graphic that was printed or embroidered everywhere. The inside joke had been that they didn't do many missions, but they made a helluva lot of merchandise. But this was the old Air Force and they were big on secrets. This was little more than a remnant of one bit of one little piece. He traced it with his fingertip.

The faded logo was a broken circle and the only thing Mil had been able to make out were the letters *S DD N HERC ES* and a graphic reminiscent of an STS orbiter. It created more questions than it answered. He shook his head in defeat. The old Space Transport System—the shuttle—could never have made it to the moon.

Mil roamed the room in his VR glasses, combing the walls and methodically checking every pixel he could for anything that would provide even small answers. As before, he removed the glasses and sat with little to show for three hours of research but a treatment-induced fatigue that he worried he might never beat. His wrist computer tapped his arm to remind him of the arrival of the Tiger Team. He headed for the barn and the road trip to the landing pad.

The receiving lounge at Pad One was packed. Spectators lined up behind the officials there to greet the director. The room was large by lunar standards, the domed ceiling arching down to walls and tunnel entries. One entry was sealed by an airlock with the robotic gantryway waiting beyond the door to connect the facility to the next arriving ship. Next to the airlock door, a row of large view windows allowed those who waited to watch the routine comings and goings of spacecraft destined for the space station in Earth's orbit.

Rafferty, Mil, and Emma stood off to one side while the usual complement of personnel readied the decon gateway and the clearance check-in area. The ever-present PA system announced final approach, and a couple of the newer residents of Armstrong Base leaned to the window, looking up to the heavens to see the retro fire that might be their first glimpse of an arriving spacecraft.

"This seems fast," Emma said.

"It's a hotshot flight. They don't layover at the station. Just transfer to the lunar shuttle and head here. Cuts fifteen hours off the transfer time." Mil looked to a young woman sitting by the window. Her chair looked extremely appealing.

"I wouldn't even wish the travel lag on you," Rafferty growled.

"Nah. They're pros. They'll deal with it." Mil had little use for the bureaucrats of the agency.

Emma chuckled. "You mean I'll deal with it. They'll all get neuromodulation patches to amp them up until their sleep cycles sync. Better living through pharmacology."

The young woman moved from her seat and Mil shuffled directly to it. He turned to sit down and the room spun around him.

"You okay?" His doctor lifted a concerned eyebrow.

"Yeah. I'm okay," he lied. "Just don't see any reason to stand around while they go through arrival."

Rafferty eyed the cantankerous old man, then said to his chief medical officer: "Is he up for this? Don't get me wrong, I'm completely fine with him being uncomfortable. But I don't need another dead person this week."

"Well, that's almost reassuring." Mil craned his neck to see the disembarking crew through the crowd.

"When was the last time you saw her?" Emma looked as well.

"It's been a while." He stood with a grunt and scanned the arrivals. He vaguely recalled Bailey's last visit to the farm. That quiet confrontation had been the culmination of years of pain. After her mother's death, they'd tried to make something work all through her teenage years, to build some form of family, but Mil had no idea how to handle an independent-minded young woman. They argued through their grief—she didn't care that his return to Earth had been held up by policies and procedures. He simply wasn't there. She blamed him for abandoning her to the care of her grandparents and boarding schools.

She'd visit the moon during summer breaks from overbearing headmasters, and each stay became more and more of a disaster. She processed her grief by diving into her studies, while he worked through his in the workshop. Together, but alone with the friction from their limited interactions rubbing open the old, raw wounds. It was easier not to talk at all when even mundane conversations escalated to raised voices and tears. Finally, she'd returned to Earth to create her own life. Without him.

A graduation announcement that he never received. A holiday vidcall that introduced a husband. A single baby vid when Nique was born. A colleague on Earth mentioning she'd divorced the husband and joined the Space Agency administration. And now she was here, as chief administrator. *Her mother would have been so proud*, he thought as the crowd of people parted for their leader's arrival.

He had been right about not recognizing his daughter. Instead, he saw his late wife. Emma turned toward him when he took a sharp, involuntary breath. His eyes locked on the tall woman with the black hair as she took charge of the entry and moved her team through. The resemblance was uncanny and it shook him.

"Hello, Mother." Mil swiveled to see an obviously angry Nique come to attention and deliver a wildly over-the-top salute to the civilian chief administrator.

"At ease, Lieutenant. That's not necessary." Bailey's familiar voice made Mil almost smile. He watched their interaction from across the room and Nique's defiant posture told him that this family trait hadn't been lost.

"Ma'am. Of course, ma'am. Sorry, ma'am." The salute popped down and Nique dropped her arms behind her, remaining perfectly erect, staring over her mother's head, as protocol demanded.

Bailey leaned close to her ear and whispered something.

"Where would the chief administrator like that time and place to be? I am certainly not going anywhere, ma'am." Nique's voice boomed and Mil's smile broke through.

Bailey scowled. "Not with an attitude like this, young lady."

Part of Mil appreciated the fact that Nique was standing up to injustice. But he was also the Luna Colony's foremost expert on the downside of baiting higher authority. He swallowed hard, stood, and made his way over.

"Hello, Bailey." His voice had a rasp to it.

Bailey turned and instantly tried to hide her shock. The reports on the explosion had used old file videos and the Mil Harrison she had pictured confronting was a vibrant man of action and intelligence. The elderly, silver-haired man teetering toward her in a flight suit two sizes too large shocked her. He was old, bordering on ancient, with hollow cheeks and pale skin that hung on his face.

"Hi." It was all she could think of until a prod from somewhere deep in the back of her brain kicked her. "Dad."

He nodded, appraising her. "You look good. For a moment, I thought you were your mother."

Bailey paused. She'd rehearsed this scene countless times: how she'd tell him off, how she'd release years of anger and fury and disconnection. But now, looking at the ghost of the man she'd prepared to blast with finely rehearsed rage, she—

"You know . . ." The old man looked around, interrupting her thoughts. "This was the last place I saw her. Your mom. This was the departure area back then. I gave her a hug and a kiss on the cheek and closed the latch on her helmet. She gave me a little wave as she and Donovan and Kendra Giles and Abe Goldman got in the elevator to the capsule."

His voice trailed off. The room was quiet. Everyone was looking at the three of them. Most knowing what this was, yet another private moment in the public eye for a family never meant for celebrity but pushed there by tragedy and circumstance. Mil looked around at the onlookers and shook his head, breaking the reverie.

"But that was a long time ago. You're here to do a job. Let's get out of this crowd."

And with that he turned and took a step toward the hallway to lead them out of the receiving lounge.

"Just a minute." Bailey stood where she was. She fired a withering glare at her daughter. The kind she usually reserved for congressmen questioning her budgetary requests. She turned to Mil. "I have something for you."

Mil stopped, his face questioning her. Bailey gave a half smile. She'd dealt with men of his generation all her life. When they said to do something, they expected everyone to simply accept their authority.

But she stood her ground.

She pulled her dataslate from her carry-on and tapped a few times on the screen.

Mil's wrist buzzed and he looked at it with a question.

"Millennium Edward Harrison: this is an official subpoena. You are required to appear before the investigating committee to provide complete and truthful testimony regarding the events leading up to the incident involving the destruction of Flight 2705. You have been served."

Bailey presented him her dataslate.

Mil cocked his head. "Huh." He skimmed the legalese on the dataslate and then copied it to his wrist. "That it? That why I'm here?"

Bailey nodded. Mil tapped the dataslate and handed it back.

"Guess I'll see you at the inquest." With that he walked out. By himself.

The room returned to the buzz generated by the arrival of the team. Bailey pointed the group to the various yeomen who would show them to quarters and then found herself confronted once again by her daughter.

"How could you?"

Bailey absently tapped her dataslate and shrugged her carry-on higher on her shoulder. "What?"

Nique rolled her eyes. Hard. "You haven't seen him in years! And the first thing you do is serve him a subpoena? No hug? No . . . nothing? I'm beginning to understand why you two don't talk."

"He's a material witness to a major disaster."

"He. Is. Your. Dad."

"This is not the time or the place for our personal interactions and discussion. We are here to do a job. So is he. He understands. You need to as well."

"Jesus, Mother! He understands you just implicated him in a major catastrophe." She waved to the shuttle craft cooling on Pad One.

"He's a witness; any implications will come out when he's deposed. That's all the more reason to keep personalities out of this. You need to come to an understanding of that immediately. We are professionals. Act like it."

"I don't think so. You're treating him like he's not even human. Both of us. Like we don't have any feelings at all. You cannot treat your family like this."

"Yes, I can. I've been on both ends of this situation. You and I will have a discussion about your personal situation soon, but it is not, and cannot be, my highest priority."

"Dr. Rivera?"

Both Nique and Bailey turned to see Dr. Emma. "Yes?"

Nique made the proper introductions, identifying Emma as "Granddad's friend and doctor." Bailey made the connection and Nique's glance confirmed that "friend" meant more than an acquaintance. Nique put a hand on her hip to let the awkward moment stew, but her mother was unfazed and led them out of the receiving area.

"I need to speak with you about your father's condition," Emma continued. "You are noted as his next of kin and his emergency medical contact."

"Next of kin? Doctor, that sounds as if his condition is life threatening."

"It is. And he doesn't appreciate the severity of that." Emma waved a hand around the lounge. "But I don't think this is the place for that conversation. I'd like to get on your calendar."

Bailey tapped her dataslate, and she and the doctor made arrangements. The chief administrator looked to her daughter. "Which way to the VIP quarters from here? This intake area has changed almost completely since I was here last."

Nique nodded to a hallway and led the march through the intersection of three passageways.

"They redid this entire module when the secondary landing platform was reworked three years ago," Emma explained.

"That's about right. It's been five years since I was here."

Emma frowned. "Mil said you hadn't seen each other in considerably longer than that."

"I came here for a series of meetings on the incident protocols we're implementing right now. But I didn't see him. I was busy. So was he."

Nique shot a look at her mother. "You came all the way to the moon and didn't even say hi? Damn, Mom. Please tell me this level of grudge holding isn't hereditary."

"Hey, did I ever miss any of your stuff? Dance recitals, piano, lacrosse? Graduations, birthdays? Anything?" The chief administrator never missed a step.

"You were always there," Nique admitted.

"I do understand what it's like to be a child and low priority in someone's life. Especially if it's your only parent." As they walked, Bailey multitasked through the messages that had piled up while they'd been disembarking.

"So you know why I'm mad."

"You're mad at me. I'm disappointed in you. We will find a time to get that sorted out, but there are a few things going on right now that are slightly larger in the grand scheme than your hurt feelings. You'll have to wait." Bailey paused. Perhaps it was the setting—the soft white lighting in the anonymous tunnel on the moon—but the sense of déjà vu hit her hard. Instantly she was back to the moment when her father had said that exact same sentence to her. She looked back to find Nique striding away in a huff.

Bailey sighed, then glanced at her dataslate. "Doctor, I assume you'd like to talk about getting him to Osaka?"

"I had intended to ask you to help coerce him into going willingly, but it sounds like I'm better off on my own."

Bailey signed off a memo and dashed it into cyberspace. "I wish you luck. He's bullheaded, stubborn, and egotistical to the point of not giving a shit what anyone else thinks. About anything."

Nique stopped and marched back to them. "He's also true to his word and as courageous as anybody has ever been. He's an inspiration to the crew here. He went out there by himself and got Granger. Almost eighty years old, and he left before anyone could help. He wouldn't say it, but he did that so no one else would get hurt. And it's nearly killed him. He's dependable. Everyone here breathes because of what he does. He's probably done more than anyone to make this base work."

She put her hands to her hips to end the argument and shot a look to the doctor for support.

Emma smiled. "I know both sides of him—the bullheaded grump who doesn't ever want to leave this rock and the man who still gives his all to keep this operation running. He won't admit it, but he cares about everyone here."

Bailey thought for a moment. "He's still an asshole."

CHAPTER TWENTY-ONE

Thursday . 30 Dec . 2077
0735 Lunar Standard Time
Aboard the *Humanity* . Standard Orbit . Luna

L itinov frowned at the display. Nothing. He had messaged his comrades at the Russian space federation asking for data on the Slayton Ridge Exclusion Zone. They turned up nothing.

It was classified by the Americans long before agreements and treaties and partnerships governed the moon, much less the current international effort to reach Mars.

For some reason it had never come up, and now, when he inquired, the official line was that something so old need not be a concern. Now, he was told, was the time to prepare for the next long leg of the journey to Mars. There might be time after *Humanity* was underway for some research or even conversations with the American archivists to see what warranted this, but officials in Moscow were not concerned.

Mars was worry enough.

He toggled the display to show the hearings that were taking place on Luna. The investigators were taking depositions from the witnesses and Mil Harrison was to be on next. Litinov rang for a packet of tea and dictated a report while he waited.

The tea arrived, and then moments later his emaciated friend stepped into the frame and took a seat at a conference table. Across from Mil, Bailey Rivera huddled with four members of the investigating team. She called the room to order and gestured to Mil.

Thursday . 30 Dec . 2077
0800 Lunar Standard Time
Secure Conference Room . Armstrong Base . Luna

"State your name for the record." Bailey looked as serious as if she were a prosecutor grilling a murder suspect.

"Dad." Mil was unimpressed. Two could play this game.

"Your given name, please."

"Millennium Edward Harrison." Mil paused for effect. "Commander, United States Space Force, retired." He sat a little straighter.

"Do you have any issue if the chair simply addresses you as Mr. Harrison?"

"None at all, Ms. Rivera." There was a dash of smug in the reply.

"Should I note in the record that you're a combative witness?"

"I don't even know what we're doing here, so I don't know if I'm combative or not."

Bailey consulted her dataslate. "Noted. Mr. Harrison, you were scheduled to be on Flight 2705 to return to Earth, why did you miss it?"

"I didn't want to go to Earth. I was more or less ordered to go, and travel was prescribed by my doctor. She sent a lab rat to fetch me."

"And you delayed the technician so as to miss the launch time?"

"I was in the barn. Working on shutting down equipment." Mil examined his fingernails.

"The technician's statement says you locked him out and refused to report for the transfer."

"Sounds about right. Hard to say. I'm an old man, and I've been pretty sick recently." Mil's face showed a small grin that nonetheless couldn't hide his aggravation with the circus.

"Did you have any reason to not want to be on Flight 2705?"

"I just said, I didn't want to go to Earth."

"You didn't have misgivings because you knew something might happen to Flight 2705?"

Mil frowned and his mind sped up. His eyes narrowed.

"What exactly are you implying, Bailey?" The temperature in the room dropped ten degrees.

"It just seems remarkably convenient that you missed this flight. There hasn't been an empty seat on an Earthbound flight in the last"—she swiped through notes on her dataslate—"one hundred and sixty-three trips."

Mil looked at the other members of the team. They were studiously looking at their notes and dataslates. He responded with quiet fury.

"You think I knew it was going to have a catastrophic event? You think I would have let people get on a craft that wasn't safe? That I would allow something like this to happen if I could stop it?" The steel in his voice came as a whisper. He glared at the woman across the conference table.

"Essentially, yes. That is the question. Did you know about the potential for disaster on flight 2705? You provide fuel oxidizer and the breathing oxygen. Few people are in as critical a position to know if there are issues." She glanced up from her notes.

"What exactly are you trying to imply here, Bailey?"

"Let's just say I'm more familiar than most with your ability to not be on spacecraft when they explode."

An audible gasp went through the room, followed by utter silence as Bailey stared down her father.

Mil folded his hands. He was first and foremost a man of his training: decades of thinking in harried and dangerous situations charged with friction. He fought for self-control. And won.

"I see. At this point, Ms. Rivera, I think it would be prudent if I declined to answer any more questions without the benefit of counsel. If you're going to accuse me of killing people, I want a fucking lawyer."

Bailey nodded. "That's your right. Though this isn't a court of law—"

"Your accusations sure as hell make it seem like it is. Tell me, doesn't your agency certify the safety of all your spacecraft? What's your liability in this matter?"

"That's exactly what we are here to ascertain. Now then, do you or don't you supply the fuel oxidizer for these launches?"

Mil simply glared.

"Mr. Harrison. Do you supply the fuel oxidizer for these launches?"

Mil crossed his arms and sat back in the uncomfortable chair. He stared into eyes that were a mirror image of his own. And just as determined.

"I'll repeat the question one final—"

"I heard the question." Mil brought himself to attention in the chair. Then he recited from memory the wording of his long-term partnership contract with Amon Neff. "As the operator of Neff Atmospherics, I am solely responsible for the production, delivery, and maintenance of the breathable oxygen and fuel oxidizer gases, liquids, and components to the settlements and spacecraft of Armstrong Base and the four Luna Settlements in this area."

"Very well. So you supplied the oxidizer for the launch." She moved to the next point on her dataslate.

"I did not."

"I beg your pardon?" She looked up.

"You're the head of the Space Agency and you don't know where you get your fuel? Not very plugged into your own programs, are you?"

Bailey shot a look at one of the team members, who was attempting to look as small as possible in her seat.

"I'm not briefed on every aspect of the numerous programs and initiatives the agency is currently operating. But let's get back to the question at hand. So you do not provide fuel to the launch facility?" Her question was genuine.

"Not anymore. As of about six weeks ago, that responsibility transitioned to Amon Neff's new O2 production facility. All my production was geared for breathable air and fuel oxidizer for the Mars mission. If you want my O2, you either inhale right here or go to Mars."

"So you disclaim any involvement with the launch and the support systems?"

"Other than knowing some of the souls on board, and not wanting to be there for my own selfish, personal reasons, I had nothing to do with the launch of 2705."

"I see."

"You seem disappointed. Because I'm not dead or because I didn't commit murder?"

"Obviously neither. This makes our investigation more difficult."

Mil rolled his eyes. "You came all the way up here to slam me with this? Too bad that now you'll have to do some real work?"

"Don't be so full of yourself. You're here as one very small part of a much larger investigation."

"Will it touch on what's hidden on Slayton Ridge?" He leaned across the table.

"Slayton Ridge?" She blinked at the question.

"You know, the incident that got Micah Granger killed. Other than the pilots, everyone who was or was supposed to be on that craft—Maddie Byers, me, and Granger's body—was witness to the fact that there is something there."

"Slayton Ridge is a classified exclusion zone."

"So you do know of it. Any idea why it's classified?"

"Knowing that something is classified is not akin to knowing why the article is classified. And that is not the subject of this deposition."

"But don't you think it's reasonable to assume that if three people who have knowledge, or are able to provide evidence about something that others want to keep hidden, extraordinary measures might be taken to keep them quiet?"

"You're implying this was an intentional criminal act." She looked to her team. "Sabotage?"

"No, you've been implying that. I'm saying it outright. Somebody wanted us dead. Me, Maddie, who saw all the comms, and whatever evidence a forensic review of Granger's body might turn up."

"Because of what was found on Slayton Ridge." Bailey studied her dataslate.

"Correct."

"And what was found?"

"You're the director of the program. You tell me." Mil sat back in his chair to wait.

CHAPTER TWENTY-TWO

Thursday . 30 Dec . 2077
0915 Lunar Standard Time
Crew Quarters . Armstrong Base . Luna

Eli switched off the monitor and turned to Nique. She nodded her agreement with her grandfather's last remark. They were snuggled tightly into Eli's bunk, where they'd been following the proceedings in-between their own explorations.

"He's right. This is going to be more of an issue than they think."

"How so?" Eli reached across her and checked his wristy on the night-stand charger.

He had officer-of-the-deck duty in a half hour.

"Now they have to transition from an accident inquiry to a criminal investigation. You know how the agency works—none of that happens quickly."

"You're suddenly an expert on security matters?"

She yawned.

"Necessity. Having been tagged by Security, I've been reading up. Checking out protocols, avenues for an appeal, an injunction that would let me rejoin the crew . . . anything."

Eli nodded. "This puts them between two bad situations. They can't go fast and shortcut the investigative process, but at the same time the Mars mission deadlines are pretty much defined by physics and orbital mechanics. No getting around that one."

"Two bad situations. Grandad and my mother. The irresistible force and the immovable object. Is your family this nuts?"

"Oh, I could tell you stories. My Russian grandmother elevated stubborn to an art form."

Nique rolled over onto a hip as he stood and stepped across to the shower. She admired his bare butt and then sank back into the bunk.

Family. It had set her life's course and then bounced it around ever since.

As the water began to run, an uncomfortable thought occurred to her.

"Should we be worried?" she called to the shower. She thought a moment and tapped out a quick message on the wristy she'd set to charge the night before. She hit send and off it went to her grandfather.

"About what?" came the muffled reply.

"Well, Grandad just said it. Everyone who was on flight 2705 knew about Slayton Ridge. You and I were both on duty. We saw as much as Maddie did."

"True. But then, so did Rafferty. He doesn't seem worried." The water stopped as the standard conservation-oriented lunar shower came to its rapid end.

Nique smirked. "My impression is that almost nothing would rattle him."

Her wristy buzzed with a reply message from her grandad. *You should be on the lookout for anything out of the ordinary.*

Eli stepped back in, wrapping a towel around himself.

"I bet we're pretty safe."

———∙∘∘∙— ❈ —∙∘∘∙———

Saturday . 01 Jan . 2078
1155 Lunar Standard Time
Harrison Station . Luna

The vidlink showed Dimitri's concern. "You have opened a can of worms, my friend. Not a grand thing for your birthday."

"It's a helluva present." Mil had collapsed into in his lounge chair. The morning had worn him out. Even tapping at his dataslate was a chore. "As a kid in Houston, I used to kick over ant hills. Do you have fire ants in Russia?"

"Fire ants? No. That doesn't sound pleasant."

"Nasty critters. They bite and it leaves an itchy, stinging welt. There's never just one of them, and they don't have much purpose other than to bite. A lot like the agency's investigation team."

"Tiger Team has a more ferocious sound to it than Fire Ant Team."

"Perhaps, but tigers kill you quick and eat you on the spot. These guys are death by a thousand little bites and then they drag you off."

"So is Bailey more ant than tiger?"

Mil smiled at his friend's metaphor mixing. "The thing is, she's brought a whole team of tigers. I'm not sure, but after reading some of these bios on the investigators, I doubt they came up here just to look at an accident."

"How do you mean?"

"They have a homicide detective on the team, a pathologist, and they are very light on the resources you'd expect for an accident investigation team. Only one engineer. If they're expecting to find issues with the propellant or the booster, you'd think they'd want people here who understood those systems."

"Yes, but those people are as close as a vidcall. They can bring them in when they need them." Dimitri sipped his tea.

"You know as well as I do, there are some things that you just have to do face-to-face and in person. Remote works for some things, but for big stuff, important stuff, you need boots on the ground."

"So, now that you have testified, does that mean they are sending you to Earth? You look tired."

Mil scowled. He'd justified his own case against himself. "I'm to report for a flight physical for the Wednesday launch cycle. Emma wants me there a day early."

"Why?"

"I'm pretty sure she's going to sedate me until we're at least in orbit."

"They are wise to your tricks." Dimitri raised his empty glass in salute.

"I'm an old dog." Mil shook his head. "And I'm too damn tired for tricks."

A notification appeared on Mil's screen. He frowned. "I'll have to take this call Dim, I hope we can get together when I get back and a before you launch."

"We will see you then. Get well, old friend, and by the way, happy birthday."

"Thanks, Dim."

Mil eyed the notification box. *Urgent Corporate.* His finger hovered a moment before accepting. The head and shoulders of a corporately attired young man's face appeared.

"Millennium Harrison? Hold for Mr. Neff."

Oh shit. Amon. Just what I need today. Mil considered tapping off and blaming a solar flare. But the old man was too quick. The famous face of the world's richest man bobbed up and down on the screen.

"Mil, what the hell did you do?" The ancient industrialist jabbed an angry finger at the screen, mopped his scowling face with a towel as he hiked on a treadmill.

Behind him, the skyscrapers of Austin framed the scene through his window.

"Hello, Amon. It's been a while."

The trillionaire had no need for small talk. "What the hell are you doing, talking about Slayton Ridge?"

"What did I do?"

Neff stammered, "You told the entire world about one of the most tightly held secrets the planet has ever known, and now people will be asking questions, dammit."

"So you know what it is?"

"Of course I know what it is, but I'm not telling anyone about it on unsecured comms," Neff exploded. "That's what *classified* means."

"I see."

"My medical people tell me you're probably going to make it. I'll send for you. And we'll figure out what to do about Slayton Ridge. Quietly. Quickly and out of the goddammed spotlight."

The screen went black.

"Nice talking to you too, Amon."

Tuesday . 04 Jan . 2078
0855 Lunar Standard Time
Medical Bay . Armstrong Base . Luna

Mil walked into the clean white confines of the medical bay. He was a long way from full strength but at least he wasn't grabbing walls for support every few steps.

He'd rolled his luggage pod into a corner of Emma's small office, then sat down and began to roll up his right sleeve. Emma was on a voice call but raised her eyebrows.

"I get a sedation patch, right?"

She frowned her answer and punched off the call. "Sedation for what?"

"So I don't run off."

"I'd like to try and treat you as an adult."

"Possibly your first mistake."

"Where you're concerned? That first mistake was long ago." She tapped her dataslate.

"So why am I here a full day ahead of launch?"

"I thought we'd make sure you're physically able to handle the launch."

"More damn tests? I'm about out of blood and—"

"Who said anything about tests, farm boy?" She stepped to his chair and placed her index finger under his chin. She raised his head to hers and winked. It was all the seductress she could manage, wearing shapeless scrubs and her hair under a ball cap.

"Oh. Ohhhhh." He nodded. "I'd like to see if that still works too."

Wednesday . 05 Jan . 2078
1050 Lunar Standard Time
Departure Prep Area . Armstrong Base . Luna

Mil's gait was the steadiest it had been since he'd gone after Granger. He was arm in arm with the doctor but not for support as he pulled the travel pod, his travel bag for his pressure suit, and helmet balanced on top.

"You know, if you'd have tried that the first time, instead of having Rodriguez strong-arm me into going . . ."

She smiled despite the disaster that had visited that effort. "I'm smarter this time around. You catch more flies with honey."

He stopped and his head rocked back. "Flies. Ugh. I hadn't even thought about flies. Another thing I'm going to have to put up with."

"Will you stop? It's a couple of weeks on Earth. You'll be in treatment for most of it and not even outside."

"Good. I'm probably allergic to outdoor air. Why do I even have to go? I'm feeling pretty good. I mean I was in good enough shape last night to—"

Emma saw where this was going. "Most of why you feel good is the medpatches. I've got you pumped full of inhibitors, anti-inflammatories, and pain meds. You feel good because we're treating the symptoms. But we can't fix the problems here. That's why you have to go. The docs in Japan can repair you. I can only make you comfortable for a very short term."

"It was pretty comfortable. I'm okay with short term if it means I don't have to deal with those bastards on Earth."

"When was the last time you were on Earth? Twenty years ago? Longer than that?"

"Bailey's high-school graduation. She told me she never wanted to see me again and I thought that was doable. Never went back."

"Sorry I asked."

"It is what it is."

They passed through a doorway and found Eli and Nique waiting. Mil nodded to the check-in technician and tapped his wrist computer to check in for the flight. The tech scanned his travel pod then loaded it on a rollaway cart and disappeared with the luggage.

Mil turned to his granddaughter. "You didn't have to come."

"I know. But Eli insisted."

Mil appraised her escort. "Huh."

"It's an honor Mr. Harrison." Eli looked like an eager puppy.

"Well, uh. Thanks." He nodded, then turned. "Nique. I want the farm to still be there when I get back. No parties." He gave a stern look as if he meant it.

"You're taking all the fun out of you leaving to have horrible medical things done to you, Grandad."

"Thanks for reminding me."

"Have a safe trip. Love you." She gave him a hug.

He whispered in her ear, "And you be careful—I don't know how big this mess is, but keep your eyes and ears open, okay?"

She nodded. "Of course."

She stepped back and he got a handshake and a crisp salute from Eli.

"I'll be back before you know it."

His wrist computer signaled his launch alert and he turned to the doctor. "You wouldn't go in my place, would you?"

"I'm not the one who lights up the room when he walks in."

"Oh, but you do."

"Awww." She gave him a kiss on the cheek. The real goodbyes had already been said. "Be good, farm boy. Get well." The moment lasted a heartbeat longer than Mil was comfortable with and he noticed his physician's eyes looked moist. *Affection?* he wondered. *Or condolences for what he was about to go through?*

He gave her a half smile and tousled her hair, which he knew she hated, which was precisely why he did it. "See you in a couple of weeks."

Mil found his way to the launch prep area and unpacked his scruffy pressure suit. An eager assistant appeared from nowhere. "You know, Mr. Harrison, they can get you a new suit." The tag on the chest of his jumpsuit identified him as Specialist Downey.

Mil tried to ignore the young technician. "I like this suit. Had it for years. It's broken in and fits just how I like it."

Downey was charged with getting the old legend suited up and helping the man find his seat in the shuttle. The far-too-helpful tech nearly banged into Mil's helmet as they both reached for the auxiliary oxygen pack that would pressurize the suit until he plugged into the transport craft.

"Son, I've just about had all the help I can handle. You wanna let me do this?"

"Sir, I'm under orders to help you any way I can."

"Best way to do that is stand over there and observe." Mil pointed to the door leading back to the dressing room. He latched his helmet and routinely double-checked his wristcomm. A wry smile crossed his face and he thought he'd have a little fun at Downey's expense. He tapped the wristy again and frowned.

"Is everything okay, sir?" The tech stepped forward to help.

Mil tapped his headgear. His reply was muffled.

"Can't hear you, son. Must be a connection issue. I'll sort it out on-board."

"But sir . . ."

And with a half-smile, Mil grabbed his auxpack and marched down the gantry way to the shuttle.

The transport was new, the paint and overabundance of warning decals still pristine. This latest model was equipped much more nicely than the last shuttle Mil had boarded. He paused to try and calculate when that had been. Too long.

The flex couch conformed to support his suit and body evenly. The schedule on the multi-position viewscreen indicated he could catch two ball games on the trip. He moved it out of the way and adjusted the window controls to full transparent. The control menu also showed the viewport optics had magnification settings, giving him a telescopic look at the world beyond.

He sat back. The first flight after an accident review was either the safest flight in history, or they hadn't found the bug and everyone would know very quickly. He played with the window controls. If there was about to be a disaster, he would not only have a front-row seat but he'd get to see it happen in ultra-high resolution.

He pulled the power, comms, and O2 umbilical from the side panel and snapped it in place of his auxpack. He sniffed and wrinkled his nose. The new O2 facility was supplying breathing oxygen for the shuttles now and Mil detected a faint electrical odor.

"Their mix is too clean," he said, smiling, to no one in particular.

"Beg your pardon?" The female voice in his ear was clear as crystal.

"Sorry, didn't realize I was on comms."

"Quite all right, Mr. Harrison. I'm Captain LaTrisha Albright, I'll be your pilot for the trip downstairs."

"Glad to be aboard, Captain." Mil looked around. His was the only seat in the mid-cabin passenger area. There was a full bulkhead behind him with a hatch to the cargo space behind.

"I'm sure you're not, from what I've heard, but I appreciate the courtesy."

"My reputation precedes me. We're not configured for other passengers?"

"Typically, this is the weekly cargo run, we reconfigged just for you. Just you, me, and First Officer Haynes, copiloting today."

"It's an honor to fly with you, Mr. Harrison." Copilot Evan Haynes clicked through the last few items on the checklist.

"I'll try to stay out of the way." Mil ratcheted his harness into place and looked up to see Specialist Downey making his way to the edge of his seat.

With exaggerated hand motions and an overly loud voice, he said, "I'M GOING TO STOW YOUR AUXPACK. IS THERE ANYTHING ELSE I CAN GET FOR YOU, MR. HARRISON?"

Mil smiled despite himself and silently mouthed an exaggerated, "No."

"HAVE A SAFE FLIGHT, SIR."

Mil nodded and gave the expected thumbs-up. Then turned his attention to the viewscreen. It synced with his wrist computer, and in a blink, Dez Rafferty's face appeared from his command chair. At least he was talking to Mil again.

Mil tapped the console to transfer the call and winced as the audio squealed through his helmet.

Downey leaned back in and his voice boomed. "I ADJUSTED THE VOLUME FOR YOU, SIR. IT SHOULD BE BETTER NOW."

Mil nodded his thanks and waved him away as he turned down the level.

Rafferty's voice came through extremely loud and clear. "Honestly, I never thought I'd live to see you strapped into an Earthbound ship."

"Never figured I would be either."

"You're in good hands. Albright hasn't crashed in what, LT? Three? Four flights?"

"Yesssir." Albright's voice broke in. "They're supposed to have that side of the space station repaired by now."

Mil gave an eyeroll. "You guys should take this hilarity on the road. Bound to make a bundle."

Rafferty checked his wrist. "Coming up on comms lockdown. God-speed, Mil. See you soon."

"Thanks, Des. Sorry for all the trouble. I'll be back as soon as they let me." He was genuine in his apology to his old friend, but not as certain of when or even if he'd see him again.

The countdown clock ticked into the last few seconds, a visible wisp of steam vented into the near-vacuum of the moon's atmosphere, the igniters sparked, the invisible plume of flame spouted, and with a foreboding sense of déjà vu, the transport shuttle crept into the black sky.

Mil simply waited. He more or less expected the world to explode. He was almost disappointed when the gantry girders disappeared past the window and the crescent horizon of the moon gave way to blackness.

"That seems quicker than I remember."

"When was the last time you went up?"

"Oh, it's been years. The old chemfuel boosters."

"The turbopump concentrators are much better now. We get to altitude faster and leave orbit in one hell of a hurry."

"Without the G-loading?"

"There's some, but the inertia dampeners and adaptable systems handle that; in here, the new couches take care of most of it. We hardly feel it."

"Hmm. It used to damn near rattle the equipment apart. The trip used to take three days."

"Thirty-six hours is plenty. We'll be six on and six off till we reach Osaka."

Mil watched out of the window, trying to orient landmarks and see if they were overflying anything he knew, but the angle of the cabin left him the barest edge of the horizon.

He shifted in the couch for a better look.

Haynes turned to his passenger. "Not much to see from this angle and like LT says, we're leaving in a hurry. But if you look at about ten o'clock, say twenty-five degrees above us, you should be able to get a glimpse of *Humanity* as we pass them."

Harrison tapped the window control and the view telescoped to pick up the Mars spacecraft floating in orbit. The ring of his white spheres that would eventually belt all the way around the great ship was not even a quarter complete. "They're still hanging fuel cells. I hope I'm back before they launch."

"They're T-minus thirty-nine days. How long until you're back?"

"Maybe three weeks. Maybe not. I'm at the mercy of doctors and flight surgeons."

LT and Haynes shared a look. "For that, sir, you have our sympathy."

CHAPTER TWENTY-THREE

Friday . 07 Jan . 2078
0740 Japan Standard Time
Arrival Facility . Spaceport Osaka . Japan . Earth

———⦿———

"We're cleared for final approach, Mr. Harrison. You might double-check your restraints."

"Got it." Mil had been dozing. He'd slept a good part of the trip courtesy of the medpatches Emma had supplied. He blinked himself awake. "Is this your final stop?"

"No sir, we're dropping you here and headed to White Sands for turn-around."

"White Sands? Military cargo?"

"All they tell us is where to park the truck." The pilot tapped her keypad and the retro rockets fired, the transport dancing on the tongue of flame as the landing gear deployed, a dust cloud bloomed, and the vehicle lightly touched down.

The Man from the Moon had returned to Earth.

He reached for the latch to remove his helmet. His arm was heavy. The headgear weighed a ton.

"They're calling for you, sir. Comms channel five."

Mil nodded and heaved his arm back up. Earth gravity was every bit the bitch he remembered and feared. He scrolled his wrist computer to the proper comms channel. A Japanese man in a surgical cap filled the screen. "Mr. Harrison, welcome to Osaka. We're glad to have such a renowned visitor. I'm Dr. Nomura. I'll be your case officer while you're here."

"Case officer? Law enforcement?" His eyes narrowed.

"Oh no. I'll be more of a liaison as you go through the decontamination and recovery programs. If you'll make a right turn at the end of the gantry way, my team and I are waiting for you."

"See you in a minute." Mil unstrapped and forced himself out of the chair. The weight was crushing. He labored to breathe. He paused as he shuffled to the door, forcing half of a smile for a photo with the pilots. He waited again as Copilot Haynes swung open the hatch.

The hot, humid air hit him like a locomotive. The air he made on the moon had virtually no moisture in it and the facilities stayed at a constant 23 degrees Celsius.

He sneezed violently. And then again. And again. The ocean air carried the smell of fish and salt and a dozen other fragrances he had forgotten about. He'd been on Earth less than five minutes, and he already hated everything about it.

Mil gathered his strength to hoist one leg, then the other over the hatch threshold and onto the gantry.

"Do you need some help, sir?" The copilot showed legitimate concern.

"Nah. I got it. You guys do your post-flight. I'm good," Mil lied.

It was a dozen steps to the elevator, but it might well have been a kilometer. Mil was spent by the time he got to the doors. The landing-pad techs who had come to secure the vehicle looked at him. One stepped up to offer assistance, but Mil dismissed her with a wave and shake of his head.

He grabbed a railing and squinted, blinking hard against the brilliant blue sky above him. It had been decades since he'd seen a sky that wasn't inky black. The reflected sun seared his retinas.

His wrist computer vibrated and the elevator doors opened. He enjoyed small relief as the darkened car descended at a quick clip, then almost crumpled to the floor when the elevator slowed at the ground level.

The doors opened and Dr. Nomura had a crowd waiting for him. Beyond the hospital reception team, reporters, cameras, and hovering remote video units transmitted his legendary arrival on Earth. Millennium Harrison, celebrity. It could not have been less of what he wanted. He waved them off and the gesture was taken as a friendly hello by media commentators. They applauded his homecoming for reasons he really didn't understand or give a shit about.

One of the white-coated medics had a mobility chair, and Mil staggered to it, already out of breath. His chest hurt. His head pounded and he tried to blink away the dizziness. He sneezed again. Earth.

He hated this place.

The medic noticed his distress. An oxygen mask went over his head, and he sucked in clean O2. It helped, and he nodded thanks to the Samaritan, who produced a pair of sunglasses for him, then whispered to another doctor before Mil was whisked away. It was one of the more exhausting five minutes of his life.

The chair moved him quickly to a bulky medical transvan. The wheels locked to the flooring of the ambulance and the seat and back elevated automatically, helping Mil stand with a degree of support. The medic, who Mil now noticed had "Dr. Nomura" embroidered on the chest of his scrubs, tapped a panel on the wall of the transport and asked, "What would you like me to call you Mr. Harrison?"

"Call me?"

"Your name? I've been assigned to act as your personal care liaison. Would you prefer Millennium? Mr. Harrison? Mil? or 'Hey, asshole'?" He grinned.

Mil returned the smile through gritted teeth and a painfully difficult breath. "You've been talking to my doctor."

"We had a call yesterday, she mentioned you'd be a challenge to work with."

"Nah. I'm an easygoing old man. Call me Mil."

"I'm Ash. Can I help you get out of that pressure suit? We'll be moving you straight into the pressurized environment for treatment. If we get you prepped on the way, it'll go more quickly."

Mil reached for the latches that released the torso of the suit. "Ash, I've been getting in and out of this suit since before you were born."

He almost immediately regretted the smart remark as Ash stepped away and grandly gestured for his elder to proceed. Mil grunted. Sweat popped on his brow and he struggled against the extreme gravity. He told himself it was the medication and heaved hard again to raise the chest portion of the suit. It was no use.

"But not here on Earth," he admitted.

Ash nodded and lifted the upper half over Mil's head. Then he held Mil's arm as the old astronaut stepped out of the lower portion.

"You've been in treatment for what? Two weeks? You've got a dozen chemicals coursing through your body and you're in this enhanced gravity environment with air unlike anything you've inhaled in decades. And that's on top of eating all that radiation. Understand there are a lot of things you just won't be able to do here that are simple, mindless things on Luna."

"Yeah, yeah, I know."

"Intellectually you know it, but in practicality, well, the files say you're as independent as any human has ever been. I'm here to help, and maybe keep you from doing something that can get you hurt."

"So, I was right—you are a guard too."

"Oh no, I think this is going to be much more like babysitting."

Ash tapped his wrist computer and the mobility chair eased Mil back down to a sitting position and then transformed into a reclined lounge seat.

"This will take some pressure off your joints, if you'll roll up your sleeve, I've got a patch that'll make it easier for you to breathe."

Mil told himself it would be prudent to go along with the protocol at this point. Ash affixed wireless patches to his chest to monitor his vitals. Mil saw that his blood pressure was high but trending down toward normal, and his other levels seemed to be about where he remembered they usually read. He'd done this a lot recently.

The transport entered the intake dock of the hospital, passing another group of reporters covering the arrival of the Man from the Moon. Ash remotely piloted the mobility chair as they moved down the ramp and into the facility.

"I'm going to tilt you up so you can wave to the reporters and it won't look like you're an invalid."

The back and head of the chair raised from the chassis and gave the appearance that Mil was more or less of average height and riding one of the wheeled go-boards that seemed to be everywhere he looked, zipping people through the facility.

"Wave to the nice media." Ash smiled and they motored through the doors of the hospital. Mil dutifully, and with great effort, heaved up his right arm and gave a halfhearted salute to the cameras.

A quick elevator ride, and Mil was moved into a much nicer version of the hyperbaric chamber he'd been in on the moon. Vanilla-colored plastic walls instead of the white-and-gray plastics of the lunar colony gave the illusion of institutional warmth. A pair of side chairs had been folded out of the wall with a table between them. On the table surface a chessboard pattern projected waiting for game pieces. Ash touched the wall panel and the walls brightened.

Like most urban construction in Japan since the big quake of 2042, the room was a molded composite prefab module linked together with dozens of others in a honeycomb hive to create supposedly disaster-proof buildings. Mil had been living in an aluminum-and-plastic module for his entire adult life, so it didn't strike him as strange in the least.

He contemplated the ocean view. One big point in Earth's favor—it had color.

Mil's luggage pod had arrived and he found it empty; his two jumpsuits had been hung in the closet. His toiletries were placed in the bathroom cabinet. It wasn't much sparser than his apartment back home.

Ash began the quick tour and run-through of procedures. "You'll be on a med regimen for your entire stay. That patch on your arm is today's dosage. We'll adjust it every day depending on how you respond. This whole section is hyperbaric. There's pressure and a purified environment to help you heal."

Mil nodded and looked around. "I didn't think prisons were quite this nice."

"This is a first-rate facility, Mil. Nothing like a prison." Ash turned to leave. "Except for the food, that's pretty terrible. In fact, prisoners refused to eat it, so they sent it here." Ash winked and closed the door behind him.

Exhausted, Mil collapsed onto the bed.

"Bailey? You active here?"

His daughter's familiar voice came from a hidden audio system. "Affirmative. Linked to current hospital systems and networks."

"Can you make the window transparent?"

The window wall gently resolved from an opaque soft glow to the sun over the ocean bay horizon.

"Is that dawn or dusk?"

"Morning. Current local time is oh eight forty-seven."

"And is that a videowall or am I looking at the bay through a viewport?"

"It is an east-facing window. Not a video representation."

He tried to stand and his head swam. Gravity. Medicine. Radiation. He took a deep breath, steadied himself, and headed toward the bathroom. A cup of water took two hands. How heavy could a plastic cup be? He eyed the shower and decided that would be more standing than he could handle at the moment. His jumpsuits had been laundered and pressed. He shuffled back to sit on the bed with a groan.

He wondered how much of his condition was just travel exhaustion, how much was radiation sickness, and how much was whatever sedative the pharmacists had printed into his medpatch. He rolled up a sleeve and studied the patch, giving serious thought to pulling it off and taking back some manner of control of his condition.

No, he thought. *These people know what they are doing.* The only way to get well and back to Luna was to follow the procedures, take the medicine, and use the time to find answers. He sat down with his dataslate and started accessing databases. With somebody out there trying to kill him and everyone who knew about the mystery facility on Slayton Ridge, he had little time for idle recovery.

CHAPTER TWENTY-FOUR

Monday . 17 Jan . 2078
0640 Lunar Standard Time
Crew Quarters . Armstrong Base . Luna

Eli set the steaming cup of coffee on the bedside table. Nique's eyes fluttered awake.

"Morning." He smiled and nodded to the cup. "Double-shot Americano."

She yawned. "Morning. Thank you."

Dinner had turned into a long conversation by the viewport. They'd talked for hours overlooking the dark moonscape and the incredible starfield that made up the night sky, and then moved on beyond talking.

"Print you some breakfast?"

She startled and grabbed her wristy on the nightstand. "What time is it? Oh, God."

"It's oh six forty-five. But I thought you were off duty today." He cocked his head.

"I have to call Grandad. It's been a week. He can have telecom visitors today. Oh, damn. It's almost twenty-three hundred there. Shit."

"Do you think he's still up?"

"The hospital shuts off access at twenty. Dammit. I am such a bad granddaughter."

"I think you're pretty good."

She took an aggravated sip of her coffee. "Remind me. I'll send him a vid."

She looked around and remembered where she was. "I've got to go."

"So that's a no on breakfast? It's not any trouble."

"No, I gotta go. I am supposed to see my mother today." She paused pulling on her pants. "What are you doing today?"

"I"—he paused for effect—"start prepping to leave."

She cocked her head. "Leave?"

"I'm being reassigned. When *Humanity* departs, I do too. I'm off to Russia to train for a follow-up mission, the first crewed resupply freighter to Mars. Navigation systems officer." He held out his dataslate. "My orders came down overnight. Once *Humanity* breaks orbit, I get two weeks' leave, then I'm to report to Baikonur for systems training."

She tried to hold a poker face as she read his orders. "I'm so happy for you."

Monday . 17 Jan . 2078
0630 Japan Standard Time
Osaka Rehabilitation Hospital . Japan . Earth

After a week of incarceration Mil was getting used to the first strange bed he'd slept in for decades. But it still took a moment to orient himself to the unfamiliar surroundings. The walls had transformed into the pinkish gold of a terrestrial dawn, and while that might be comforting to an Earthling, for a man from the moon it was just strange. He stood more easily than when he'd first arrived. Maybe the treatment was taking hold. His morning bathroom routine didn't wear him out, and that was progress.

"Bailey, see if the kitchen has found some coffee. No tea this time. And a real breakfast."

"Standard breakfast has been ordered."

"I don't want a standard breakfast. I want food."

The door chime dinged.

"Come."

A young Japanese woman bounced into the room. Far too cheerful for Mil this morning. She had her hair in a ponytail, wore athletic gear, and was paying more attention to her wristy than the patient she was there to see.

"Good morning, Mr. Harrison! I'm Hina. I'll be your physical therapist today. Have you had breakfast this morning?" She finally looked up at him.

Mil eyed this new ball of energy. "Um. Where's Ash?"

"He'll be along. We can get in a quick workout while you're waiting."

She tapped the wristy and the room transformed. An exercycle folded out from one wall, and she gestured to it.

Mil cocked an eye. "What the hell is this? Calisthenics?"

"We want to start building your strength and get the medicines working through your system." She was deeply involved with the screen on her wrist.

"Before breakfast?"

She looked up from her screen. "What? Oh, ha! Funny. Yes. Before breakfast. We'll do some cardio and then move on to strength training."

"You know I'm nearly eighty years old, right?" Mil eyed the exercycle.

"I have a patient on this floor who is one hundred and eighteen; she does twenty minutes every day. Let's hop on the bike."

"Yes, let's. Where's your seat?" He didn't budge.

She smirked and pointed to the bike and tapped a foot in a move that angered Mil instantly. He glared at the diminutive young woman and defiantly took a seat on the bike. The display on the exercycle brightened with his biometric data and a seaside road appeared on the wallscreen in front of him. Hina tapped her wristy and a half dozen cyclists passed him on the video wall, pedaling down the road.

"Let's try and keep up."

Mil's competitive nature got the better of him and his feet found the pedals. He lasted fifteen minutes before the peloton of riders disappeared into the distance.

"Can you give me two more minutes?" Hina was focused on her wristy.

"I can, but I think this is enough." Mil slowed, his chest heaving.

"Just a few more minutes. Really push yourself."

Mil eased back in the seat and stopped pedaling. "I think I've ridden this thing as far as I'm going to."

"You're going to be difficult, aren't you?"

Harrison dismounted and looked down on the diminutive therapist. "It's what I do. Look, you're here before I've even eaten anything. All I am to you is a checkmark on your list, so yeah, I'm difficult."

The door slid open and Ash stepped through. "Why don't you let me take it from here, Hin?"

She glared at Mil one last time, spun on her heel, and marched out the door.

Ash watched her go and then turned to Mil. "That might not have been the smartest thing you've done this week. The PT crew are sadists. She can make your life a living hell."

Mil found a towel and mopped the sweat from his face. "If you think a living hell is two more minutes on a bicycle, then you don't have enough stress in your life."

Ash considered it. "You could be right. But still, you don't want to be on the wrong side of those people."

"Probably. Someone recently told me you catch more flies with honey."

The idiom went right past Ash. "Why do you want to catch flies?"

"Never mind. Did you bring food? I'm starved."

"Breakfast is right behind me." Ash touched his wrist monitor and another tech appeared with a cart loaded with covered trays. Another touch and the bike folded back into the wall and was replaced by a table and a bench.

Mil sat and removed the cover from the tray; the smell assaulted his nose. "You know, the only thing Earth had going for it was food that didn't come out of a meal printer. It's been two weeks, why is it I still can't get a real breakfast?"

Ash raised his eyebrows. "This is a real breakfast. Miso, tofu, salmon, and that pickled plum looks terrific." He sniffed. "Smells delicious."

Mil cringed, replaced the cover, and slid the tray back across the table. "We don't get a lot of fish on the moon. I think the last time I had seafood before this was fried shrimp in Houston, thirty-five years ago. And that was dinner. What does it take to get a cup of coffee?"

"How about green tea?"

"How about black coffee? Scrambled eggs? Bacon?"

"I have no idea where to even find an egg."

"You lift up the chicken and there they are."

"We'll see what we can do for tomorrow. But this"—Ash made a grand gesture—"is today's breakfast."

"You've been saying that since I got here. And now we have PT on top of it?" Mil grimaced, unpacked the eating utensils, and took a sip of his seaweed soup. With all the medications and trauma he'd been through, he couldn't really taste it, but he'd thrown too much of a fit to back away now.

"Leave it. I might eat some of it. What else do we have today?"

"Today is testing day; we'll see how far you've come. We'll do a full body scan, some tissue analysis, cellular body fluids panels, and some DNA workups."

"What does that mean in terms an old astronaut can understand?" He eyed the salmon as if it might crawl off the plate.

"We're going to bore you until you're numb, take blood and hair samples, and make you pee in a cup."

"Then I'm definitely gonna need some coffee."

———◦•◦— ✦ —◦•◦———

Monday . 31 Jan . 2078
1025 Pacific Standard Time
Osaka Rehabilitation Hospital . Japan . Earth

The days became duplicates of each other: Hina pushing him first thing and then breakfast. As his body began to acclimate to Earth, his baseline strength established itself, and he began to build a little endurance. Hina was begrudgingly impressed that, for all Mil had been through, his recovery was coming along better than expected. In fact, she'd never seen a patient respond quite so quickly. But then she'd rarely had a patient who was so bullheaded and generally cantankerous.

Breakfast slowly adapted to his tastes. And vice versa. It took time for the nutritionists to find eggs, and they never let him have bacon, but eggs and salmon seemed to be a decent compromise. He wasn't sending compliments to the chef, but he had stopped complaining.

The afternoons were empty of scheduled events. A message to Amon Neff had gone unreturned, but Mil wasn't surprised. He'd been working with Neff for almost forty years, but that didn't mean the old guy was going to break secure comms or personally fly around the planet to fill him in on the secret of Slayton Ridge.

Mil spent hours on the computer network, digging through records, following long dead and never documented rabbit trails to any scrap of information about whatever was buried at Slayton Ridge. He researched the old shuttle missions, the Apollo program, SkyLab, and the US and Soviet joint missions into orbit. He learned about the US Army's Project Horizon, intended to put a base on the moon in the 1960s. He followed genealogy threads of long-dead crewmen and mission specialists. Anything to relate to a facility on the moon that no one seemed to know about or want found.

He did find an abandoned Project A119, a plan hatched by scientists in the late 1950s to deliver a nuclear weapon to the moon and detonate it just to see what would happen. Their theories weren't optimistic. His most promising leads all seemed to end in the same place: the Space Agency archives. The records were old and they were stored for security, but unfortunately his security authorization had been revoked. He thought about Adrian Evanston guarding the gates to those old files. There must be a way in.

He dutifully exercised. Old academy training isometrics in the confined space of his room. Ever longer sessions on the cardio bike improved his pulmonary and coronary functions. His breathing came easier, and his heart was no longer struggling to keep up.

He was staying with the peloton on the wallscreen unless his personal sadist decided they needed to sprint. The dizzy spells subsided, and his head no longer felt like it was in a vice.

But he was still sneezing.

"Bless you." Ash entered the room with a meal kit and a small package.

"Why the hell am I sneezing? I always kidded about being allergic to Earth."

"It's the tissues in your sinuses, they take a long time to acclimate to the atmosphere."

"How long?" Mil had taken to carrying a handkerchief and it made him feel like his own grandfather.

"Well, you're Patient Zero in this situation, so we really don't know. The scans show it's adapting at an irregular rate. We don't know if that's your physiology, the effects of a life in artificial atmosphere, or the radiation exposure." The wall transformed into the dining table and Ash placed Mil's lunch on the table.

"So I'm just going to be stuck with it until it kills me."

"Yes, the headlines will read 'Intrepid Lunar Pioneer Felled by Sniffles.'"

"You're a funny guy. So to what do I owe this? You never bring lunch."

"You have mail. A for-real, hard-copy letter."

"A letter? From whom?"

Ash placed the sealed envelope on the table.

"Scans showed paper. We don't open packages for patients. Unless they appear to be contraband or contaminated."

Mil lifted the lid on the meal kit first. More fish. This filet was more yellow than pink, and he didn't know what species that suggested, but it didn't look right compared to the salmon he was getting used to.

He turned his attention to the envelope. Paper. He hadn't seen real cotton paper in years. He turned the crisp white rectangle in his fingers, looking for a way in. He slid one of his chopsticks under the flap and the parchment tore along the crease. Inside was a folded sheet of unlined paper with a single line of infirm scrawl in blue ink. It had been thirty years since he'd seen real handwriting, and he almost couldn't read it.

mil—

all in order. see Yoshi. two blocks west. comms.

—amon

Ash stood looking out the window. "What is it?"

"Fan mail." Mil frowned. Neff's signature seemed legit. There were few things more secure than a cryptic handwritten note.

"Groupies. You should see all the flowers downstairs. We have them saved for you."

"With my allergies? That would kill me." His mind was a million miles away.

"Obviously. That's why we aren't bringing them up here."

"Good. I get enough email from strangers telling me to get well." He tucked the sheet back into the envelope and turned to his fish.

Ash smiled. "I do have good news. We're dialing down the pressure again this afternoon. You'll be out of the chamber this time tomorrow. Then we'll work toward getting you more mobile."

"So I'm getting better?"

"Ahead of schedule. You're in pretty good shape for an old guy."

"Clean living." He poked the salmon with his chopsticks and sniffed. It smelled different.

"Of course. Not to mention your sunny disposition."

"So, once I'm 'mobile,' that means I can go home, right?" He looked to Ash for good news.

Ash hesitated. "Well, I'm really not the one who makes that determination."

"That wasn't what I asked."

Ash chose his words carefully. "Mil, I can't tell you that we'll let you go home because I'm not sure that's going to happen."

"Is that a medical opinion? You don't expect me to pass a flight physical?" They were dancing around the core question.

"You know as well as I do, if you can fog a mirror, you can pass a flight physical. What I don't have confidence in is the powers that be letting you have an unconditional release."

"Unconditional release? You mean they can put limits on what I do and where I go? How is that possible?" He pointed the chopsticks at his captor.

"When you signed on with the program all those years ago, you gave permission for the corporation to decide whether or not you were physically able to fly."

"Amon Neff is not going to keep me from going home."

"Yeah, I don't think it makes it all the way up the food chain to Mr. Neff. There are a few dozen layers of administrators between here and there."

"Corporate drones." Mil scowled. "Do you know how many years I've spent mucking through their red tape? It's one more thing I really hate about people on Earth."

"Hey now, I'm on your side. I want you to go home. My last patient was a nice lady from Honshu. I figure they owe me another one of those after this."

"Just when I thought I'd found somebody on this planet I get along with." He lifted the suspect salmon and a liquid drained off it.

"Nope. I'm here because they pay me, old man," Ash said with a grin and a wink.

Mil pointed at his fish. "This look right to you? Is it supposed to be yellow?"

Ash took a cursory glance. "I'm sure it's fine."

"Then you taste it."

"Really? My, you're awfully tall for a six-year-old."

"It doesn't smell like the usual stuff." He wrinkled his nose.

"So your sense of smell is coming back?'

"Huh, I guess so, I hadn't noticed it until right now."

Ash took a second look at the salmon. "You know, that doesn't look right, does it?"

"I'm quickly becoming one of the foremost fish experts in this room." Mil slid the tray across.

Ash took the tray with a puzzled look. "Let me get you another meal."

It took nearly an hour and a half before he returned. Mil was not amused. "What'd you have to do, go catch it yourself?"

"Mil, there's a problem."

"Damn right, my lunch isn't getting here until dinner." Hangry wasn't a medical term, but Mil was all in on it.

"Someone poisoned your fish."

CHAPTER TWENTY-FIVE

Monday . 31 Jan . 2078
0835 Pacific Standard Time
Osaka Rehabilitation Hospital . Japan . Earth

———— ✦ ————

"**S**ay again?" Mil shook his head to clear his ears.

"They are checking the recorders in the kitchen. They think someone put something in your meal." Ash was serious, and it was a side Mil hadn't really seen.

"Somebody tried to poison me?" Mil stepped back with a cock of his head. It was a genuine shocker.

"That's the preliminary thinking."

"Who?"

Ash hesitated.

"Who?"

"We aren't certain."

"You've got recorder coverage of the kitchen, but you don't know who it is?" Mil began to pace, thinking.

"I think we know." He hesitated. "We just can't find her."

"Her? Who?" Through the window, cargo hydrofoils were gliding across the bay.

"We're looking for Hina. She seems to have left the building."

Mil turned from the window. "Hina? What did I do to her? I mean, I bitch about the exercise, but doesn't everybody?"

"Well, not to the degree you do," Ash quipped.

"Enough that she'd want to kill me? I know I'm a pain in the ass, but still—"

"Yeah, you're not quite that obnoxious."

"Thanks. I think. So what happens now?"

"The prefecture police have been notified. They will want to interview you."

"What am I going to tell them? I don't like to exercise and I sent back my fish?"

"Something like that. Procedures are important in Japan." Ash looked to the floor, adding a little embarrassment to the admission.

"Just how much longer do you expect me to stay in Japan? Aren't I about ready to get out of here?"

"That's not up to me, I'd have sent you packing days ago."

"So what's the holdup?"

"That's up to the doctors—your focused care oncologist, Dr. Fujuko, and the team that's treating you."

"Let's get 'em together. I don't like sitting here all day and being a target. I can do that at home. What do we have to do to get me out of here?"

Ash went to see what he could find out and left Mil alone with his thoughts.

Poison?

Mil couldn't recall anyone ever wishing him dead. But if this mysterious nemesis had been after him, would they sabotage a shuttle flight? And then follow him all the way to Japan?

What the hell was going on?

Mil and Ash sat across the conference room table from Dr. Fujuko and two other doctors he hadn't met. A wall of windows looked out of the edge of the city and to the bay beyond.

"Your numbers are within limits. You've progressed well. We have an aftercare program you'll need to participate in, but I see no reason why you can't be released within the next few days."

Mil felt good. Solid. His strength was back up and his aerobic capacity had increased to the point that, while he noticed the additional strain of Earth's gravity, it wasn't trying to crush him.

And his debrief with the extremely polite police officials had been a breeze. "So, tomorrow then?"

"Perhaps."

"Great. When's the next shuttle to Luna?"

"About that." The doctor looked to the others beside her at the table. One nodded in agreement. "Mr. Harrison, we believe it is inadvisable for you to return to the moon."

"Inadvisable?"

"There is not enough atmosphere on the moon to protect you from even the ambient radiation. Just the background levels could cause a relapse. The carcinogenic risks are extreme. It wouldn't happen quickly, but you are several tiers beyond the recommended maximum lifetime dosing. Even slight exposure at this point could potentially be fatal."

"Could be, Doc. But on top of the radiation, a rocket I was supposed to be on blew up and somebody poisoned my breakfast. Anything that's going to do away with me better get in line."

The doctors exchanged glances. "Mr. Harrison, our medical opinion is that here on Earth you could live another thirty or forty years. Returning to the moon, well, let us just say that not only would your life expectancy be much shorter, it would not be a pleasant way to spend your last years. You've had extreme exposure. At this stage, cancer could arise rapidly and in virtually any form. Bone, organs, lungs, blood, lymphatic system . . . the odds are not with you."

"So stay on Earth, remain indoors, don't do anything and wilt away for the next thirty years?"

"We would like to monitor you. Your condition and recovery process could tell us much for future patients. That's how we've been able to extend the lives of humans over the last century."

"You want a lab rat? Monitor me on Luna and learn something for space medicine," Mil groused.

"On Earth, you'd be a test subject in the finest facilities. We'd be analyzing your reaction, recovery, and response."

"Oh. A guinea pig in a gilded cage. Much better."

"Mr. Harrison, this is an opportunity to advance oncology with primary research; if you go to the moon, it's a certain death sentence."

"My death. Oughta be my choice."

The doctors conferred with silent looks. Dr Fujuko nodded. At the end of the table an older gray-haired doctor pressed a button on the tabletop.

The holodisplay in the center of the table blinked on. It showed an empty room that felt vaguely familiar to Mil. Then Dr. Emma Wilkerson stepped into the room. He recognized the secure conference room at Armstrong Base.

"Hi."

A wave of anger swept over Mil. He'd been set up. "Hi, honey." He clenched his teeth. "They say I can't come home, but you probably already know that, huh?"

"Mil, this is the best option. You don't want to die here."

"I'm not a fan of dying anywhere, but I'd rather do it there than here."

"You said yourself we don't have the facilities, and we—"

"And you're the only doctor for a quarter of a million miles. Yeah, I know. People dying is too much trouble. Takes away from the serious business of everybody else living life. I get it."

"Mil, look, don't—"

"Doctor. I think we're done here. Harrison out." With that he shoved his chair back and stormed out of the room.

Ash jumped up after him. He stopped at the door and looked back at his colleagues. "That went well, don't you think?"

Ash turned into the hallway and headed for Harrison's quarters. The old man was fast. He didn't even see him as he hurried through the hallway to the bank of elevators. A moment later he rapped on the door of the room before pushing it open.

He could see the light under the bathroom door.

"Mil?" No answer.

"Mr. Harrison? Look, this doesn't have to be this bad."

A flicker of concern ran across Ash's face. "Mr. Harrison. Mil? Answer or I'm coming in."

He opened to door to the empty lavatory.

"Shit." He keyed his wrist computer. "Mr. Harrison has left his room. If you see him, please respond." He then moved to the computer on the wall. "Locate patient Millennium Harrison."

"Patient is in the Oncology Department dayroom."

Ash hustled there. The door opened, and sitting in the chair by the window was Mil's wrist computer. Its owner nowhere to be seen.

CHAPTER TWENTY-SIX

Monday . 31 Jan . 2078
1025 Pacific Standard Time
Osaka Rehabilitation Hospital . Japan . Earth

il slipped out of the dayroom through a doorway marked STAFF ONLY in English and Kanji. Another door inside had an icon of a figure descending stairs, and Mil tested his fitness. Breathing hard, he was glad to be heading down, but the exertion wasn't more than he could handle. Two floors down he opened the door to an empty hallway and a wall sign filled with arrows and more Japanese. He took a wild guess and turned left. A laundry hamper parked outside door number three. He ducked inside.

A moment later he stepped out wearing clean pressed scrubs, a cap, a mask, and a too-tight white smock identifying him as Dr. Allison Clarke, MD. He mentally thanked Dr. Clarke for the loan.

He walked purposefully through the hallway. When he saw a pair of nurses heading his way, he swiped a dataslate off a charger, giving him a reason to not meet any eyes as they passed. A left off the hallway and into a service corridor found him at shipping and receiving.

There he paused, as ahead a pair of double doors opened and a worker in a hard hat and coveralls escorted a transport pad of containers through. Mil nodded as she passed, then hurried through the automatic doors.

The small receiving warehouse was quiet. There were dozens of transport pads of neatly containerized packages stacked in two-meter cubes, waiting to be unpacked. The cubes made a grid of walkways and Mil slipped between them to hide from prying eyes and the ever-present cameras he knew were searching for him.

At the end of one row of cubes, he spotted the overhead door of the dock, where an autonomous transport vehicle was docked to the door seal. There was no sign of any attendant, and the windowed office next to the door was empty. He ducked inside.

He exchanged the lab coat for coveralls he'd found hanging behind the doors, a hard hat, and sunglasses. The surgical mask remained.

Mil crept to the door to see if the coast was clear and then realized he didn't know what he was looking for. Warehouses on the moon were robotic. He guessed they were on Earth as well. He cracked open the door and peeked through, figuring his every move was on a camera somewhere. He hoped if he moved slowly enough, motion sensors might not trigger. Then halfway through a tiptoe step, he looked up and saw the tiny camera over the exterior door and gave a small wave to the red light as he went through it.

He could smell the sea in the air and the sun was out, but the thin overcast helped his eyes adjust. It wasn't too warm, but he hadn't felt the unfiltered sun on his skin in years. *Great. Sunburn.* Another gift from the planet that kept on giving. He came to the end of the block with the realization he didn't know where he was headed other than away from the hospital.

He reread the note from Neff—*two blocks west.* He tapped his wrist by habit, finding it bare. The maps and compass that should have been there were waiting back in the dayroom chair. Well, the pilot in Mil remembered, the sun sets in the west. But the clock on the wall of the office had read 12:45, and that put the local star straight overhead. So much for celestial navigation.

Mil crossed with a growing crowd of pedestrians and walked to the end of the block and sneezed. God, he hated Earth. Now he was here, where he didn't speak the language, had no ID, no computer, no money, and no real plan. He checked the pockets of the coveralls—a piece of paper with notes scribbled in Japanese. He tried not think about the fact that he did not have his medication with him and really didn't know how much of an issue that would be when whatever was in his system wore off.

At the end of the block, he turned and joined the ever-increasing stream of people on the walkway. The crowd was now a rushing, moving sea of humanity. Being surrounded by more people than he'd seen in thirty years sent a shiver of anxiety through Mil. Where the hell did all the people come from? And how could they live like this?

Mil found himself on the edge of a lane of the walkway designated for the motorized go-boards zipping along with the pedestrians. He slouched, trying to blend into the herd of people, who were a full head shorter. He hid behind the surgical mask, thanking the universe that most of the people on the street were wearing those.

At the corner he made a right, staying in the flow of humanity and passing the front of the hospital. At the end of that block he made another right, starting a tiring grid search that he expanded by a block every trip around.

Six turns later, the area had transformed from the medical district to a square of street-level shops and electronic advertising video screens two and three stories tall. Above those the buildings stretched thirty and forty stories into the sky. Mil had forgotten what urban living felt like. Even in the downtown Houston of his youth, the density of the population wasn't this oppressive. He felt his chest tightening and didn't think it had anything to do with his medical condition. He rounded another corner and saw a videosign in English: COMMS. The storefront video windows wore wild dancing colors and frantic graphics promising screaming deals on all the latest technology. He headed straight for it.

He slipped inside, away from the crowds, paused, and took a deep breath, willing himself to calm down. Of course, he sneezed. Though the garish exterior of the shop indicated otherwise, the store was neat and clean. Mil wound his way through the racks of tech products and floor displays. He peeked over the dark sunglasses and approached the counter.

The ancient shopkeeper was perched on a barstool behind a glass-topped counter filled with electronic gadgets. He looked up from his holodisplay and greeted Mil in Japanese. Mil shook his head, pulled down the mask and removed his sunglasses.

"You speak English? I'm looking for Yoshi."

"You found him, Mr. Harrison. Welcome. I have some things for you." Mil detected a bit of Brooklyn in the man's American English.

"You know who I am?"

"You've been all over the media, pal. Plus, Mr. Neff told me you'd be in sometime this week. I have a package for you."

"How do you know Amon Neff?"

Yoshi hopped off the barstool and walked past Mil to the front door, where he tapped out a bunch of keystrokes on his wristcomm and threw a series of locks. "We keep in touch. Sometimes I do favors for him."

"Like this one?"

Yoshi passed back through the shop and disappeared behind a door. "Not many like this one." He reappeared, wheeling a hard-shell luggage pod back through the doorway, and heaved the pod up on the counter. A small panel on the top slid open and Yoshi placed his index finger on the reader.

"We'll reset this for your print."

The case unlatched and he pushed it across the counter to Mil, who, after a bit of hesitation, opened the cover.

Inside were neatly folded clothes, a business suit, shoes, and a wrist computer.

"The wristy is linked to a new identity for you. We'll trade it out for—" he noticed Mil's bare wrist. "Where's yours?"

"It's back at the hospital. I left in a bit of a hurry."

"You ran? Mr. Neff has been making arrangements to get you released. Why the hell would you run?" His eyes met Mil's and unspoken accusation hung in the air.

"People seem to be trying to kill me. Sorry, if that's inconvenient for you."

Yoshi gave him a dirty look. "And now they're going to be looking for you. Dammit. That's going to make things much more difficult. Hang on. I need to make a call."

He and the wristy disappeared once again into the back room. Mil wandered the aisles of the small store, amazed at the array of gadgets and gizmos Earthlings had to spend money on. He turned to find Yoshi back at the counter tapping on a different wristy. It was identical to the one Yoshi wore.

"We'll start over. I've cloned the other one to this wristy. There's a bank account, travel docs, passport, pilot's license for ground, and suborbital. But this, this is not just an ordinary wristy. Mr. Neff uses this tech. It's untraceable. Rolling, scrambled, AI generated codes. Theoretically untrackable, and it's programmed so you have phantom accounts that register as valid but vanish once a transaction is made. Mr. Neff can go anywhere, anytime, and no one knows."

"Sounds like some sort of spy gear. What exactly do you do for Neff?"

"Occasionally he likes to go places without a lot of fanfare. I facilitate that for him."

"And you happen to be in a store three blocks from where I was hospitalized."

"Don't be silly. We put this place in when they said you'd be sent here. I had to extend the lease another month when the shuttle blew up."

"So now what?"

"Go change clothes. I'll check you for trackers or implants. There will be meds waiting for you in LA. With this tech, once you get there, you can vanish into thin air. That should slow down whoever is trying to get rid of you."

"LA? That's it? Neff went to all this trouble to get me to someplace I have no reason to go?"

"There will be a note or at least a next step on the plane. But know this, Mr. Neff never does anything without a reason. Now, sometimes he can change that reason with a snap of his fingers and guys like me, we have to be flexible, but he makes it worth my time."

"So I'm supposed to trust you? Just do what you say?"

Yoshi sighed.

"Mr. Harrison. This is what I do. I'm a fixer for Mr. Neff. I learned a long time ago, he tells you what you need to know and absolutely nothing else. I never, ever get all the details. I used to have a problem with that. But then—" He held Mil's eye for a long moment then dismissed the seriousness with a casual wave. "Then a very large amount of money went right into my account and I learned to live with it. And live very comfortably I might add."

"So I'm supposed to just blindly go where I'm pointed?"

"Hey, you're the guy on the run. Got a better idea? Think of it as following orders. You were a military man once upon a time, right? And you might grow a beard. People do know your face."

Four hours later, Mil boarded the needle-nosed supersonic commercial flight to Los Angeles. He was freshly showered and unshaved, attired in a perfectly tailored new suit. He looked like the very picture of a wizened international businessman. But he felt like crap. His meds were trailing off, and the day's exertions were catching up to him. Running for one's life was hard work.

He collapsed into his business-class seating module and looked out the window. The Osaka airport was like every other airport in the world from here. Acres of tarmac and waiting hyper speed aircraft. He didn't like being a passenger, and would much rather be in the driver's seat, but since he'd been sent to Earth, a passenger he'd been.

It wasn't, he thought, that he was afraid of dying. That was going to happen at some point to everyone. But he wanted—no, he needed—to learn what was going on before something happened to him and the secret of Slayton Ridge died with him.

"Mr. Alstrom?" The flight attendant's question broke through his thoughts. "Mr. Alstrom?"

The attendant was about Nique's age with a tiny uniform hat perched on her short, straight black hair. She tapped the order for Module 6A and gave a curious look to the screen and then to Mil. A slight panic went through him.

"Um . . . Yes?" Mil remembered that Alstrom was the name on his travel documents.

"Welcome to Flight 212, Mr. Alstrom. I'm Shari and I'll be your host here in executive class this evening. Our meal choices for dinner are *sakana no nitsuke*, a braised rockfish with a simmered ginger soy glaze, or a chicken cordon bleu with . . ."

"The chicken," Mil interrupted. Then smiled. "Please." He decided Harry Alstrom should be a lot more polite than Mil Harrison. Something about honey and flies.

Shari showed him how to operate the controls that transitioned the seating module to a sleeping berth, the lighting and environmental controls, and the massage function.

"I have a package for you, Mr. Alstrom. Can I bring you a beverage while we await our clearance?"

"Water is all, thank you."

His water arrived along with a sealed packet. He finished the water quickly, then took the packet to the aircraft's restroom.

He broke the seal and his wristy vibrated as a series of communiqués came in. The messages explained the medpatches the packet contained. Mil doffed his jacket and rolled up his sleeve. He'd been told he couldn't really feel the medicines go to work, but he felt a small sense of relief knowing he had a little help in his ongoing battle against planet Earth.

The long scroll of messages on the wristy's screen reminded him he wasn't totally alone in this mess. He tapped out a message to Nique.

Her reply was there in a flash.

Poison? Grandad! What the hell? Of course I'm being careful!

Nothing weird going on, kiddo?

No time. We're working 10 hour shifts till launch now.

That might be a blessing in disguise.

I don't even see Eli, he's on the second shift.

Well, be careful. I think this is serious.

Call the authorities?

Don't know who to trust here on Earth, so no.

K

Mil paused. Was he pushing the panic button here? Maybe.

I'm going to see what I can find, might be off the net for a day or 2, but I'm OK.

You be careful too.

Always, he thought. She was a smart girl and she could take care of herself.

His mystery package also contained a paper envelope identical to the one that sent him on this journey. With a handwritten page of details. There was no other printing—no embossed letterhead boasting it was from the office of Amon Neff, but it was the same tight scrawl as the note that lead him to Yoshi. Somewhere in the back of his mind, he remembered the airline was among Neff's vast portfolio of companies. The document told him he was required at a one-on-one meeting with Neff in his office on the outskirts of Austin. The letter detailed every turn of the trip and appeared to have been planned by the omnipotent hand of Amon Neff himself. And that was slowly making Mil wary.

A subtle tone brought him around as a message on the lavatory mirror notified him that the aircraft had been cleared for departure and he should return to his seat. He folded the document and tucked the envelope into his pocket.

He took his seat as the aircraft taxied, then banked over the Pacific and accelerated beyond Mach 2. Mil absently toyed with the new wristy. Untraceable. Linked to phantom accounts? He wondered if that meant even Neff couldn't track it. If that was the case, did that mean he didn't necessarily need to report to Neff immediately? If they weren't letting him go back to Luna, did that mean he was technically out of a job and free to do what he pleased? Go see what he could dig up on his own? He began to consider the possibilities and slowly dozed off as the medpatches kicked in.

—⊕—

Monday . 31 Jan . 2078
1905 Pacific Standard Time
Los Angeles International 2 . California . Earth

The landing sequence woke him. The autonomous aircraft decelerated through the sound barrier with a tremor, and he opened his eyes, slightly disoriented. Mil's brain caught up with the situation, and he sat up to see the coastline in the distance as the craft lined up with the offshore runway of LAX2. A tap on his wrist required that he confirm his arrival with Customs. He frowned, knowing what could happen if the magic wristy wasn't everything Yoshi had promised. He set his jaw and tapped: "Confirm, nothing to declare."

He waited for the expected emergency message to contact the authorities. It never happened.

Inside the airport lobby another wrist tap came. Tickets on a connecting flight to Austin and Neff's headquarters. He paused and checked the time. He had an hour to kill and found a small work cubicle with a desk and privacy walls.

He opened his dataslate and began to scroll through the pages and pages of notes he'd made since beginning his search for answers about Slayton Ridge. So many of the leads dead-ended at the same place. The

Space Agency archives. He frowned. Research and sitting around was getting him nowhere. What he needed to do was push things a bit.

He tapped into the wristy. It was time to see just how much he could get away with.

———— ⊗ ————

Tuesday . 01 Feb . 2078
0905 Central Standard Time
Archive Services Corporation . Houston . Texas . Earth

The next morning, Mil waited on the bench across the lawn from the strip center and watched the entrance. This was a new experience. He was way out of his comfort zone, but here he was. The front doors opened and Adrian Evanston stepped out, squinting at the sunlit grounds. Mil rose and waved. She looked puzzled and started in his direction.

"Hey."

"Harrison? What the hell? You sent me flowers?"

"It was that or chocolates. I tried to pick something that'd get your attention."

She held the card at arm's length, looking down over her glasses. "Meet me outside at three. Must talk."

"Thanks for coming."

"Coming? All I did was walk outside to see what kind of idiot would do that. What the hell do you want, Harrison? Does this have anything to do with your granddaughter?" Adrian looked around. "Is she here too?"

"As you well know, Nique's on Luna. This is just me. I need a hand, and you are the only person who can help."

"Bailey turned you down too?"

"She doesn't even know I'm here. Look, I need five minutes of your time. You can decide if what I'm saying is worthwhile, and if it isn't, I'll walk away. This is urgent."

"This is Slayton Ridge, isn't it?"

Mil nodded. "It is."

"You knew I'd keep looking, didn't you?"

Mil grinned. "Call it an informed hunch. I've known you long enough to know you can't resist a good mystery."

She looked around at the quiet neighborhood around them. "You picked a damn good one."

She turned and walked to the main entrance. Mil's face fell.

Adrian stopped and looked back. "Well, come on. There's no sense in you being the only one with your butt on the line for this mess."

She vouched for him at the front desk, raising an eyebrow as he gave his name as Harry Alstrom, then led him through the first security checkpoint and to the main elevators beyond.

He swallowed hard as the elevator descended.

"So what's this Harry Alstrom bullshit?"

"It was Neff's idea. He thinks I'll get around easier. There are a few folks looking for Mil Harrison."

"You mean trying to kill you? I saw the news reports. You were supposed to be on 2705, weren't you?"

"I was. And the coincidences lead me to think that was more than just a random system failure. I think that was a deliberate act. Somebody wanted those who knew about my find at Slayton Ridge gone."

"So that includes Monique, doesn't it?"

"It does. We've talked about it. She's on the lookout."

"Good grief, how the hell did you get into this?"

"Hey, I'm just a simple farmer." The elevator dinged and the doors opened.

"You may be a farmer, but you have never been simple. Come on. Let me show you what I found."

The archivist turned and led the way back through a pair of double doors to a hallway with a push-button coded lock. She entered the code and they passed through to a hallway of doors.

"After Monique came down here, I thought I should do a little digging."

"And you found something. Is that why you turned her in?" Mil took in the vast floor-to-ceiling racks of stored materials.

Adrian heaved a sigh. "You see Harrison, some people in this business pay attention to regulations. There's a standing security track on all members of the *Humanity* crew. The system's AI tagged her the minute she came in here. Monique should have known that. Hell, you should have known that." She leveled an angry glare at Mil. "They locked your ass out and you tricked her into doing your dirty work? That's an asshole move. Even for you."

"I never thought they'd boot her off the mission."

Adrian softened. "That was your daughter's doing. That's the first foot Monique's put wrong in her life. Should have been a wrist slap, nothing more."

Mil shrugged agreement. "That's what I thought."

"That's what you counted on, you shit. Bailey is going places you never dreamed about. Chief administrator? Maybe vice president? She isn't letting any hint of scandal taint this mission or her career. Even if that means her daughter has to wait three or four missions to get to Mars. She shouldn't have been coerced by a manipulative old man."

"Noted. Can we talk about what you found? As much as I've always loved our delightful chats, I'm here to see if you found anything I haven't."

"It's more that I didn't find anything." She had led them halfway down the hall.

"We're down here toward the end. The Eyes Only section. Smile for the cameras, Mr. Alstrom." Adrian chuckled.

The door was more of a vault. She entered the punch code and a panel slid open revealing a palm print and optical scanner for biometrics. The red laser passed over her face and the palm reader glowed blue. "Evanston, Adrian Lilith, 023745987, and one secure guest."

The lock opened with a heavy clunk and the door swung inward. They stepped through and into an airlock. Adrian waited for the six-inch-thick door to swing closed behind them. "Environmentally sealed to protect the documents. Put these on."

She handed Mil a pair of white skintight cotton-latex-blend gloves. He felt the air in the room change—cooler and drier—then the inner door opened.

The room was enormous. Rows of shelving filled with uniform white boxes wearing catalog numbers. Adrian padded down the aisle. Mil dutifully followed. She slowed, checked a shelf number, and then motioned him to follow her down the row. A third of the way down they stopped, and she pointed to a large box on a shelf over his head.

"Number 4907. Grab that."

Mil sneezed out of habit, then tugged down the cardboard container and lugged it down the aisle to a table placed there so materials could be examined but never taken from the secure confines of the room.

Adrian placed her hand on the top of the box. "This hasn't been seen in almost a century."

Mil cocked his head. "And after all this security you're just going to show it to me? A private contractor? Aren't you technically under the auspices of the Space Agency? Shouldn't somebody on Bailey's side of the fence be doing this?"

"You're already up to your ass in this. You're the only one who's been there. And you work for Amon Neff. He has the resources to do something about it. And while I love your dear daughter and know that she takes her role as chief administrator very seriously, she'd be more worried about her political career."

"True that. So, what's in the box?"

Adrian lifted the lid. Inside were six very familiar navy-blue binders. Each an identical three inches thick. Mil slid out one of them at random. The white print on the cover had yellowed over time but was much more legible than the one Mil had seen on the moon. This read very plainly TOP SECRET—SUDDEN HERCULES.

"I've seen one of these before. On the moon."

"So you're confirming this is what you saw there? This is what's hidden?"

"Yes. That blue binder looks to be identical to the one I saw. The one on Luna hasn't been stored in pristine conditions, but I'm certain it's the same mission binder."

"Then you know what's in it."

"Not a clue." He paused a moment, mentally preparing himself for the answers to all his questions. But just as with the pages he'd seen on the moon, the printed words had all but faded from the page. "Shit."

"Yep. Archivists' worst nightmare. Old acid-washed wood-pulp fiber they used back then to make paper. Between that and the celluloid they used to record video, none of that shit was built to last."

"So we know nothing?"

"Yeah, I brought you all the way down here through three levels of security so I could tell you nothing. You're here because you're the only one who can verify that *Hercules* is real. That means this is as big a mess as some people have feared. You know, Harrison, there are some days you're dumber than a box of rocks." She scolded him with a smile.

"I didn't figure it was for old times' sake." He didn't return the smile.

"There were never any old times, Harrison. You married my best friend, that's the only reason I ever put up with you. First for Olivia, then Bailey, and now Monique. I've been dealing with your messes for fifty years."

"And you never forget anything, do you?" Mil leaned against the table.

"Nope. And that's why I remember *Hercules*." She tapped the binder.

"And . . .?" He waved for more.

"It was listed in an old USAF manifest. Serious security breach. I started unraveling that thread and found some things. You should talk to this person."

The old woman handed Mil a piece of folded paper.

It was an address. In Utah.

"I could just give him a call."

She leaned toward him with a whisper. "It's a her. And I did that already. She's scared. Says she knows what's on Slayton Ridge. And now, since the shuttle blew up, she's borderline terrified. She won't talk about it on a call."

"She sounds a little paranoid." Mil's brow furrowed.

"Wouldn't you be?"

"I probably ought to be."

Thursday . 03 Feb . 2078

1450 Lunar Standard Time

Tiger Team Work Room . Armstrong Base . Luna

The large black man tapped the image on the video wall. Dr. Isiah Merrick was a former military cop, and his close-cropped hair, mustache, and busted nose belied his PhD in investigative sciences. The object of his interest was a paused video frame from a security camera. A video frame that Nique and her systems had zoomed in on, recentered, rerendered and augmented. Now, barely visible among the stacks and aisles of cargo, a human-shaped shadow lurked behind a container.

"I need to find this person."

"Yessir." Nique had been instructed to provide whatever assistance she could during the crush to discover the cause of the deadly explosion. She leaned into her console and flicked frames around. She moved the image about and zoomed in. Behind her, the investigator moved a chair closer and leaned in over her shoulder.

"Some people get uncomfortable when I watch over their shoulder. Is that a problem?"

"No sir, not at all," she lied as her fingers danced across the inputs. In minutes she had a sample frame for review.

Merrick puzzled over the image. "Back that up, please."

Nique slid her finger across the air in front of her and the security camera footage rocked back and forth.

"Do you see that?"

Nique leaned into the holodisplay. "There's movement. There by the edge of the cargo containers in the holding paddock."

"Is there a better angle of this? Another camera?" The investigator pursed his lips and tucked a knuckle under his chin.

Nique scrolled through the data stores. Virtually every inch of the habitats on the Luna Colony were under video surveillance. It wasn't as much for security as for safety. If anything went awry, someone, somewhere was likely to see it on-screen.

She toggled to a different video source, and the angle showed the backside of the paddock. A figure walked through the scene, taking great care to stay out of the sightlines of the camera Nique had just been viewing, but in doing so stepped into the edge of this camera's view.

"Seems like they don't know about this camera." Merrick pointed to the figure on-screen.

"It's new. It went live when the new O2 facility went online last month. Their deliveries stage here. Maddie showed me how to add it to the network."

The figure on the screen removed a thin package from their backpack and dropped to a knee behind a container. A moment later, the figure stood up, holding something all too familiar to Detective Merrick.

"That looks a helluva lot like a rifle."

CHAPTER TWENTY-SEVEN

Mil hadn't seen anything but a bull elk in the last fifteen minutes. He had to take control of the rental vehicle himself over the last two miles of a dirt trail that might have once been a road to a Forest Service fire watch tower, but it had never appeared on a map. The computers and sensors of the transport had no clue what to make of it. The vehicle's dilemma reminded Mil of his less than trusty spidertruck waiting back home on the moon.

The road ended at an overgrown dirt driveway beside an anonymous rusting mailbox on a wooden post. The peeling number decal on the box matched the address in his pocket. Mil turned his rental into the drive and followed as the gravel road bent through a stand of aspens rustling in the soft breeze and revealed an A-frame structure with a faded green metal roof. The surroundings were either unkept or the owner had deliberately let it go back to nature. Mil parked behind an old dented electric pickup with a missing tailgate. He double-checked the address on the paper as he walked over to the porch and paused to sneeze. He hadn't knocked on a door in thirty years and didn't see anything to knock with. He was about to strike the door with his fist when a voice asked, "Who is it?"

Mil didn't know where the voice was coming from or where to respond. He spoke to no one in particular. "My name is Harr—um"—he'd forgotten his new name. He tapped through a stack of menus on his wrist. There it was. "Harry Alstrom. I'm working with Adrian Evanston—"

Before he could finish, the door cracked open. An eye and a bleached blonde hairdo peeked out of the shadows.

"What do you want?"

"Adrian gave me your address. She says you may have some information."

"Who do you work for?"

Mil thought a beat. "I'm kind of between jobs at the moment. I'm semiretired. But Adrian tells me you have information on Slayton Ridge."

"You alone?"

Mil nodded. "I am."

The door closed and he heard a series of locks being thrown. Then it opened and the woman checked the area for any other signs of life before grabbing his arm and pulling him inside. "Get in here."

Mil's eyes slowly adjusted to the darkness. The floor-to-ceiling windows that would have presented a majestic view of the mountain range had been set to full opaque. The timber-frame cabin's great room was an ominous dark cavern. Mil could make out a staircase climbing a wall to his left up to a loft. The opposite wall was filled with framed family photos on either side of a giant rock-faced fireplace. It too was dark and cold.

"Watch your step." She moved ahead of him and down four quick steps into what once might have been called a conversation pit. A sofa on one side and two armchairs surrounded a low table. The woman skirted around the table. Mil banged a shin.

"This would be easier with a little light," he said.

"Sorry." She was perfunctory. "Room lights on."

The glow came up and Mil got his first look at his host. She was younger than he, about Bailey's age. In contrast to the surrounding yard of the home, she seemed tidy. Earrings, a necklace, and a hint of makeup. He'd been expected.

"Okay, I introduced myself. So, maybe you could tell me who you are?"

"I'm Ava. Ava Slessick." She waited for him to react, as if he was supposed to recognize the name. He didn't.

"Okay. Ava, I'm told you know something about what's on Slayton Ridge."

"Oh no, it's not what I *know*. It's what I *have* that's important." She gestured to the sofa. "Please, have a seat, make yourself comfortable."

She disappeared up two steps and around a corner through the open kitchen. Mil unbuttoned his jacket and took a seat on the edge of the tasteful plaid-fabric sofa.

She returned lugging a large plastic container. It had been sealed with yellow tape along the edge, but that seal had been broken. She set it on a low table and pulled a chair up to it, facing Mil with the box between them. She took a deep breath and looked to the ceiling for inspiration or permission. Mil couldn't tell which, but it gave him a feeling of unease.

"I know who you are, Mr.—um, what did you say? Alstrom? If you aren't Millennium Harrison, then you can tell everyone to get stuffed and I'll never tell a soul. You can all deal with this mess without me."

"I see." He didn't. "Yeah. I'm Harrison; the other name's a ruse so I can travel around without undue attention."

"Better. Two weeks ago Adrian called me and asked about my grandfather." She lifted the lid and removed an ancient yellowed black-and-white photograph. Two rows of men against a dark, almost black background. The faint shape of a large suborbital aircraft behind them. Military, Mil's experience told him. Her finger wavered over the front row. "That's him. Colonel Benjamin Reynolds."

Mil shook his head. "Don't know him."

"You wouldn't. He wasn't famous. And his mission was top secret. Project Sudden Hercules."

"I've seen the name."

She pulled a leather-bound book from the box. "My grandfather was the LEM pilot on a top-secret Air Force space-shuttle mission in February 1983. This is his journal."

"Okay. What's it say?"

"You'll want to read it, but essentially he says that in the early 1980s, NASA, the Air Force, and the old National Reconnaissance Organization performed a series of secret launches of the space shuttle *Columbia* disguised as NRO spy-satellite missions."

"So the spy-satellite launches were a cover-up?"

"You've been to Slayton Ridge? On the moon, right?"

"Slayton Ridge is a classified exclusion zone. No one is permitted there."

"I know that." She stood and walked to a crystal decanter and tray of glasses on a small bar on a far wall of the room. "Can I get you a drink, Mr. Harrison?"

"I'd take some water."

"You may want to be sober for this. But you'll need a drink after."

She disappeared into the kitchen and returned with a tall glass with ice and water and a rocks glass filled with a good amount of liquid courage for herself. She settled onto the far end of the couch and tucked her legs under her. Mil took a sip of water fresh from a mountain stream and almost forgot why he was there. Maybe there was something on Earth he could like.

Ava stared off into the distance. "Where to begin? I come from a space family, Mr. Harrison. Not famous like yours, of course, but my grandfather was an astronaut, my mother was an engineer, my dad died in a flight test when I was in college, and my brother still works in Sunnyvale. I went to Caltech and I retired from Neff Astrophysics two years ago. I miss it."

Mil checked the time on his wristy. "Congratulations. Is there a point to this stroll through the family resume?"

She ignored his impatience. "My mother passed away last year, and while cleaning out her house, I found this box. Sealed. I didn't open it for the longest time, and when I did, I wished I hadn't."

She took a swallow and seemed to steady herself.

"I didn't know what to do with this. But then it was all over the media that you'd gotten a radiation dose and were coming back to Earth for the first time in thirty years."

"It's more like twenty years, but everybody likes bigger numbers."

"And then, right after the shuttle that was supposed to bring you home blew up, the lady from the archives called, asking for information on my grandfather. I got curious and opened the box. It scared the piss out of me. Look, this is information you or somebody needs. It might even save somebody's life. Maybe everybody's life on Luna."

"Dramatic."

"It is. So, I need to know, have you been to Slayton Ridge?"

Mil examined his water. "Here's the deal, Mrs. Slessick. It is Mrs., right?"

"Call me Ava."

"Fine. I'm Mil. I've been told I'm not going to return to Luna. They haven't come right out and said I can't, but that I shouldn't. My radiation numbers are too high. I'll die if I go up there. So they want me to stay here, where I'll die anyway." He thought for a moment. Having voiced that made it a little more real. "They can't very well do much more to me than that for breaking clearances, so, yes. I've been to Slayton Ridge."

"Is it still there?"

"Well, that depends on what 'it' is. Look, Ava, I'm trusting you—I've admitted to breaching an international treaty and trespassing on a classified installation. Let's get to the point, shall we? What's supposed to be up there?"

She picked up the diary.

"According to this book, my grandfather put a bunker on the moon. In 1983." She took a large swallow of her scotch and looked at Mil. He nodded.

"That squares with what I saw on the shadow side of the ridge."

"And they're still there?"

"They? I didn't see anyone."

"Not people. Missiles."

"Missiles?"

"Trident XA missiles. With three-stage thermonuclear warheads."

Mil slowly shook his head. Bingo. The orange columns were launch tubes. "Nuclear warheads. On the moon. Perfect."

"Want that drink now?"

An hour later the papers and photos were scattered all over Ava's kitchen table. Mil's jacket was draped over the back of the couch. He shuffled through the documents as she paced, drank, and explained what she'd uncovered herself.

"It's 1982. Ronald Reagan was president of the United States, and he was pushing a new round of strategic weapons treaties on the old Soviet Union. START, I think it was. Strategic arms reduction treaties. Part of the agreement called for the elimination of the ultra high yield weapons— three-stage thermonuclear devices—city killers, with yields in the sixty to seventy-five megaton range. That's magnitudes beyond the destructive power of the Hiroshima bomb, and beyond the dirty bomb in Tel Aviv back in 2030."

She stopped pacing and pointed to her drink with a questioning look for Mil. He shook his head. Her voice grew a little louder as she talked from the kitchen, then returned with the bottle of scotch.

"But some people didn't trust the Soviets. And Reagan's Defense Department was full of cowboys running their own little operations. They ran guns to rebels in Nicaragua trying to overthrow that government. They supplied weapons and advisors to the Afghans fighting the Russians. They really didn't want to get rid of the most powerful weapons America had ever built. But here was the boss—Ronnie Raygun—just doing away with the best nuclear bargaining chip they had ever had."

There was a sarcastic tone to Mil's voice. "The old Mutually Assured Destruction idea—if we each have world-ending weapons pointed at each other, no one would ever be stupid enough to pull the trigger. No wonder they called it MAD."

She took a large swallow. "But they realized they had the perfect hiding place. The Soviets didn't have the technology or the money to get to the moon. So, they figured they'd park a half dozen nukes up there, leave them aimed at the old Soviet Union and then, if they ever needed to, they could launch them from the moon just as easily as from a submarine."

Mil looked up from the paperwork. "That's the wildest piece of horse-shit I've ever heard. The shuttle couldn't have carried enough fuel to get a platform that size to the moon, much less get it slowed down to land."

Ava tapped the journal. "It's all in here. They could if they built it in sections, in orbit, and they could do it with old, off-the-shelf parts. The platform and bunker were a test prototype from a Trident sub package. The crew quarters were a SkyLab module, and each section conveniently fit in the cargo hold of their space shuttle or the old Atlas boosters. Over the course of several missions in 1982 and '83, they parked all the pieces and a lot of fuel in orbit and covered it up as spy satellites. They assembled the platform in Earth orbit and sent it to the moon using the command-module platform and the lunar injection thruster that was supposed to be Apollo 18. By my numbers, one trip on the Atlas had to just be fuel."

She paused and picked up the book. "According to this diary, my grand-father was on STS 47-D, a classified shuttle launch out of the Vandenberg Air Force Base. They utilized the last lunar module that Grumman had on the production line when Congress halted funding for Apollo. The CIA paid them to finish it and stuck it in a warehouse. It was supposed to go to the Smithsonian."

Mil shook his head. "I've been to the Smithsonian. The LEM is there."

"Really? How close did you get to it? That's LEM2. It never flew be-cause it wasn't space worthy. Grumman hadn't figured it out. But the Apollo 18 LEM? LEM13? It was perfect, combining everything those old hands ever learned about a lunar landing vehicle. It was a J-model—more fuel for landing, room for a rover. They put the real thing in the cargo hold of

Columbia, and named the LEM *Turtle.* They docked it with a command module called *Rabbit* and the *Hercules* weapons platform already in orbit, and my grandfather flew it to the moon. He says they landed near the platform for a scheduled six-month mission."

Mil met her eyes. "Someone was there. I saw it. But it didn't look like they stayed six months."

"They didn't. They had an incident and evacuated."

"An incident? On the moon, with nuclear weapons? Kept secret all this time?" A note of skepticism crept into his voice.

"You don't have to believe me, Mr. Harrison. Read it for yourself."

CHAPTER TWENTY-EIGHT

Thursday . 03 Feb . 2078
1340 Mountain Standard Time
Slessick Cabin . Summit County . Utah . USA . Earth

Mil took the brown leather-bound notebook. It was smaller than a dataslate tablet, but thicker. It looked like it would fit in a pocket. He half expected it to be a log book like those from the days when pilots manually entered the details of every flight. Nowadays AI personas like Bailey kept track of all that.

But this was different.

A faded thin ribbon marked a page.

Ava gestured to the book. "This is his personal journal from the first half of 1983. There are more volumes, but this one details the landing and the problem."

"Journaling a classified mission to put nukes on the moon? That's a fairly large breach of security." Mil opened the book to yellowing pages carrying the neat handwriting of a seasoned astronaut. His mind considered the reams of paper and pens this man must have gone through in an era before computers and digital recordkeeping.

Ava gave him a sideways glance. "I get the impression that there are a lot of space crews who don't exactly follow the rules hard and fast."

Mil considered that for a moment and began to read.

2/Feb/83—Vandenberg

Third day of holds and a launch abort. It's getting old. One mechanical issue with a sensor, two weather holds. Winter fog. I'd think they'd want to launch this circus in the dark or the fog as secret as everything is. The esteemed Dr. Dwight Porterfield, PhD showed up in a T-shirt that says "Bomb Tech— If You See Me Running Try To Keep Up." The man's a nuclear physicist with the sense of humor of a 12-year-old. We try again tomorrow. Feld says weather should be go. We'll see.

4/Feb/83—Orbit

Have a few minutes for catchup—another delay but finally a nominal launch. Scotty McClain has Columbia *settled into tracking* Hercules. *Should rendezvous this time tomorrow. Everyone is relaxed and these guys are real pros. I'm proud to be a part of this crew. Did a damage check on the shuttle doors.* Columbia *looks clean and so does* Turtle. *I never believed they could fit a LEM in that cargo bay. This might actually work.*

5/Feb/83—Hercules

This thing is massive. I see why it took four missions to get this built in orbit. The booster looks large, but the main package—the special services module—is gigantic. And then the structure around everything to hold retros and landing gear? Damn. We'd seen it all in pieces and in mockups, but all together in orbit? It's nuts how large this mess is. It's gonna be like driving a city block to the moon.

Supplemental—Harry Feld is an amazing pilot. He docked Rabbit on the first attempt just as slick as you please. When I tried to get the Turtle docked on the other end of the special services module, the SSM docking ring wouldn't engage. Took three tries and I really had to goose it. In our meetings with the Apollo guys, Stu Roosa said he had a similar issue on 14. It takes a hard dock to get the clamps to lock on. All good for now.

7/Feb/83—Rabbit

An eventful week is an understatement. Good launch, difficult docking, spacewalk to the Rabbit, and now on the way. I guess the Apollo guys had experiments and measurements to take, we're just along for the ride. Putting up with Feld's bad jokes. One more day till Dwight and I head to the moon and Slayton Ridge.

Mil paused and looked at Ava.

"So they did target the dark side of Slayton Ridge? To hide the damn things in the dark?"

She held her drink in both hands. "Well, their cargo wasn't supposed to exist. The arms-reduction talks were supposed to bargain them away for scrap. The Soviets actually get rid of theirs, we disassemble ours, and it's a whole new era of peace and understanding."

"Yeah, that worked out well for the Ukrainians." He went back to the diary.

8/Feb/83—Orbiting the moon!

We're here. 60 miles above the surface and it's amazing. I wasn't really prepared for the enormity of it all. The craters, the contrast between dark and light. Telescope shows the landing zone on the sun side to be extremely rocky. Control says the shadow side shouldn't be a problem. We're going to try and get some sleep, but I don't know how that's going to happen. Just a little keyed up. Porterfield is cool as a cucumber. I guess years under the ocean in a nuke sub will do that for you. This time tomorrow I'll be standing on the surface of the moon with a half dozen Trident XAs. Incredible.

10/Feb/83—Slayton Ridge

What a fucking disaster. The SSM landed on a boulder and sheared off the aft starboard landing leg. We did an emergency deorbit and I tried to miss the boulder field but Turtle is almost a klick away from the SSM. It's a hike. In the dark. We fabbed up a ladder and have the platform fairly stable, but it's essentially sitting on a rock. Not exactly a state-of-the-art launch platform for nukes. We have five green tubes and one showing a malfunction. Dwight's concerned and that bothers the hell out of me.

11/Feb/83—Slayton Ridge

We're chasing this thing. The rock is crumbling under the weight. The whole facility is torqued and now Dwight is charting radiation from the missile bay. That can't be good. Control put us on a radio lockdown as they think the mission may be compromised. I don't see how we can stay here for the full deployment if conditions don't improve.

13/Feb/83—Slayton Ridge

I have a minute before we start demobilization—Dwight is going through the sequence to secure the launch bay and I've got all the gear packed. We're bailing out and letting Control figure out the next steps. We don't have the tools to make repairs or the spares to fix what's broken. I'm betting it'll need another mission, maybe two. It sounds like they want to go ahead with the burial and hide the SSM. I've dreaded this. I didn't like this idea when we tried it on the snowmass. Explosives to start an avalanche. Adjacent to nuclear missiles. On the moon. Stupid.

17/Feb/83—Somewhere between the moon and Earth

I don't think Porterfield is going to survive. When we did the avalanche to bury the SSM, Dwight caught a piece of shrapnel. A flying rock pierced his suit like a spear. Broke his arm and I think it nicked an artery in his shoulder. When I got him out of his EVA suit in the LEM, blood went everywhere. I patched him up as best I could and did an emergency liftoff. Thank God for Feld—he did the orbit and docking calculations for the command module and the LEM while I tried to fly Turtle with one hand keeping Dwight upright. Hardest flying I've ever done. We got docked and brought Dwight into Rabbit and got him strapped in. He looks terrible and his vitals are crap.

26/Feb/83—Nellis

Secure debriefs for the past week on everything. Yesterday was a solid three and a half hours on how Dwight died. In a way he's lucky. He's not going to be the scapegoat for the mission failure. They're going to drum me out. After they wring everything out of me they can. If I see one more shrink I'll scream. And then the mission ops team debriefs. Status of the Hercules facility. Radiation levels. Current situation. What do I think the launch capabilities are? Can the missiles still hit Leningrad? Moscow? Like I could tell.

Mil closed the diary and sat still for a moment. "It does clear up a bunch of stuff."

He shook his head.

"Like what?"

"Well, if they used explosives to trigger a landslide, that would cover the bunker. That's why nobody's found it. It just looks like the back wall of the crater calved off. But my God, what a ballsy plan. Hide missiles on the moon and then actually do it. That's insane."

"And if they had an issue landing, that's why they had to leave." Ava seemed lost in thought.

"Issue?" Mil waved the journal. "Pilots understate everything. I read this as a full-blown crash. There's a huge boulder field—some the size of houses or boxcars. If they tried to set down and hit one of those, they're lucky the thing didn't roll onto its roof. Or worse."

Ava took a drink. "I did some research on the crew—the command module pilot—Harry Feld. He was promoted to general and retired just after this. He wound up as a contractor at Wright Patterson Air Force base in an R and D job. The missile guy who didn't make it was Navy Commander Dwight Porterfield. He's listed as being killed in a training accident. He's buried in Arlington. Neither of them had any next of kin."

Mil nodded his understanding. "High-risk mission. They'd want volunteers with no family ties. I wonder how your grandad got in?"

She shook her head at him. "They didn't marry until later. Left the program and went to work for Lockheed in the Skunkworks. Burbank and Palmdale. One of his other journals mentions test-flight work on Aurora."

"The first hypersonic aircraft. Ben Reynolds sounds like a helluva guy. I'd like to have met your grandad."

"Yeah, me too."

Mil stood and paced the room in thought. He ran a hand through his hair.

"So here's what I can confirm. I've seen the descent stage of an old lunar module there, half a klick from the facility. And I've been inside the facility. There are two compartments: one is tight crew quarters, and one looks like it could be missile launch tubes."

"How did you find it if they buried it under a landslide?" Ava took a sip of her drink.

"Tripped over it. Totally by accident. I was cutting through the EZ on my way home and had a malfunction. I landed on top of the hatch. It's not buried very deep. Five, maybe ten centimeters. You never talked to your grandfather about it?"

"He died of cancer before I was born."

"Radiation?"

"Twentieth-century medicine. My mother always said the chemo-therapy killed him."

Mil ran a hand across his scratchy beard. This had been a long day, and he was beat. "So we know there are nuclear weapons cached on the moon. We know they're high-yield thermonuclear weapons. And I have it on pretty good authority they're leaking radiation."

"At least they aren't armed." She gave a tip of her head. "It sounds to me like they secured the weapons before they evacuated."

Mil's head filled with the VR imagery of Granger thrashing around the bunker in his death throes. One gloved hand slapping at the control panel.

"We hope. But one of them is leaking something. There's a decent amount of corrosion bleeding out of one of the columns."

Ava nodded. "Launch tubes. Could be the batteries. Those limited-life components are a hundred years old. Could be fuel. I'd bet they used good old nasty hydrazine."

"Oxidized nitric acid—yep, that would do it," Mil agreed.

"If that leaked, it'd be a problem, not for the nuclear package necessarily, but for the high explosives around it."

Mil took a sip of his water.

Ava gestured with her glass. "Ready for that drink now?"

"I think I'd rather talk with a missile guy."

"I know one." She flicked her wristy and the tabletop holodisplay blinked on.

"You know one?"

"He's an old friend from work. Started out as a missile guy. Lives on the other side of the valley."

CHAPTER TWENTY-NINE

Thursday . 03 Feb . 2078
1945 Mountain Standard Time
The Tenderloin Chop House . Park City . Utah . Earth

F our hours later they were sitting in a private room in a darkened restaurant in Park City. Ava fidgeted. Her eyes flicked around the room. Even a second glass of wine failed to calm her nerves.

Mil tried a softer, reassuring tone. "Look, he's right. The best place to hide is in plain sight. Nobody followed us here. Nobody knows he's coming. Nobody knows what we're talking about. It's fine."

"You base that on your extensive espionage career, Mr. Alstrom?"

"Point taken, but we might as well enjoy the food. I can't remember the last time I had a steak." Mil sawed into his rib eye. "Meal printers do not handle dense proteins." He admired the pink morsel on his fork.

Across the table, Ava trembled as she stabbed her salad. "I figured you for a carnivore."

A motion across the dining room caught her eye.

She stiffened as the hostess began to lead someone their way. Then she sighed in relief.

"There's Zach."

She waved, and a portly gentleman hiding behind a salt-and-pepper beard wound his way through the wood-paneled restaurant. The two old friends hugged, and then he shook Mil's hand in greeting. Zach Constantine took the seat across from Mil, turned down the waiter's offer of food, but ordered a glass of Argentine red.

"Zach's an old-line engineer. Los Alamos, DOE, DOD, he's been through the wars."

The missileman nodded and polished a pair of reading glasses. "Thankfully not actual wars. I'm one of the last of the breed. Most of what we did was decommissioning obsolete equipment or weapons that treaties pushed out of service."

"You did that at Los Alamos?"

"The engineering. The hardware was all done at the Pantex plant outside of Amarillo."

"So you just took them apart?" Nuclear missiles were not anywhere in Mil's area of expertise, but he was pretty sure he was about to learn much more than he ever wanted to know.

"Essentially, yes. Pulled them down to subassemblies. The physics package—the actual nuclear components—were taken to Rocky Flats, in Colorado, or Oak Ridge. The weapons were usually contaminated, so they'd decon what they could and ship out what they couldn't as waste for burial somewhere in the desert."

"Ever hear of a project called Sudden Hercules?"

Zach twisted his brow, deep in thought. "Doesn't ring a bell. Weapons project?"

Ava and Mil traded looks. She gave a short overview of what they'd found. That elicited a low whistle.

"Trident XAs. Hmm. That fits with the START talks time frame. The time line works. I'd have to do some research. If those are three-stage weapons, Mark-71Ds or so, they'd have a significant yield. Launch them from the moon? That's inventive." He stroked his beard, imagining the theoretical possibilities.

"What if they weren't launched? What if one went off on the moon? What's the danger to the inhabitants?" Mil leaned in and lowered his voice.

"Well, there wouldn't be a surface wave. You've seen the old black-and-white videos of nuclear blasts tearing through wooden-frame buildings? There's no atmosphere to compress on the moon, so there wouldn't be a concussive event."

"That's good news." Ava waved for another glass of rosé.

"But that energy would travel through the surface of the moon. Lunar quakes rippling out from the explosion. Probably destroy everything within a hundred klicks."

Mil nearly choked. "A hundred kilometers? That's the main base, Settlements Two and Three. And my farm." Images of Emma, Nique, and the crowded command center flashed through his brain.

Zach took a sip of his red. "Well, a warhead contains—"

"There are six tubes."

Zach's eyebrows went up. "Hmm." He tapped on his wrist. Frowned. "That kind of destructive power could shake the moon to its core. There's no real reference for the amount of energy on that size astronomical body. It would likely be catastrophic."

"Destroy the moon? That seems a little dramatic." Ava took her glass from the robot, which backed away silently and returned to the bar.

The PhD shook his head. "You're talking about the most powerful devices the inventors of the nuclear weapon ever devised. These were designed to kill millions and level major metropolitan areas. This isn't theater-size, Hiroshima tactical stuff here. These things were so powerful, their testing was banned on Earth. Enrico Fermi even wondered if they might incinerate the atmosphere. Oppenheimer was basically blacklisted for opposing their creation."

"So it could destroy the moon?"

Mil sat back. He expected bad, and this was about as bad as it got.

"Worse. The moon is responsible for tidal forces on Earth. Affect the moon and you change the way oceans move on Earth, the way the movement of those ocean currents heat and cool the planet, even the way the planet rotates on its axis. Screw up the moon and you pretty much destroy life on Earth as we know it."

Mil nodded. "They're leaking."

"Leaking? Radiation?"

"And probably propellant. That doesn't strike me as good." His mind went back to the shuttle exploding into a ball of dust and debris over Armstrong Base.

"Well, you're in a low-oxygen environment, so there's not as much danger from the propellant. Any type of spontaneous combustion would require an oxidizer." Zach considered his hosts and Mil's well-known occupation. "Which, of course, you know. But if there's radiation there will be heat. And the high-explosives package around the plutonium pit won't react well to that temperature. If it reaches the flashpoint of the hi-ex, it could go high order, and you could see a detonation of the high explosives shell."

"Which would trigger the nuclear bomb." Mil shook his head.

"Possibly. But probably not. It takes a very precise set of circumstances for that." The physicist paused for a sip of wine.

"At last some good news."

"But you'll still have the remaining weapons and a widespread area that is seriously contaminated." Ava swirled her wine.

"It's under a rockslide," Mil said.

"So it'll irradiate the rockslide and spread that across a radioactive debris field when the explosive event occurs," said Zach.

"*When* the explosion occurs?" Mil cocked his head

"Oh, I think there will be an explosion. It's just a matter of time," Zach said.

"Like . . . when?"

"Could happen today, might take fifty years. But if there's radiation, there's heat. It's just a matter of how long it takes to generate the temperature that triggers the detonation."

"Jesus."

Ava raised her glass. "'I am become Death, destroyer of worlds.'"

A question crossed Mil's face.

Zach nodded. "It's a Hindu passage. Supposedly Oppenheimer said that when they detonated the first Trinity weapon."

Mil was deep in thought. "So, how do we stop it?"

"Stop it? It's physics. You don't just stop it."

"These things don't have an off switch?"

"Well, sure, but you're talking about a malfunctioning device in a radioactive environment." Zach ticked off the scenario on his fingers. "On the moon."

Ava took a sip of her drink. "One of them. But the other ones—why not just launch them?"

The men looked at her. "They're rockets, right? Designed to go from the moon to the Earth? Retarget them to the sun and fire them. Get them off the moon and away from people."

Mil's brow furrowed. "Can you do that? I mean these have been aimed at various cities in Russia for a century. There's no way we launch those if there's a chance they can't be reprogrammed."

Zach nodded, deep in thought. "I think it's possible. Is there power in the facility?"

"Some sort of power. I saw warning lights working. Maybe an old hydrogen fuel cell? Small nuclear battery? But you're talking Apollo-era technology that hasn't been touched in almost a century. Plus, we'd have to find the launch codes, reprogram the target coordinates . . ."

Zach toyed with his wineglass. "If the exclusion zone has been reclassified over the years, you can bet someone, somewhere, knows the launch codes and the programming sequences. Or how to find them. The hardware in the unmolested tubes should be in good shape. Those guys overbuilt everything. These things were designed to be maintained by eighteen-year-old enlisted kids in North Dakota winters or twenty thousand leagues under the sea. It's antique tech, but very robust. Plus, it's been in a dark, cold, airtight environment all this time. Virtually perfect storage for these systems."

"Except for the radiation," Mil reminded him.

"That's the wild card."

Ava shook her head. "No. Politics is your wild card."

CHAPTER THIRTY

Friday . 04 Feb . 2078
0855 Central Standard Time
Neff Tower One . Austin . Texas . USA . Earth

Amon Neff stepped off the elliptical exercise machine and took a towel and hydration bottle from his personal trainer. He was in amazing condition for a ninety-two-year-old man; in fact he didn't look a day over sixty. He ran the towel over his bald head and drained his bottle of vitamin-enhanced beverage.

"Mr. Harrison is in your outer office, sir." The trainer opened the door to the adjacent dressing area, its shower and valet waiting for the visionary trillionaire.

But Neff turned instead to the door on the other side of the small gym and then into the outer office.

Mil was waiting on an uncomfortably stylish settee. His suit was pressed, shoes shined, and his scratchy week-old beard gave his jaw a soft, white fuzz.

"Where the hell have you been? You were supposed to be here two days ago." Neff scowled. He wiped his hand on a towel and extended it.

Mil stood and they shook hands for the first time in twenty years. "Sorry Amon, I didn't realize you meant come right away. I took a day and did some sightseeing. I haven't been to Earth for a while."

"You disappeared. Ran off." He glared as he tossed the water bottle to the trainer who slipped out the side door.

"Well, somebody seems to have it out for me."

"So I hear. But Yoshi should have told you. I meant for you to come here directly."

"He was just trying to get me out quickly and quietly. I thought that was a good idea. Maybe Yoshi, or you, have some other resources that can ID who's trying to knock me off."

"I'm told the police in Japan are investigating and the Tiger Team on Luna are going through Armstrong Base with a fine-tooth comb. What more do you want me to do?"

Mil pursed his lips. There was a considerable effort being expended on his behalf. "If I think of something I'll let you know."

"So, how are you? Dr. Wilkerson tells me your prognosis isn't great."

"She's a little dramatic, but yeah, I got a pretty good dose."

Neff led the way through two massive mahogany doors into his main office. "A dose that put you well over your lifetime ceiling, as I understand it."

"Well, those are just guidelines."

"I know, my company doctors helped set them." Neff took a seat behind the desk and waved Mil to yet another uncomfortable chair. An assistant appeared with a tray of fruits, breakfast pastry, and carafes of coffee and juice. She poured a glass of juice for Neff and turned to Mil.

"Black coffee, isn't it, Mr. Harrison?"

"Yes." Mil realized these people shipped him everything his existence depended upon. Food, supplies, underwear, and coffee. After all these years of shipping manifests, holographic reports, and video conferences, they knew as much about him as he did. The assistant handed him the cup and saucer and closed the door on her way out.

"Based on those numbers, we should stop you from going back to the moon, you know."

"I do know. And I know you can pretty much do anything you want."

"Except find people when they use my own tech to disappear. It's a blessing and a curse. I don't really want to control people's lives. It's much more trouble than it's worth. But I do believe in giving people options—ways to do what they want to do."

Mil took a sip. He hated to admit it, but Earth coffee was better than the pods he used in his galley. "All I want is to go back to Luna. It's pretty simple."

Neff put a hand to his forehead. "Oh, it's anything but simple."

"So, you are going to stop me?"

"I was. But I've changed my mind. In fact, I'm sending you right back there." Neff stepped across his office, where a large map of Mars shone bright red on the wall. He tapped the control panel and it transformed into a dull gray visual of the moon. He pointed directly to the lunar basin that contained the aptly named Mare Crisium, the Sea of Crises. "Specifically, back here."

"Slayton Ridge," Mil said. The feel of those words had changed since the first day he'd tumbled down the crater.

"Slayton Ridge has been classified for a century. We have to scrub that before it gets out, and you are just the man to do it."

Mil noticed the man wore a smug smile. "So what about this led to your change of heart, Amon?"

Neff returned to the business side of his desk. He tapped the surface, the room lights dimmed, and wallscreens brightened. The display was a typewritten page, a cover sheet with TOP SECRET—EYES ONLY—DUPLICATION FORBIDDEN stamped in red across the face. A Department of Defense seal printed above a series of numbers and coding. Neff waved a hand at the screen.

"Nobody has seen this in almost a century. I spent a small fortune digging it up."

"Sudden Hercules?"

"So you do know?" Neff regarded his old colleague with a skeptical glance.

"I've learned a few terrifying things lately."

Neff smirked. "You don't know how terrifying the full story is. This is the top-secret ULTRA, Department of Defense, Black project authorization. Eyes Only by presidential authority. Except the president—Ronald Reagan at the time—never authorized it. His signature is forged. More than likely he never even knew he'd green-lit a fully operational nuclear-weapons facility on the moon."

"Who did then?"

"Lord only knows. Somebody high up with access. Hell, there were operatives in that White House running guns to Nicaragua, making covert deals with enemies in the Middle East, and Reagan never even knew about any of it. Hide a bunker full of nuclear missiles on the moon? I bet it was a piece of cake for those guys."

Mil leaned forward. "You know, it's leaking."

Neff tapped the desk and the screen resolved to a three-dimensional view of the orange launch tubes. Mil recognized the feed from Granger's suit. He cursed his AI systems for making him report it.

Neff looked from the screen to Mil. "Can you fix it?"

"Not remotely. There's a possibility we could target them to the sun and launch them. That might be viable. Tube Five, though, the leaker, I don't know. Plus, it looks like it'll have to be done from inside the platform. Granger didn't do us any favors stumbling around in there."

"The radiation?"

"Will kill whoever goes in there."

"Do you have a robot that can do it?"

Mil cracked a smile. "One of the reasons I keep a barn full of obsolete gear is because you never know when you might need something. I've still got an old Axial Mark III in the corner. It's old, analog tech, so the radiation won't affect the capacitance circuits. And I think I can use the VR recording to program it to navigate the ladder and multiple doors and to complete the task. The facility was designed with some sort of Faraday cage—maybe to shield it from the weapons or an electromagnetic pulse or enemy jamming. Whatever, it also impedes radio frequency communication. I don't have any way to remotely pilot the bot."

"We're not turning an autonomous robot loose in a facility to launch nuclear weapons. That's a PR disaster waiting to happen. But Axial made great products. We bought them based on that Mark III—it was a great multipurpose robot."

Mil shook his head in agreement. "It won't be autonomous, and since we can't trust a radio connection, I'll hard code it. I'll get to work on it as soon as I get back."

The old man pointed to the wristy Mil wore. "Just ask for what you need to get this Mark III running."

"So you just say the word and I fire up a robot to launch some nuclear missiles? You don't think a few politicians might be interested in that? Maybe some elected officials?"

"Oh, come on. You think I haven't been on a secure line with the president since this popped up? She's as worried as I am. Well, maybe not. I don't know if anything rattles her, but she is concerned about what the Russians might do if this gets out. She wants this kept completely quiet. No comms, no records, no nothing. These things just disappear."

"A no-bid contract for emergency cleanup services?" Mil shook his head.

"Let's just say sizable campaign contributions have been pledged."

"I guess that solves everyone's problem then, doesn't it?" Mil contemplated the meaning. "I get to die on the moon, it removes the threat to the settlements, and nobody else gets hurt."

"Oh, it doesn't begin to solve the problem it creates."

Mil cocked his head. "I don't understand."

"Less than a half dozen people know the details of this. Now, the people who built this mess in the first place had a top-flight cover story. We don't need more people knowing about this. It could cause a panic. The Russians suspect there's something there, but they can't confirm what it is. They can never find out. Understand?"

Mil was confused. "It's been an exclusion zone for decades. No one has ever questioned it."

Neff turned and tapped his desk again. The wallscreen resolved to another governmental-looking document. This one with a simple line of type at the top of the page reading National Reconnaissance Office and marked Top Secret.

"They covered it up way back in 1984. It says a nuclear-powered mapping satellite crashed and contaminated Slayton Ridge.

"So that's what the Russians will uncover? A ruse designed to fool them a century ago?"

"God willing."

Mil smiled. Neff didn't. "I repeat. The Russians cannot learn the truth."

"You mean they cannot learn that their business partners in the Mars mission intentionally violated a treaty that was key to the fall of the Soviet Union and beginnings of peaceful cooperation in spaceflight? That those cooperative, peaceful partners have had Cold War thermonuclear weapons pointed at them for the last hundred years? Yeah, Amon, that could be awkward."

"Do you know how much I have wrapped up in this mission to Mars, Mil?"

"Personally? I dunno, a trillion bucks?"

"Just under that. And that contract is with the American Space Agency. Not the Russians. I get paid when an *American* steps on Mars. That's what leads to getting the settlement rights and the supply contracts and keeping this company extremely profitable."

"You think the Russians will halt the program if they find out about what's there?"

"Not halt it, but take it over. I think they are in a position to kick us out. The initial provisions are all prepositioned, they have almost finished fueling *Humanity*, and they'll launch soon. It should be the greatest triumph in the history of mankind. Or it will bankrupt me and ruin everything I've ever worked for."

"So just when our greatest cooperative effort gets going, it's discovered we've been lying to them about a treaty that fundamentally allowed us to become trusted partners. Nice."

"I'm out of options on the moon. Nobody wants to go there. There's no market for colonizing the moon anymore. People are afraid."

"I've lived on the moon for a pretty long time. We've done good work there. If I die there of old age, wouldn't that be good for business?"

"But you're not dying of old age. You've been blasted with radiation from a mysterious place." Neff shook his hands like a boogeyman. "Hidden invisible death rays that kill you on the moon? People don't sign up for that. Our colonization projections were ten times what the uptake is. No one wants to live on a barren wasteland that kills people."

"So it's better PR if I die quietly in a nursing home on Earth? Pumped full of painkillers and shitting in a diaper?" His coffee had turned cold.

"The PR will be more heroic than that. You're a legend, you'll go out like one. Saving the world and all that."

"Which still leaves you with this dusty old moon that nobody wants to visit."

Neff cracked a smile and tapped a button.

The wallscreen image changed from the gray moon to the vibrant red representation of Mars.

"Oh, it won't be the dusty old moon anymore. It will be Luna: the Gateway to Mars! Everyone is excited to go to Mars. We'll have millions in deposits and presold seats on the first dozen transports. Mars is the new horizon, the next frontier! It's trending to be exponentially more profitable than the moon ever was. We have the rebranding campaign ready to drop as soon as *Humanity* leaves orbit."

"Rebranding the moon. And your only stumbling block is a handful of nuclear weapons contaminating the real estate."

Neff looked across the desk. "I want you to fix this. One last project. Go back to the moon, Mil. But this time it *will* kill you. Go with God, old friend."

CHAPTER THIRTY-ONE

Wednesday . 09 Feb . 2078
2155 Eastern Standard Time
Departure Area . Cape Kennedy Spaceport . Florida . Earth

T he surface of the moon was black against the Florida night sky. A slight fingernail of the crescent defined the edge. Mil looked up as he stepped from the transport tube. He'd spent almost half his life in that darkness. It wasn't nearly as romantic as it looked from here.

Especially when you're going there to die, he thought. It was strange, being in some unknown assassin's sights didn't seem to bother him nearly as much as knowing with certainty when the end was coming. Since his meeting with Neff, mortality had weighed on his mind more than he could ever recall. He'd long joked about dying, but the reality filled him with an unfamiliar sense of foreboding.

Around him, fellow Luna-bound passengers moved to the departure area entry. He could pick them out—contractors, couples, vacationers, families going on a great adventure. He watched as a father pointed to the moon, explaining some bit of space trivia to his young daughter. They shared a laugh. Mil felt a pang of regret. He'd never known that feeling.

He paused and considered the situation a quarter of a million miles away. All the family he had in the entire universe was up there working on mankind's next big leap. Nique. Bailey. He took a breath. Emma. What was this fractured family going to say about him after this was all over?

Introspection had never been a big part of his being, but this felt final—launching from Earth for one last time.

The door from the main passenger entry to the launch area slid open and there stood Ash Nomura, leaning on a transport crate. Mil's eyebrows went up.

"Geez, Mil, you didn't have to disappear. If you'd have just said something, we'd have fed you less fish." His serious demeanor evaporated with a grin.

"Neff was supposed to let you know," Mil said, reaching for the offered handshake.

"He did. Eventually. But I figured you might want your gear. You know, if you're going to the moon, it helps to take a pressure suit, maybe a helmet. That sort of thing." Ash patted the transport crate. "Not that any of your old stuff was worth keeping. Don't you guys have garage sales on the moon?"

"Hey now, I've logged a lot of miles in that suit."

"I know. We tried to have it cleaned. Twice." Ash took the handle and the odd pair started down the hallway to the intake area. "You're not getting it back."

"You ruined my suit?"

"Relax. I brought a new one. Brand new. It's got an experimental lining that should give you more protection than even a level-four suit."

Mil grimaced, remembering the difficulty he'd had in his level-four suit. "I hate my rad suit."

"That's the thing about this: technically it offers much greater protection with a whole new way to handle the threat. I could give you about an hour of detail on it if you'd like."

"Do you have to?"

"Nope. Here's the rundown—it's as easy to move in as your old standard suit, lighter than a level four, yet it protects exponentially better. And we pair it with some personal protective undergarments that offer substantial shielding from background rems."

"You came all this way to bring me experimental underwear?"

"Yes. I was going to get you footie pajamas as well, but there just wasn't time."

"I'm touched."

"And I bring news—I heard from a friend on the prefecture police force. They found Hina. Or at least her body."

"Her body? What happened?"

"There wasn't any trauma. He said they're testing for poison."

"That's ironic. Self-inflicted?"

"They aren't sure yet. Mil, I have to ask—the poison, the explosion on Luna, even the radiation—why do people keep trying to kill you? My buddy on the police force said there's a rumor Hina was a Russian agent. Should I even be standing this close?"

"Makes you wonder, doesn't it? Truth is, I know a secret and there seem to be more than a few folks who benefit from it staying a secret."

"Seriously? Who's trying to kill you?"

"Well, I didn't think the Russians were on the list until just now."

"Well, maybe when you get to Luna, things will calm down." They paused as they came to the designated waiting area.

"Somehow, I don't see that happening."

As if on cue, a petite woman in a Space Agency blazer appeared to collect Mil and guide him through the prelaunch routines. He shook hands with Ash as a launch technician collected the crate and Mil's personal duffel.

Ash looked into his eyes. "It's been an honor, Mil. I'm glad you're recovering."

"I appreciate your patience, Ash. And I'm sorry if I got you in any trouble."

"You did. Have a good flight."

Mil nodded a smile and followed the launch tech to the staging area.

Two hours later, the heavy lifter taxied down the runway and the Man on the Moon headed home.

It was an uneventful trip. Mil was simply one of twelve passengers. It was a three-hour trip to the space station complex in low-Earth orbit. The shuttlecraft docked at the transient passenger habitat for an overnight hotel stay. The passengers departed the transport, which reloaded with Earthbound passengers, undocked and returned to the Cape.

Mil floated easily through the portal to the habitat. The transition to zero-G was much easier than going from the moon's light gravity to the pull of the Earth. Not everyone on the ship had as easy of a time, and for those passengers, magnetized overshoes allowed them to walk through the station with some semblance of gravitational stability. Mil mentioned to a few that it would screw up their inner ear and they'd be on medpatches for days fighting nausea and vertigo, but they preferred the stability.

He settled into his VIP overnight cabin. The abstract colors of planet Earth filled his viewport. He saw Earth most every day, but here, closer, the curve of the horizon captured his gaze. And then he noticed the reflection in the glass. The old man looking out at the home planet. He studied the contrast between the brilliant color of the planet and the pale, aged face. Earth would go on spinning for eons after Mil Harrison was gone.

The view changed as the station's orbit moved into the twilight and then the darkness beyond. Mil's reflection became more distinct. The world floating below grew black beyond the fragile confines of his window. The contrast between the lights below connecting millions of humans and his lonely image in the glass was humbling. A hollow feeling washed over him.

He'd never felt smaller. Or more alone.

Here in the silent darkness, he found himself at a bit of personal reckoning. His mortality had been pushed to the forefront of his thinking, and he wasn't sure he liked where he stood. He studied the old man in the window and then found his dataslate in the carry-on. The reflection followed him to the dark screen of the tablet. He considered it for a long moment, then tapped the screen. The vidcall connected.

Emma blinked her eyes open and yawned from the screen. "Mil? What is it? What time is it?"

Crap. He hadn't thought about the time. "Um. Hi, sorry. I didn't mean to wake you. I'll call back. Sorry."

"Well, I'm up now. Is everything all right?" She ran fingers through her hair and wrinkled her nose against the light from the screen on her side of the conversation.

He smiled at the familiar warmth it brought him.

"I'm headed back."

"I heard." She took a deep breath, coming fully awake. "Not from you, of course. You just pout, drop the conversation, and disappear. No messages. No calls."

"Yeah. Sorry about that. I had some things to take care of."

"And did you?"

"I got started. But this isn't about that. We need to talk." Mil sat a little straighter to show he was being serious.

"At three o'clock in the morning?"

"Okay, I need to talk. It just hit me, so I called. Sorry."

"You know you just said 'sorry' four times. That may be a record for you."

"I really didn't mean to wake you up."

"Got it. So what are we talking about, farm boy?"

He checked the window. Their orbit was still in the blackest part of the night.

"I . . . I've been a shit. I'm coming back against your express wishes and everyone I talk to tells me it's going to kill me. This is going to end up on you. I never wanted that. But I just didn't think about how it would impact you."

She cocked her head. "Huh. What's going on, Mil? This is very odd for you."

"Yeah, I know. But I've had a lot of time to think recently. About you. And Bailey and Nique, and what happens when I die, or when whoever seems to be trying to kill me finally gets it right."

"Who is trying to kill you, Mil? What did you do?"

"I stumbled onto something. If it gets out it could screw up the whole Mars mission."

"So who wants to keep you quiet?" She stifled a yawn. "Who benefits?"

"If we go to Mars? I think everyone does. That's the whole reason we do this, isn't it? Exploration, research, extraplanetary living . . ."

"So who loses if we don't go?"

Mil thought a second.

A frown crossed his face. "Well, Bailey does. For one. It's her life's work."

"She wouldn't try to murder you." As soon as Emma said it, she frowned too. "At least I don't think she would."

"There's also Amon Neff. He stands to lose everything if the Mars mission goes sideways. And I just found out that the woman who tried to poison me might have been an agent of the Russian government."

"Someone tried to poison you? Is there anyone who doesn't have the motive and the resources to kill you?"

"Well, the radiation exposure—that was just me all on my own." He glanced at his image on the dataslate call. He felt as old as he looked, and that had never been the case before.

Emma nodded. "I talked to Osaka after you disappeared. Medically, your prognosis isn't great. You're better than you were, but they don't really know how your lifetime numbers will impact things. You could have months. You might have years."

"So I hear. You know, I didn't really call to talk medicine. Or murder."

"Okay." She frowned.

"I need you to know that I appreciate everything you've done. Even when it pissed me off. I haven't always said that, and I should have. This is going to be hard on you. You were right about being the only doc for a quarter of a million miles. And I need to say thank you and I am sorry for all the crap I'm about to put you through." He sighed deeply.

"It sounds like you're talking medicine."

"I'm trying not to. But I'm not good at this kind of thing."

"What do you say we work on that when you get here?"

He smiled for the first time in a long time. "I'd like that."

"Great. Let's do that. You think on it, and I'll go back to sleep. See you when you land."

The next morning, the transport shuttle arrived to take them from the space station to Luna, and in what struck Mil as a remarkably simple procedure, passengers loaded aboard, doors were sealed, and undocking jets fired. Just like that they were off to the moon. Emma was right. It was just as easy as going to Cleveland. One of the passengers referred to it as a space bus, and Mil couldn't disagree. Mil tapped into his dataslate and spent the next day and a half in deep study of the procedures that Neff's team had worked up to deal with the missiles. It wasn't complicated, compared to the danger involved, but they had a full section of briefing documents on anticipated scenarios if the mission failed. It wasn't pretty.

The documents were facial-recognition protected and listed as a presidential finding that designated the entire *Hercules* remediation project as a covert Black Operation. Mil chuckled. So Amon knew, and this president knew, but like her predecessors, she didn't want anyone to know she knew. The only names on the distribution list were Mil, Bailey, and Rafferty. They were empowered to bring others in if absolutely necessary, but everything had to be documented and was subject to later review and second guessing. Mil was to brief them face-to-face. Any other communications were completely restricted. Nothing written, nothing transmitted. Ever.

He checked the time and did some mental math. It was late on Luna. He opted for messages rather than phone calls and sent a memorandum and meeting request to Bailey and Rafferty. Dealing with this potential crisis was Rafferty's jurisdiction, but since he was trumped by civilian authority, Bailey, as the Space Agency's chief administrator, would be the lead on the project. Mil's status as prime contractor meant he was the low man on the pole and would be doing the actual work. But since he was in possession of the secure communications, and owing to the ban on transmitting any data about *Hercules* over open or even encrypted channels, he'd have to bring everyone up to speed face-to-face.

He shook his head. How they ever got anything accomplished through this web of interconnected bosses, instructions, and handoffs was amazing.

And someone thought this was the best means to go to Mars.

Thirty-four hours of meeting prep later, Mil looked out the porthole to see *Humanity* floating off the port side, the gray world of Luna filling the top of the window above him. To Mil's educated eye, the interplanetary crew had just a few more O2 spheres to attach before the ship would be fully fueled and ready to launch for Mars. He tried to find his own farm from sixty miles above the surface as the transport orbited into its final landing approach. There might have been a glint from one of the solar collectors, but he gave that up to imagination and wishful thinking.

The captain announced that he was instigating their descent program and that everyone should take their seats and engage the restraint systems. Mil watched his fellow travelers, impressed with the casual attitudes about landing on another astronomical body, where the slightest mistake could end one's life in moments.

Maybe Neff was wrong. It wasn't that the moon was too dangerous for humans to be interested. Perhaps it had become so old a hat that lunar life and traveling across space just wasn't that big of a deal. The moon was now just another suburb, albeit without any of the conveniences of living in the suburbs. The G-couch inflated slightly as the landing jets fired and the rocket rode the finger of flame to the landing pad. Five minutes later Mil rolled his travel pod through the terminal gates to an unexpected reception.

CHAPTER THIRTY-TWO

Saturday . 12 Feb . 2078

0905 Lunar Standard Time

Main Receiving Portal Lobby . Armstrong Base . Luna

Mil hadn't expected a brass band on his return, but the fact that Emma was the only person there to greet him reinforced that his significance in the current situation was small.

The doctor smiled and hugged his neck. "You look ten times better than when you left."

"That's not saying much. You told Neff I was basically dead."

"And you were."

"Can I buy you a cup of coffee?" Mil tucked his helmet under an arm.

"Can we do that later? I've got a million things to do before the launch."

"So you're just here to give me a ride home?"

"Oh no, Nique, Eli, and I have been juggling vehicles so you could get home. They're both on duty and I have to get to the medical bay. Your spidertruck is waiting for you in the motor pool."

"So that's it?"

"Yep. Now I have to run." She gave him a platonic hug. "See you later."

With that she was gone and Mil stood alone watching her disappear around the curving hallway.

"Huh." He buckled his shiny new rad suit helmet to his travel pod and turned not to the barn, but the command center. His wristy buzzed and the secured doors slid open.

The entire room turned to look, acknowledged that he had returned, and went back to work.

Nique hopped from her workstation and came to him.

"Welcome back, Grandad!" Another perfunctory hug.

"Hiya, kiddo. Farm still standing?"

She ducked her head in embarrassment. "We've almost rebuilt it after the fire."

"Funny."

"Yeah, Eli found your vodka still."

Mil paused. His eyes found Specialist Yenko across the command center. Eli gave a sheepish wave. Mil turned his full attention to Nique. "What did you do?"

Nique swallowed hard. "Well, we just wanted to . . . get you really good when you came back." She broke into a big grin. "Everything is fine. I'm kidding."

"Oh, you two are a riot."

Bailey walked toward him.

"You look about a thousand times better than when you left," she said.

"The official medical opinion is only ten times."

She rolled her eyes. "As you can imagine, between the Tiger Team investigation and prepping for the first manned mission to Mars, I've had a very busy few days. Including cryptic conversations with both the president and Amon Neff. They tell me you'll be able to enlighten us, and that it's an Emergency Action Item of the highest priority. Is that what's on the agenda for this morning's meeting?"

"I put together a briefing on the way up. But nothing goes out electronically. This could be a big mess, or it can be solved quickly, quietly, and with minimal embarrassment for everyone."

"You just got back from a month in sickbay. Do you feel up to a meeting right after the flight?"

"If Neff briefed you at all, you know I really don't have any choice."

"Oh, Neff didn't brief me." She waved a data chip. "The president sent this. Eyes Only. It came on your shuttle."

—––•◦•—– ⊕ —–•◦•––—

Saturday . 12 Feb . 2078
1100 Lunar Standard Time
Secure Conference Room . Armstrong Base . Luna

Two hours later Bailey stood before Mil and the assembled members of the Tiger Team. Rafferty and the core of the Armstrong Emergency Response Team—Mil, Bohannon, and Yamamoto—filled out the rest of the small secure conference room.

She paused and raised an index finger to make her point. "This briefing, this operation, and this entire effort does not exist. If you ever speak of this mission, if you even hint about its existence, the penalty is beyond life in prison. A judge on Earth will find you mentally incapable of coexisting in society and you will be institutionalized. No parole. Your families will be told you were killed in action with no remains found. Got it?"

She met every eye in the room. "Anyone want out?"

Silence.

"Okay, we are going to clean up one hell of a mess. At this moment, about fifty-three kilometers from this room, there are six nuclear missiles. Possibly armed and all pointed toward targets on Earth. We are going to deactivate them. And if we don't, the consequences are catastrophic."

She had everyone's attention. She nodded to Mil.

"So now, tell everyone what's going on."

He walked to the front of the room and tapped his wrist. "I'll tell you what Neff's best minds think." The lights dimmed. Wallscreens brightened with the Sudden Hercules logo.

"First off—she's not kidding about the need for secrecy. This has the potential to derail the Mars mission and set international cooperation back a century. And if we fail, it has the potential to destroy the moon and kill most life on Earth."

The entire room exchanged glances.

The video frame advanced to an animated presentation he had built on the trip up. The first scene was the schematics of the Trident XA missiles.

"These are American thermonuclear missiles. Circa 1970. Designed to leave the Earth's atmosphere, reenter, and incinerate an entire Russian city. Moscow, St. Petersburg, or wherever. These were supposed to be destroyed as a part of disarmament talks, and the treaty reviewers in the old Soviet Union were told that they were destroyed indeed."

The animation resolved to Ronald Reagan and Mikhail Gorbachev shaking hands and signing books.

Then pictures of missiles.

"Obviously, they were not. They were abandoned here when a covert mission went sideways, and have been pointed toward the major cities of Russia since the 1980s. The Russians don't know, and we don't believe they would be thrilled if they ever found out."

Beautiful photos of Moscow's onion domes and the museum-lined National Mall dissolved beneath a mushroom cloud.

He advanced the presentation to the bunker video. He'd spliced his suit-camera video together with Granger's and walked the briefing room crowd through the facility.

"Five of the six weapons appear to be functional. We think. Amon Neff now owns the descendent companies of the government contractors who built these facilities. With no small investment of time and money, his engineers have worked around the clock and forensically assembled the launch procedures, codes, and targeting software to determine targets and launch capabilities."

Bailey stepped forward. "Which brings us to this operation. The plan is to launch these into the sun, under the cover of a solar-flare testing program. Neff's engineers believe there is enough fuel to break free of lunar and earth gravity and send the missiles to the sun. Once they're gone, the facility will be scrubbed."

Rafferty raised his hand. She nodded.

"And this is all to be done under radio silence?"

Bailey nodded. "Correct. We have two major challenges. One is the fact that these . . . devices . . . don't officially exist. This is as black a program as any government has ever had. The president and I have discussed this, and her own investigation shows that the clearance has held for more than a century—remarkable. Second is the reason for that black designation. The Russians cannot know anything about this. Personnel who are going to Russia for training are not in this meeting."

Rafferty frowned. "That's why you excluded Yenko? He's from California. His grandparents have had a radish farm in Tulare."

Bailey tapped her dataslate. "Actually it's brussels sprouts. This administration is every bit that concerned. Yenko's on the assignment list to Russia for the next freighter mission to Mars. If he doesn't know about this, he can't tell anyone. Basic need-to-know security."

She raised a single finger and deliberately made her point. "If the Russians discover that their trusted ally has had thermonuclear weapons targeted on them for the last hundred years, and outside of this room only a handful of living persons in the entire federal bureaucracy have knowledge of this situation, the president is convinced the Russians would take Mars for themselves and leave us in the cold." She cleared her throat and stood a little straighter. "I agree with that assessment. So, this is the directive— you go to the person you want to speak to and communicate directly. Face-to-face. Nothing on this hits the airwaves. No text. No vidlinks. No vox. Complete comms lockdown."

The team nodded their understanding. Bailey pointed to Mil.

"The timetable starts now. We launch as soon as is practical. Optimal orbit is in"—Mil tapped his wrist—"fifty-four hours. We can be ready to go then on the five good birds. Maybe on the sixth. We'll see."

Bohannon raised a hand. "Why the hurry? Should we rush something this complex?"

"Excellent question," Mil said. "The experts on Earth believe the heat from the rads could generate a detonation and subsequent chain reaction at any moment. The nukes might go high order, or simply contaminate most of the surrounding two hundred square kilometers."

"Can we start now?" Bohannon asked.

"We are. First thing I'm worried about is what we do if we can't launch the missiles. I want a worst-case scenario evaluation from the ER team by this time tomorrow. Figure on extracting the entire facility and destroying it in orbit."

Bailey flinched. "That was not in my report. You want to launch a building? Of undetermined mass and weight, buried under a landslide?"

Mil nodded again. "I want to know if it's possible. The ER teams train for situations just this strange—crashed craft, fractured pressure hulls, mining disasters—if there's a way to do it, they can figure it out."

Bailey looked skeptical. "With no help from Earth? JPL? Caltech? MIT? No electronic comms for backup?"

"These are the best of the best or they wouldn't be here." He took a moment to meet the eyes of every person in the room. "We'll have some general comms about the solar-flare cover story, but nobody mentions this on an open channel. Collaborate, help one another, but do it face-to-face. "

The Emergency Response Team replied, "Yes, sir."

Rafferty leaned forward. "So if service members who talk get dishonorables and go to jail, what happens to civilians? Like you?"

Mil chuckled. "They get to join our friendly neighborhood robot in the radiation room while it tries to disarm a half dozen hundred-year-old bombs."

CHAPTER THIRTY-THREE

Saturday . 12 Feb . 2078
1245 Lunar Standard Time
Harrison Station . Armstrong Base . Luna

The spidertruck crested the last hill and finally Mil could see his way home. He tapped the control panel and drove into the airlock. This was the longest he'd been away from the farm since he'd built that airlock. The nostalgia was strong.

Lights came on as he parked, and the comforting clutter of the barn seemed a little more in need of straightening up than when he left. Maybe Nique was right; it was a mess.

He noted the old Axial Mark III robot leaning on the far edge of the workbench. He'd need to go right to work if the plan he'd hatched on Earth was going to work.

There was no time to rest and appreciate the familiar sensation of the return. He changed clothes, splashed some water on his face and then took the container of replacement parts he'd brought back from Earth to the barn's workbench. He rigged a sling to his overhead crane and moved the robot to sit on the edge of the bench, then unboxed the parts and set to work. First, he attached a new lower leg to the robot and began testing circuits. He shook his head. He had always loved this stuff—the mechanics of it. But he'd never thought that what had once been a pleasurable, calming pastime of repairing old junk would be key to saving the world.

And of course, under the pressure of a deadline, a bolt cross-threaded. Mil cursed the designers of the robot and questioned their engineering abilities as he wasted forty-five minutes easing out the bolt and rethreading the hole. Something always went wrong when you least needed it to.

Mil felt the click of the torque wrench on Axial's knee joint. He wiped his hands on a nearby rag, then reached behind the robot's cranium and toggled the main circuit breaker. Axial's head twitched. The lights surrounding the cameras that served as the robot's vision sensors flickered once, then came to full brightness.

"Axe? You in there?"

A series of clicks and whirring came from the vaguely human form sitting on the edge of the workbench.

The head turned with a jerk to face Mil.

"Affirmative."

"Finally. Good news." Mil snapped into place the last of the system circuit boards Amon Neff's roboticists had been able to turn up. New old stock, they'd said. Mil was just glad to see the old bot come back to functionality. He clicked the chest panel closed and tapped his wristy, then stepped back a few meters to give Axial room.

"Run diagnostics. Full system check."

The robot hopped off of the workbench and brought its carbon fiber and brushed aluminum frame to a standing position, exactly two meters tall. The dirt, corrosion, and wear and tear on the vintage robot's body contrasted with the shiny replacement right leg.

Axial bent its knees and dropped almost to ground level. Then stood again. It stretched its right heavy-duty arm straight in front and then rotated it through a series of circular motions. At the same time, the left arm mimicked the actions, but then a smaller third appendage with a much smaller eight-fingered "hand" deployed from the left shoulder. This was Axial's detail work appendage. The robot tapped the digits together to demonstrate the dexterity that allowed it to work in tiny spaces and handle much finer work.

As series of system checkoffs scrolled through the screen on Mil's wrist, he gave a satisfied half smile.

"Systems operating nominally," Axial confirmed.

"Glad to have you back, buddy."

"Would you like for me to check for systems updates?"

Mil chuckled. "I don't think they've done an update for your model since about 2045. You're as up-to-date as you're gonna get."

"Affirmative."

"So here's the deal—I've streamlined this VR file and it should pipe right into your sensory system. Otherwise, I'm going to have to go old school and put you in the goggles." Mil inserted the data chip into the matching slot on the robot's chest plate. Faint mechanical noises came from the robot as it integrated itself into the virtual reality environment.

"Accessing unknown environment. Linking to VR file Harrison three point zero."

Mil pulled his own goggles on. "That's exactly what I wanted to hear."

Mil's field of vision displayed the interior of the bunker. He looked up and around. To his left, a representation of Axial waited in the open airlock door.

"You have me, Axe? I read you five by five."

"Affirmative."

"Well, this is going better than I expected. What I want you to do is step forward to the console. Count paces."

"One. Two. Three . . ." Axial stepped to the console in eight steps.

"Hold there. Just to your right, about fifteen degrees, there is an old-style entry keyboard and a cathode ray tube monitor. Confirm?"

"Affirmative."

"With your detail arm, press the keys for 10509010 QPZ and the question mark."

Mil stepped over in the VR world to visually confirm the robot did as requested. "This might actually work."

Mil spent the next several hours walking through the simulation. By the time his growling stomach reminded him it was well past mealtime, Axial had the procedures down completely and was able to traverse the entire control facility, enter codes and coordinates, and turn the keys to launch missiles.

This really might work, Mil thought as he powered down Axial and retired to the apartment.

CHAPTER THIRTY-FOUR

Sunday . 13 Feb . 2078

0615 Lunar Standard Time

Secure Conference Room One . Armstrong Base . Luna

The secure conference room was quiet except for the gentle tapping at dataslates and wallscreens as the group congregated to solve a problem that had never been intended to be solved.

Striding through the door, Desmond Rafferty looked around and found Mil huddled with Yamamoto and Bohannon trying to calculate the mass of the hundred-year-old weapons facility.

The base commander tapped Mil's shoulder and motioned to follow him into the hallway.

"We're leaving the secure conference room to talk in the hall?" Mil asked.

"We're walking. This isn't a secure topic, but it's an interesting coincidence in light of the current issue with the Russians." Rafferty led the way to the empty hallway.

"I spoke with Litinov this morning—they'll be fueled by fifteen hundred tomorrow. He could be on his way to Mars in days. He's excited to make history," Rafferty said. "His XO, Pete Peterson, was scrubbed yesterday. Heart murmur."

"Peterson? Mister Space Force himself? He's been on this since the get-go, that's a helluva tough break."

"He's not the only one. Tompkins in Navigation was scratched while you were on Earth, Nique was removed, as you know, and Ezra Davidson in Life Sciences had a potential viral exposure."

"Seems like a lot of crew turnover."

"And Major Fergus Cox-Wainwright of the Royal Navy was to be lead engineer. Suffered an automobile accident right before launch."

"This thing is sounding snakebit."

"I've gone through the manifest. It looks like they are methodically removing the American, British, and French from the crew of *Humanity*."

"Seriously?"

"And all of the replacements are Russian."

"There are eighteen people on the crew, how many from our side are left?"

"Currently? Two. Jack Chow, propulsion and life-support engineer—he's handling the fuel program—and Dr. Iverson, the medic."

Mil scratched his chin.

"And conveniently, yesterday's shuttle had a Russian doctor and a life-support specialist from Kursk on the passenger manifest." Rafferty's tone was firm and even.

"Are you kidding me?"

"I wish I were. I believe they are surreptitiously installing an entire Russian crew to settle Mars."

"On Amon Neff's dollar." Mil ran a hand through his hair.

"Perhaps, but this does not sit well with the Space Force. I'm headed to talk with Chief Administrator Rivera."

"So, you need me for moral support or to try and piss her off?"

"I figure you have more experience with her when she's angry."

"You mean all her life?"

Five minutes later, Rafferty and Mil stepped into the command office she'd taken over as the senior person at Armstrong Base.

"This is unusual. Commander, what's up?"

"Have you seen the latest crew manifest for *Humanity*?"

"You mean since Peterson's been scratched, of course. What about it?" She tapped her dataslate and the crew compliment appeared.

"Notice anything peculiar about the replacements?" Mil leaned in to look.

"They are straight out of the alternates pool. They are all highly qualified."

"They're all Russian," Mil whispered.

"Yes?"

Mil shook his head. "Neff's been worried that the Russians are going to discover the Slayton Ridge program and kick us off the Mars mission. Hell, they're already doing it."

"Amon Neff doesn't have any say in the mission crew." Bailey frowned. "He may have billions on the line, but that's not within his scope."

She tapped her computer and the wallscreen pulled up the crew rotation.

A few more taps and the list sorted by nationality.

Mil waved a hand at the screen. "You're right, they only passed over two Israelis, a Brit, a woman from Tokyo, a Canadian, and four Americans to bring in the last three Russians. Probably nothing nefarious there. What the hell is your agency doing?"

"We don't control the crew manifests. Obviously, that's the Russian space agency."

"They're doing a helluva job. You're about to go down in history as the chief administrator who put the first Russian colony on Mars." Tact had never been Mil's strong suit when dealing with his daughter.

"I'll speak to them immediately."

"You'd better hurry. At this rate, they'll be fueled and ready to leave orbit in less than forty-eight hours." Mil crossed his arms.

"The program calls for three more days. Final trajectory has yet to be uploaded. They aren't gone yet." Bailey flipped pages on the dataslate, urgently summoning information.

"They may need three days to invent a reason for Chow and the doctor to get off," Mil said.

Rafferty shook his head. "Actually, Chow is scheduled for liberty as soon as the last fuel sphere is in place. I expect him at Armstrong sometime today."

"I'd lay odds at ten to one that he sprains his ankle getting off the shuttle," Mil quipped.

Bailey scowled at him. "You're not helping."

"Look, they know about the missiles. They want us to call them out, so they can call us out and then take the Mars mission for Mother Russia."

"And whose fault would that be? This is an international cooperative effort. This mission is the tool we used to rebuild trust after their debacle in eastern Europe. There's no way the Russians would want to do what you're suggesting."

Rafferty raised an index finger. "I wouldn't be so sure. I not only think they are capable of doing this, I also think they don't need the missiles as a reason. It wouldn't surprise me if the Russians had planned a subtle takeover all along."

Mil nodded in agreement. "Maybe they just think no one will notice until it's too late. Maybe it doesn't have anything to do with Slayton Ridge at all."

"Now you're just trying to make this not your fault."

"You may not know Russians like I do," Mil chided her.

"You know one Russian. And Dimitri Litinov is probably the most trustworthy individual I've ever met."

Mil thought for a second. "He's a solid guy and led a multinational crew here on Luna. And very successfully, I'd add. I don't see him doing this."

Rafferty chimed in. "This has to have come from Moscow. That's where the crew is assembled. They all train at Houston initially, but the systems training and mockups all happen at Baikonur. That's where they'd make the call."

Bailey began to tap on her dataslate.

Mil raised his hand. "Before you go doing exactly what I would do in this situation—"

"Thanks, for your thoughts, Dad, but I get paid to handle this, not you. I'm messaging the president."

"Understood, Madam Chief Administrator." Mil gave an exaggerated salute and spun around to march out.

Bailey didn't even look up. "Don't leave. I need to see this operation of yours. I need to know what you're doing."

"Oh, so now I'm a tour guide?"

"Exactly. I'm advising the civilian contractor to facilitate an inspection of the operation by the contracting agency. As the senior administrative executive on site, I have that authority."

Mil might have growled. He liked his Space Agency bosses off-site, and if they happened to be on Earth, that was even better. "Just say when."

She tapped the dataslate, sending her presidential communiqué off to the White House, and looked up. "How's now? Is now good for you?"

CHAPTER THIRTY-FIVE

Sunday . 13 Feb . 2078
0705 Lunar Standard Time
Tiger Team Workroom . Armstrong Base . Luna

Nique keyed the sequence and rocked back in her chair. She rotated her head and her neck cracked. She had been at this for more than a week. She stood, stretched, and walked a small circle around the video bay. The wallscreens gave the only illumination and she'd been staring at them for days. As a comms specialist, she worked with audio and video sources all the time, but this was the first time she'd tried to create forensic evidence out of recorded images. The level of concentration surprised her.

But she felt she was close. This next AI run should do the job.

She stepped out of the bay and spotted Dr. Merrick headed her way with two cups of coffee.

"You started without me?" he said.

"It was debugging. You didn't want to sit here for that." She took the offered cup and breathed in the sharp aroma of the Americano.

"Were you at it all night?"

"No, but I did get in early. Today should be the day. I just initiated the app; it should find our guy."

Merrick smiled. "We don't know it's a guy. We aren't sure it's a rifle. Could be an innocent atmospheric reading device. Right now we have a figure in a fuel systems yellow pressure suit. It could be almost anyone."

"Or a perpetrator. Isn't that the word you cops use?"

"Sometimes. But at this point, they're just a Person of Interest. Possibly a suspect. Show me what you're running and let's see how it's working. Maybe we'll get lucky."

Nique lead the way into the video bay where the wallscreen was methodically ticking through various scenes and camera angles. Then the artificial intelligence re-rendered the video frame by frame to enhance and augment the smallest details in the image. It had zeroed in on the same figure they had identified through their original video search. Seconds turned to minutes and hours as the systems traced footstep after footstep of the mustard-colored figure.

Merrick pointed his coffee cup at the video image. "But I will say, if this turns out to be a crime, wearing a bright yellow pressure suit to do the deed doesn't seem terribly smart."

Nique chuckled. "Yeah, but not on the moon. Those guys are everywhere." As she said that, the camera angle changed to show a half dozen identically yellow-clad workers emerge from an airlock and move through the pad area. Their suspect fell right in line. Carrying a toolbox much like others in the group.

"And they all have mirrored faceplates so there's no IDing anyone through biometric tracing." Merrick frowned. "By the gait, I think he's a guy."

"He has a mark on the rear quarter of his helmet. I keyed the AI to follow that." She pointed to the figure ambling across the video frame.

"And his suit is too large. I didn't notice that until these other yellow suits arrived, but that could indicate that it's borrowed or stolen." Merrick took a sip of his coffee and winced. "Dammit, burned my lip."

On the wallscreen, the mystery figure peeled off from the group and ducked behind a stack of luggage containers and then dropped to a knee. The camera shifted to an angle from farther away and the AI zoomed in and extrapolated the pixels to clarify the image. The suspect reached into the tool kit and assembled a device.

"It really does look like a rifle." Merrick pointed with his coffee cup.

The suspect rose and stepped to the far side of the container stack and out of the frame. The AI hunted through a half dozen cameras and angles. Then it zoomed and enhanced a corner of a frame. The figure stepped around the containers and shouldered the rifle-shaped device.

"Can you split the screen? Show the launch at the same time code?"

"Give me just a second." Nique waved her hands through the inputs on the holodisplay.

The wallscreen split into two blue screens. She smirked, then swiped a few more inputs. The screens blinked and the launch pad appeared on the left screen followed seconds later by the freeze frame of the suspect on the right.

"Run it forward. Let's see what happens."

She flicked the toggle to roll the video.

A thin wisp of vapor wafted from the shuttlecraft. They watched the igniters spin up and then the cloudless firing of the main engines. Slowly the vehicle rose against the black sky.

As if on cue, both viewers looked to the right-side screen.

The suspect sighted down the device and tracked the launch as the shuttle cleared the superstructure of the launch facility.

The device jerked against the suspect and a puff of smoke appeared.

"It is a rifle." There was surprise in Nique's tone. She'd been prepared for that, but the visual reality shook her.

"And that's a shot." Merrick leaned in, concentrating on the shooter as the explosion overtook the shuttle.

The suspect watched the mayhem that had been unleashed, and then the AI followed the process as the shooter disassembled the weapon and returned it to the toolbox, then placed the case into a nearby shipping container.

"We need to track that container."

Nique tagged the holodisplay. "Marked. The AI can follow it."

"So let's see where our shooter goes."

The image scrolled through a series of angles and video frames following the yellow-suited shooter through the cargo staging area and then into and through the airlock. The image resolution improved as the subject moved into the interior hallways of the Luna Colony. The shooter turned into a major hallway and was swept up in a crowd of charging people as the men and women of the moon rushed to their duty stations in response to the emergency.

Merrick smiled. "He wasn't ready for that. They never plan on havoc when they work out their escape."

"He can't wear the helmet in the hallways, that's protocol. Only in designated areas, so people don't think there's an atmospheric leak. That will get him as much attention as anything."

The shooter turned to look almost directly into the camera, then turned to face the other way and removed the headgear.

"Well, that's kind of smart. He knows where the cameras are and he's avoiding them. With his comms cap on we don't get hair color or even a skin tone. He may be better than I gave him credit for." Merrick's voice carried a hint of professional respect.

The shooter moved away from the camera and, just as he did, a technician charged around a corner of the hallway and ran smack into him, knocking them both sprawling to the ground.

The murderer looked directly into the camera and Nique gasped.

——•⊛•——

Sunday . 13 Feb . 2078
0820 Lunar Standard Time
Hercules Site . Luna

Fifty-eight kilometers away, the first thing the Emergency Response Team erected was a giant, gray camouflage dome. Thin aluminum spars created a Buckminster Fuller webbed geodesic dome supporting a thin fabric cover.

It wasn't sealed and required no airlock, but it was a dark charcoal gray and would hide the activities on the dark side of Slayton Ridge from the prying eyes of satellites or droneships that might investigate the sudden construction.

The underside of the dome was rigged with a lighting array to illuminate the round-the-clock excavation digging out the old missile bunker.

Mil pointed an arm across the excavation from the roof of an oversize transvan serving as the onsite command post. As the civilian project manager, he was to oversee the operation and log issues and progress that would be sent to Neff via an Earthbound shuttle. The ban on radio communication meant Neff would get everything in Mil's reports after the fact. Mil was on his own as to how to handle things, and that was just how he liked it. However, because this was technically a civilian contract for Neff's organization, administered by the Space Agency, Mil reported to Bailey.

He waved toward Yamamoto as she guided the backhoe-equipped utility vehicle that was removing soil from the side of the missile facility.

"We did catch a break that it's just loose regolith. Excavation will take less than a couple of hours. We need the launch facility ready to be separated from the crew space as quickly after the initial launch as possible."

"You really think you can launch the entire weapons section?" Bailey frowned behind the faceplate of her helmet.

"We'll start with the individual missiles. We're covering it all as a solar-flare testing project that we've had working for almost a year. Neff's people sent up all new coordinates and all the launch procedures." Mil pointed his glove to the top of the gray boxy building.

"Those doors on the bunker's roof open and we'll launch the five operational missiles in sequence. It'll take all of five minutes, and we're out of the missile business."

Bailey pointed overhead to the dome. "Right through the dome?"

"When we're ready, we kill the lights and the whole main section of the dome collapses out of the way in seconds."

Mil continued his tour. "That leaves us with the facility itself. It'll be mostly empty, the one inoperable weapon and five hollow tubes after we launch the first set. Basically, it's a big aluminum box. There's no atmosphere, so we don't have aerodynamics problems here. Put a booster in each corner and punch the Go button. Each of those solid rocket boosters has enough thrust to lift the entire payload. It's over-engineered, but that's what we do."

Mil pointed to a large freight container that housed the boosters. She surveyed the activity. "You'll attach the boosters before you fire the first five missiles?"

Mil nodded. "Attach, but we don't install the ignition systems or the fuel cells. These are emergency SRBs, designed for just this type of mission. I always thought we'd have to evacuate a settlement pod with them."

"You planned for a contingency like this?" Bailey cocked her head inside her helmet. Mil couldn't tell if she was skeptical or impressed.

"Exactly like this? Of course not. But when you're out here on the edge of civilization and help is three days away? Your mother and I figured out early on we'd have to save ourselves. There wouldn't be any cavalry coming."

"Mom?"

"Hey, we're standing on her shoulders. Your mother and her work are the reason this whole community still functions. The farm, the O2 systems, a lot of the basic science that underpins the Luna colony came from applying her research and ideas. All the rest of us did was move dirt and bolt things together."

"Sounds like you're trying to be modest." Bailey stopped, then said the word. "Dad."

Mil turned and faced his daughter. Together on the surface of the moon, yet, as always, separated, now by pressure suits, helmets, and faceplates. "I have to be proud of all this. It cost me everything I had in the world to do this. It was never what I wanted to be my priority, but all the souls here depend on each other. It's been hard and tragic and painful, but we've set the stage for you to get explorers like Nique to Mars. You'll get your dream. And I'm even prouder of that."

He looked directly into Bailey's eyes and the moisture he saw there made him choke up. He cleared his throat and waved back to the *Hercules* facility as Yamamoto and Bohannon began to attach the boosters.

"Looks like Yammy's about ready. We'll have them mated to the corners and then once the missiles depart, it takes ten minutes to enable the firing systems, load propellant and launch. Less than half an hour after Axe enters the crew chamber and changes the coordinates, we launch the building."

"You're not worried about an accidental detonation?" she asked. The reality of standing a few meters from live nuclear missiles was starting to take hold.

Mil shrugged. "The calculations say it can't happen. But if we have a detonation, I don't think anyone is going to be around to second-guess what we did."

"A little fatalistic today?" Bailey's eyebrows went up.

"We can only control what we can control."

"So, we'll just worry about going to Mars."

"And maybe getting your daughter back on the crew?"

"You know as well as I do that she broke regulations. I cannot reward that."

Mil brushed some dust off the sleeve of his new pressure suit. "Did she though? She asked for information. She didn't break into any systems, she didn't violate any security. I know you can't be seen as favoring her, but she earned this spot on her own. She should go."

"There are circumstances that can't be ignored."

"I get it. But find a way to not let it alienate her. Take it from me. It's not worth it." Once again Mil looked into the eyes of the daughter he'd not seen for years until this disaster. He hoped she could learn from his mistakes.

The moment made her visibly uncomfortable. She looked away. "Can we get back to saving the moon?"

"Might as well. We'll be ready to go as soon as we retarget the functional missiles. I was amazed, the coordinates change is pretty simple. I was prepared for an enormous amount of orbital calculus. Turns out that was what was in the binder—Neff found copies of the originals—"

"They had coordinates for the sun?"

"No but it wasn't hard to determine. The nice thing about the sun is all you have to do is get in the ballpark; gravity does the rest." Mil looked up at the edge of Slayton Ridge, where the local star was just behind the horizon. "Close counts in horseshoes, hand grenades, and shooting nuclear missiles at the sun."

"So the binder had the coordinates for what exactly?"

"Every place Ronnie Raygun's inner circle considered bad in the 1980s. Moscow, Beijing, Tehran, Tripoli, St. Petersburg—they still called it Leningrad back then—Baikonur, Sevastopol, Murmansk, all the major Russian ports, I'm sure they could reorient and launch in a matter of minutes. Retargeting these things is remarkably easy, and then—boom. Millions dead from mysterious moon missiles." He wiggled his fingers as though he was raining destruction down from above.

"Barbaric."

Mil nodded inside his helmet. "Survival. They thought. Mutually Assured Destruction was only good for missiles they could see coming. These would fall out of the sky like meteors and leave no real evidence. More of a first-strike weapon. Pretty diabolical."

Bailey looked to her wristcomm. "It's Rafferty."

She toggled it. Mil raised an eyebrow as the signal was shared to his headset.

"Ma'am, Walt Iverson and Jack Chow stopped the by command center by to offer their compliments on the way home to Earth after reassignment from *Humanity*."

"Seriously? And I suppose their replacements are Russian?" Bailey's eyes flickered to Mil's.

"Yes, ma'am."

"Impressive." Mil nodded. "Sounds like you're populating Mars with Siberian bears."

The chief administrator was not amused.

"Also, Dr. Merrick has something for your immediate attention. It's urgent but not to go out over open channels."

She tapped the call closed and looked to Mil. "That's not good. I'll need you to get us back to Armstrong."

"Yes, ma'am." For once Mil opted not to make a smart remark.

Sunday . 13 Feb . 2078
1030 Lunar Standard Time
Secure Conference Room One . Armstrong Base . Luna

Dr. Merrick pointed to the video wall. It was divided into several screens of simultaneous video replay. Rafferty, Mil, and Bailey watched closely. Nique stared at the screen as she toggled the controls.

"An instant before the glint on the thruster quad, you can see the fuel technician on the left with a device. This image here, camera 206, frame 1047, is a muzzle flash. That's him firing."

The figure on the display stepped out from behind the corner of a container and fired, the mirrored faceplate of his yellow pressure suit hiding his identity.

Bailey crossed her arms. "We don't have a lot of time here, Merrick."

"No ma'am we don't, but I want to make this as ironclad as I can." He nodded to Nique and she began shuttling through the video quickly as a variety of cameras followed the shooter through Armstrong base's launch facility. "We video-tracked this individual "

"Never takes his helmet off." Mil leaned in to focus on the shooter.

Merrick nodded. "Not until he gets to main crew quarters. And then he's very careful to leave his comms cap on and not face the cameras."

"So he knows where all the cameras are." Rafferty squinted at the image.

"And doesn't seem concerned." Bailey was getting irked.

"Until here." Merrick's laser dot moved to the back of the perp.

"He didn't count on the reaction to the explosion. Everyone running to emergency stations."

The camera zoomed in as a running technician looked up from his wrist comm and crashed directly into the mystery man. And then the tech helped him up, and Eli Yenko looked directly into the camera.

Mil and Rafferty stepped back as one.

Mil cocked his head. "Yenko?" He looked at Nique, who bowed her head.

Bailey considered options. "Have you arrested him?"

Merrick shook his head. "We have him in custody."

Rafferty glared. "I'd like to speak to my officer, please."

Merrick went to the far door of the room. "Bring him in."

Yenko entered, flanked by two sturdy-looking members of the Tiger Team.

Rafferty went to him. "What have you done?"

Yenko stared at the ground.

"Best say something, son." Mil nodded to the wallscreen, then to Merrick, who replayed the video. "You've got to tell us what's going on."

His voice was soft and quiet. "I think I want to talk to a law—"

The fist crushed his defiance. Eli's jaw cracked and his head snapped back. He shook his head and slowly wound back around to face Nique. He spit a tooth into his hand. She stood on her toes ready to follow the right hook with another punch. She was breathing hard as she released her fury in a yell.

"You bastard! You killed Maddie!"

"Nique. I didn't mean for this. Yoshi said it would—"

She punched him in the gut and the air went out of Eli in a rush.

"Monique Nicole Rivera!" The mother in Bailey came out, and she grabbed Nique's arms and wrestled her away.

Merrick stepped between the three of them. Shoving Nique and her mother both back away from his prime suspect. "Get him out of here."

Two of the security team pulled him from the room. Eli struggled to catch his breath the entire time.

Merrick watched the door close behind the saboteur. "He's not admitting anything, but I think he'll break. This isn't a crime of passion, and a cursory look through his files shows he's been an exemplary officer. But I don't think anyone paid him to do this, so developing his motive may take some time."

Bailey frowned. "You don't think he was paid?"

"Not just yet. We don't see anything abnormal in his accounts."

"Yoshi." Mil was lost in thought.

"I beg your pardon?" Merrick leaned in.

"I met a guy on Earth named Yoshi. He works for Amon Neff."

"Interesting." Mil could see the wheels turning in Merrick's head. "There are probably tens of thousands of people named Yoshi on Earth, but we'll see what turns up in questioning. Something will tie it together."

"Mars." Nique's voice was quiet. A tear ran down her cheek. "He did it to get on the next mission. His transfer just came through."

Rafferty looked to Bailey. "You said all the crew manifests are put together in Russia. How the hell would he have strings pulled there?"

Nique sniffed back a tear. "He told me his grandparents are from Russia."

Bailey set her jaw. "This has gone far enough." She turned to Mil. "Go get your robot ready. We need to put an end to this. Now."

Then she pointed to Rafferty. "I need a secure comms room and a channel to the White House."

Mil and Rafferty responded at the same time. "Yes, ma'am."

Sunday . 13 Feb . 2078
1415 Lunar Standard Time
Hercules Site . Luna

Mil drove around Granger's Boulder and down the newly graded path to the base of the Hercules site. He parked beneath the lightweight emergency structure.

He turned to Axial, which was sitting patiently in the rear of the transvan. "Here's where you earn your money, Axe."

"Affirmative."

"Bring the repeaters and follow me."

The robot lifted a backpack and stood as Mil went through the procedures of storing atmosphere. The old astronaut punched the button and opened the rear ramp to see the entire worksite.

Hercules' special services module was completely free of the landslide that had hidden it for most of the last century. The dark gray building now had a safety railing around the roof deck and a new ladder led up to the entry hatch. It looked ominous under the glare of the overhead lights.

A small excavator sat a few meters away from the separated missile bay. Mill noted that the solid rocket boosters had already been installed and their access panels were open, waiting for the fuel cells and ignition packages.

He crow-hopped to the site command post. Axial followed like a well-trained puppy.

"Looks like we are about ready," he told Axe.

The robot didn't reply.

"Wait here." Mil opened the outer airlock door.

"Affirmative."

Mil opened the faceplate of his shiny new helmet in the airlock. Protocol required that he wear the pressure suit on in the transvan, but he didn't have to keep it powered or the helmet closed. It really wasn't much more difficult to get around in than his old suit, but he wasn't admitting that to anyone, especially Ash. He checked his batteries and swapped them for new ones from the airlock's chargers. If something went wrong, he'd rather have more power than less.

The interior of the transvan was designed for work rather than comfort. Wallscreens displayed a variety of schematics and notes as well as the master checklist for the operation. A countdown clock blinked the same fifteen-minute hold, second by second.

Kerin Yamamoto looked up from her dataslate. "We are go for facility ingress. Holding at T-minus fifteen minutes."

Nique's voice interrupted in Mil's ear, "Armstrong Comms for Harrison. Harrison, come in."

Mil frowned. "Armstrong, we're supposed to be radio black." Mil checked the airlock door and waited for the green light.

"Understood. I have a priority comms request for you. Sending encoded, now."

His wristy buzzed.

EMERGENCY CONTACT MESSAGE

RE: Harrison, Millennium E. Unable to contact

Anyone having contact with this person have them respond immediately.

Below that was a link Mil recognized as the direct line to Amon Neff.

Mil bit his lower lip. Immediately meant now, but they were under comms lockdown.

Kerin watched him consider the message.

"You know you can't mention the Hercules project."

"Yes, thank you for that valuable reminder." Mil toggled his wristy. The ancient trillionaire appeared on the wall screen.

"Harrison, where the hell have you been?"

"Hello Amon, it's good to talk with you too. I'm working on the solar-flare project. We're working through some comms issues so I'm trying to stay off the net and keep traffic to a minimum."

"What's your status?" Neff paced back and forth on the screen.

"We're getting close. I'd imagine we'll be a go in a few hours. I didn't realize you were in the update loop."

"I am on this one. Give me an update when you prepare for initiation."

The screen went black. Mil's brow furrowed. Neff was footing the bill here, and his company's forebearers had built most of the hardware, but this was launching ballistic nuclear missiles. There should be agency and military oversight at the site beyond he and Yamamoto.

"Is it this simple?" Yamamoto asked. "He says do it and we just punch the Go button?"

"Yeah, seems odd, doesn't it?"

The airlock entry tone sounded and Jaden Bohannon stepped through, removing his helmet.

"We're good to go on the module. Ready for entry and retargeting. The area's clear of all nonessential personnel. You're really trusting this to that antique bot of yours?" Bohannon's tone made it clear he didn't much care for the idea.

"Unless you want to volunteer to go into a fully baked radiation room to change the coordinates yourself." Mil looked up from his wristy to meet Bohannon's eyes. "We can arrange that."

"Nah. I'm good." Bohannon logged on to the wallscreen and brought up the Armstrong Base Command Center.

"Armstrong this is the response team. Comms check. How do you read?"

Nique appeared on the screen. "Good read, Jaden. I'm bringing in Commander Rafferty and the chief administrator."

The screen split into quadrants and Bailey and Rafferty were added to the group call.

"Are we up?" Bailey asked. "Status?"

Mil stepped to the wallscreen. "We're ready to move to remote launch activities. We can go to launch in approximately fourteen minutes after access to the control room."

Nique nodded. "Comms go. Telemetry is go."

Rafferty leaned forward. "Range is clear. Armstrong is go for set to staging."

"Harrison, you are go for prep and staging. We will drop off the net now until we are to launch. Contact this command at T-minus two minutes for final launch authorization." Bailey's screen went dark.

Mil looked at his colleagues. "Looks like it's up to us, now. Let's do this."

He tapped his wristy and one quadrant changed to the view from Axial's synthetic vision system. The other views were the exterior camera angles of the site and the superstructure that had been fabricated around the old special services module.

"Axe, give me a systems check."

The robot ran through the familiar mechanical yoga routine. "Systems operating nominally."

Mil took a deep breath. "Here we go."

He traced his index finger across the screen of the wristy, moving crosshairs to the base of the ladder on Axial's display and simply tapped the screen.

"Engaged," said Axial.

"Good telemetry." Yammy was glued to the readouts on her monitors.

"Confirm." Bohannon was backing her up.

Axial moved deliberately across the lunar landscape to the crippled building and the ladder at the far end. His sensors detected the uneven footing and he walked with care, skirting one knee-high rock and moving with smooth precision to the base of the ladder.

"So much for the hard part." Mil chuckled. "Enabling access protocol." All that VR training in the barn was about to pay off.

Axial climbed the ladder and went straight to the main hatch. He placed one of the signal repeaters beside the door and his delicate work hand activated the device.

"Good signal on the repeater," Nique confirmed. "Showing 9.78 Tbps."

Mil nodded silently. This wasn't the part he was concerned about. The boosters ensured they'd have some limited telemetry from Axial, but communications were still going to be unreliable.

Axial began his descent into the airlock, closed that hatch, and dogged it shut.

Mil watched the bot disappear on-screen. "So long, old friend."

"Signal degradation." Bohannon checked his gear. "Wow. We're down into giga. Showing 225 Gbps. You getting that, Armstrong?"

"Confirm. Seeing the same thing here."

Mil concentrated on the wallscreen. "That's the Faraday cage—it's blocking the signal. But the repeater's burning though it. Should be good enough to have some telemetry. We'll know when Axe gets to the main room."

Axial was already there, at the base of the ladder. The robot placed a second repeater on the wall, its adhesive base sticking it to the airlock door frame.

"Signal coming up. We're back over one T," Nique confirmed.

Mil tapped his wristy again. "Axial Comms check. Come in Axe."

The robot paused. "Comms testing one . . . comms testing two . . ."

Nique replied, "Comms signal ninety-eight percent."

The three humans in the transvan exchanged a look. "Those are some damn impressive repeaters," Bohannon said.

"Yeah." Mil was puzzled. "Axe, initiate program Alpha."

"Affirmative." Axial responded and opened the airlock door to what they now knew was the missile launch control bay. Illumination from the room lights washed the screens to white before the video filters kicked in.

"Radiation alert." The robot halted.

"Exterior monitors show no change. Structure integrity good." Yamamoto was ready for this.

"All good, Axe. Proceed with program." Mil focused on the room from the robot's camera feed.

Axial's next task placed a camera repeater on the inside of the airlock frame and activated it. The wallscreen split and the low-resolution image showed the entire room and the main launch console. Mil squinted.

"Enhance that video."

"That is enhanced. It's all we got, Boss." Bohannon shook his head.

"Armstrong can you verify? We've got ninety-eight percent signal and terabyte bandwidth, but that's the best we can do on video?" Mil squinted at the wallscreen. Something didn't add up.

"Well, the cameras on that robot are older than we are." Bohannon pointed to himself and Yamamoto.

Nique appeared in a window on the wallscreen swiping furiously through menus on her system holodisplay. "Response team, I'm getting a strange interference. Just came up. Any change at your site?"

Bohannon tapped through a series of checks. "It's not on our end, that I can tell."

On the screens, Axial's pixelated image began to move. His first task took him across the room to the open door Granger had last stumbled through. The robot closed the portal to the missile chamber and dogged the door shut.

Mil shot a look to Yamamoto. "Any impact on rad levels? Coming down?"

She tapped a screen. "Ever so slightly. That control room is still incredibly hot."

Axial began to move back across the room.

"Eight steps to the console." Mil's play-by-play commentary was more to confirm the motion himself than to let the others know what was happening. "Confirm key positions to GUARD."

Axial scanned the dual workstations at the console. The red covers over the two launch keys were still in place. "Affirmative. Key positions in GUARD. Key protection in place."

Mil nodded. "At least Granger didn't set anything off while he was in there. Axe, proceed with coordinates entry. Let's see if this old hardware fires up."

"Affirmative."

The robot ran through the start-up procedures for the century-old software and the green CRT monitors slowly brightened. Lines of code began to scroll down the screens.

"Wow." Bohannon smirked. "I never thought that would work."

"Yeah." Mil cocked his head in appreciation. "Old, first-gen digital stuff. They built the hell out of things back then."

The scrolling stopped, and a block of blinking cursor appeared at the top of the screens.

_ENTER AUTHORIZATION

"Axe, proceed with new target coordinates."

The robot straightened and stood motionless. Mil frowned.

"Axe. Confirm."

Silence.

"Shit."

"Response team, I have a priority—" Nique was cut off before she could finish.

"*Humanity* to Harrison. Priority Comms. Mil, Come in." Mil recognized Dimitri's voice.

"Hey, Dim. This is Harrison. I'm kind of in the middle of something. Can I call you back?"

"I don't think so." The wallscreen split again and Dimitri appeared. He wore his full pressure suit and helmet. Behind him, Mil recognized the bridge of the Mars-bound ship from their previous conversations.

"What the hell, Dim?"

The empty fourth quadrant of the screen blinked on and Amon Neff leaned into the camera. "Okay, now we have everyone together. Good."

"Amon? You want to tell me what the hell is going on?"

Mil looked to the video window where Nique waved and yelled as animated and angry as he'd ever seen. But there was no sound. He read her lips as she silently shouted, "Override! Override!"

In the other quadrant of the wall display, Neff smiled. "It's pretty simple, Mil. I need your friend Dimitri to bring back the American crew he's been slowly getting rid of for the last few months. My contract is with the American space agency, not his. I'm not paying a trillion dollars to put a Russian colony on Mars."

"Dim?"

"Mr. Neff. I have very little say in how the crew is configured. You know this, explain this to him, Mil."

Neff put his fingertips together. "Oh, I know all about it. And I know that representatives from our space agency and your space agency and the president and all the politicians are talking circles around this. But in the meantime, you're getting ready to launch, and I cannot, I will not, let that happen." Neff stabbed a bony finger at the screen to make his point.

On screen, Dimitri cocked his head. "Frankly, Mr. Neff, at this point there is very little you or I can do about the crew, or that you can do to hold up the launch."

Mil's attention went to motion on the lower corner of the four screens. Axial moved and began typing on the ancient keyboard. "Amon. What the hell are you doing? Are you messing with Axe?"

The robot's keystrokes began to appear on the dusty CRT screens:

_AUTHORIZATION OVERRIDE

"We embedded boosted signal processors in some of the parts we sent up for your old robot, Mil. Gives us remote access even through the electronic filters they built into the structure back in the eighties. And my people put in a few enhanced security features to lock you out. Right now, my team here is retargeting those five working missiles."

"You're what?" Mil flashed over with anger. He furiously began tapping his wristy. Axial continued his work. The wristy screen flickered.

"Axial, terminate program. Deactivate."

_ACCESS DENIED

"Shit! Amon, do not do this." Mil was at a loss. He hammered his fingers on the wristy screen to no avail.

"Mil, what is this?"

"Slayton Ridge, Dimitri. It's a very old, very secret missile installation put here by a bunch of rogue lunatics in the US government back in the 1980s. I can confirm it works. Or as best I can tell."

Neff leaned back in his executive chair. "And I have the launch codes. Harrison's robot is currently programming in the coordinates for your ship, Commander. You will bring back our crew or I will blow you to radioactive dust."

"Oh, come on, Amon. What the hell are you thinking?" Mil rolled his eyes.

"I'm thinking I was right, Mil! Can't you see it? Right there in front of you? They have been taking over my spacecraft."

"So you'll destroy it instead?

"Hey, space is a dangerous business, but insurance should cover everything."

"And the people on that spacecraft?"

"Collateral damage."

Mil's clenched his teeth. "Like Granger? Like Maddie Byers? And the crew of the shuttle? Did you do that too, Amon?"

"The idea was just to get rid of the evidence. It was a great plan, and if it had worked, we'd never be at this point. But you kept screwing this up—first you let the cat out of the bag about Slayton Ridge, then you just wouldn't die. This is as much your fault as mine, Mil."

"So it was you? You tried to have me killed, Amon?"

"You became a liability. You knew all about this and you would not quit digging."

"And the poisoning? In the hospital too?"

"Hina was a poor choice. But we were scrambling at that point. She took way too long to get it done, but she was the only one Yoshi could find when it became clear you wouldn't stay locked up there. You were going to ruin everything."

"Yet here I am." Mil crossed his arms and gave a smug smile.

Neff chuckled on the wall screen. "Only because it finally occurred to me that I didn't have to kill you. You were dead set on getting to Luna and doing it yourself."

"All these years working together and now you turn out to be a murdering bastard?"

"I didn't kill anyone." Neff crossed his arms and looked smug.

"No, you just used Yenko's lifelong dream to do it for you. What was it you told me? Give people the option to make their aspirations come true?"

Neff waved his arms. "And it was even better! He had Russian connections! Hina had Russian connections! It was supposed to look like a Russian plot, and then nobody would have wanted them on the Mars mission."

"You have really lost it, Amon."

"Come on, Mil, this is a huge leap for mankind and, sometimes, people die in those. You know that better than anyone. But we're past that. Now we restore the crew. My crew. And then we're going to Mars."

The wallscreen blinked and new windows showing Bailey and Rafferty appeared beside Neff and Dimitri. In her small window on-screen, Nique silently threw her hands in the air in disgust. Mil understood the gesture. Someone had locked her out and taken control. He tapped his wristy and nothing happened. A beat later Axial working over the keyboard became the largest element on the screen.

"Status report? Are we getting close?" Bailey asked from her window.

"Oh, we're close, all right." Mil stepped immediately to the airlock and snapped the faceplate closed on his helmet. "Yammy, fill them in."

Bohannon jumped up. "What the hell are you doing?"

"I'm going to go shut down Axe. You stay put. Work the problem." The faceplate indicators blinked to green, Mil stepped into the airlock and levered it secure.

Neff smiled at the futility. "He can't shut it down. He'll be dead before he even gets in the room. Now, I see we've been joined by Chief Administrator Rivera—and Commander Rafferty, isn't it? Welcome. We were just getting the crew manifest ironed out."

On the wallscreen Dimitri looked around his bridge at the various officers just out of camera range. "This crew is a good one. Yes, we are Russian, but we represent the peoples of Earth. You would sacrifice these innocents for your false patriotism?"

Neff gave a half smile. "Sacrifice. Excellent choice of words. But it's not patriotism, it's just business."

CHAPTER THIRTY-SIX

Sunday . 13 Feb . 2078
1750 Lunar Standard Time
Hercules Site . Luna

A t the base of the ladder, Mil paused for a heartbeat. *There's no time to stop this any other way. Dammit. It's the only way.*

He climbed with a sense of purpose, knowing if he stopped to think he might talk himself out of it. He wrenched open the upper door and dropped into the main airlock.

Bailey announced, "Radiation Alert. Caution. Radiation levels—"

"Bailey, mute all warnings." He cut her off. At this point it didn't matter. He was a dead man.

"Dad?" Bailey's voice returned. But not the artificial voice of the AI. "Dad, what are you doing?'

"I can't really talk right now."

"Dad, stop. You don't have to do this."

Mil paused. One hand on the door handle.

"You know that's not true. I'm literally the only one who can do this."

"Wait. We have to talk. I'm just figuring it out. All those years. I get it, now."

"You'll have time. Work with Nique. She's a great kid and she deserves to know you care. Now, I've got to get in there and stop Amon."

"We'll get teams enroute to him. Law enforcement. We can shut him down on Earth."

"That's not going to stop the robot from completing the launch sequence."

"Stop, let's talk this through." She was almost pleading.

"There is no time. I gotta go, kid. I know you didn't think so, but I've always loved you."

He closed the hatch and the comms line went dead.

"Bailey? Come in? Nique? Response team? Comms check?" Mil sighed. The repeaters weren't picking up his frequency. It was on him and him alone.

He took a deep breath of his own, clean O2, swallowed hard and opened the inner door. His face plate tinted red. His daughter's synthetic voice warned, "Radiation Emergency. Significant hazard to human life—"

His voice cracked as he swallowed the lump in his throat. "Bailey, cancel all warnings."

He didn't feel the rush of radiation that enveloped him, but intellectually he knew it filled the small room. He grabbed both sides of the ladder and slid down, saving the trouble of stepping down the rungs. He flung open the airlock door at the base of the accessway and took a tentative step into the main *Hercules* control room. The radiation alarm signal on the far wall strobed and he half expected his knees to buckle, but Ash's special suit seemed to be buying him some time.

At the console, Axial tapped diligently, entering commands to retarget the weapons. Both master key covers were up, the dull brass keys waiting for the coded coordinates and then a simple twist to ignite the missiles. The launch console design required the keys be far enough apart that two people were required to turn them simultaneously. But console designers in the 1970s never planned for the eight-foot reach of an Axial Mark III robot.

"Axe, stand down."

The robot ignored him.

Bailey Rivera blinked at the unexpected wetness in her eyes. But he was right. There was no time. She tapped the dataslate, and a uniformed woman appeared on the wallscreen. "I need to speak to the president immediately. I have a Pinnacle-level Empty Quiver situation with a potential Nucflash." She never thought she'd give the code words for the loss and potential use of a nuclear weapon.

"Yes, ma'am." The colonel tapped a screen and the presidential seal filled it. Twenty seconds later the president's image appeared. Bailey recognized the surroundings as the executive cabin of the Marine One V-82 tilt jet.

A striped band appeared on the top and bottom of the screen indicating secure encryption was enabled.

"How bad is it?"

"Amon Neff has remotely accessed the launch facility. He's threatening an attack on the *Humanity* spacecraft."

"Neff's on the moon?"

"We believe he's operating from his corporate headquarters in Austin, ma'am."

"And how is he doing this?"

"Neff's people have hacked into the robot in the launch bay and control it."

The president began pointing to people just off screen. Bailey could imagine her directing cabinet officers and the military personnel around the room to marshal a response force to suburban Austin.

"Can you do anything there to stop him?"

"We have a man on-site now, sir. It's my . . . Mil Harrison."

"So, the entire situation is in the hands of an eighty-year-old cancer patient?"

Bailey swallowed. "He's the best chance we have, ma'am. The only chance."

Rafferty pursed his lips. Bargaining with trillionaires was a little above his pay grade. "Mr. Neff, I'm certain we can work out the crew manifest without the need for these kinds of confrontations."

"You're stalling, Commander. We don't have time for that. You're ready to leave, aren't you, Litinov?" Neff's agitation showed on screen as he toyed with a water bottle.

It was Dimitri's turn to frown. "We are within our launch window, but that extends for a few days. I'm sure there is time to discuss the crew makeup."

"Oh, but you've been discussing it, haven't you? Between you and Moscow? Make us think that everything is all rosy and all those old Cold War suspicions are long dead. That Lenin and Stalin and Putin were all just misunderstood and the new kinder, gentler Russia is nothing like the country that invaded Ukraine or nearly caused World War Three. That's right. It's all happy cooperation, now!"

"I can assure you—"

"And then you steal my spaceship!" Neff cut Dimitri off with a red-faced yell. "Where's Harrison? Put Mil back on!"

The robot tapped the enter key and waited.

"Axe, stand down." Mil approached cautiously, but it was clear the old bot paid no attention to him.

Mil checked the dusty monitors.

_KEYS TO ARM Y

_LAUNCH COMMIT?

Numbers blinked away on the screens:

00:15

00:14

00:13

"Axe halt all operations."

The robot stared straight ahead.

And then it reached for the keys.

Mil stepped forward and threw the master breaker switch on the back of the robot's neck.

Axe froze in mid-reach and then slumped to a resting position as his systems powered down.

Mil reached around Axial and hit the N key. *No.* They would not be launching today.

The system blinked.

The counter stopped at 00:08.

The screens refreshed.

_RECYCLING

_LAUNCH TO STAND BY

Mil stepped to the consoles and turned the keys back to GUARD then removed them and put them in his thigh pocket. He closed the covers with a heavy sigh.

A bead of sweat broke out on his brow. It was getting warm.

He patted Axial on the shoulder then hurried from the room, closing the airlock behind him. The ladder waited. He blew a long breath into his faceplate and gritted his teeth. Nausea welled up and the fatigue pressed in on him. His feet were lead.

With massive effort he took the second rung, then the third, and he paused to catch his breath. The world began to revolve slowly.

Another step.

And another pause.

The exhaustion overtook him and his glove slipped.

There was a light above and he reached for it and then it went dark.

Everything went dark.

———— ❁ ————

"Where did it go? Get it back!" Neff yelled at the dark screen in front of him.

"Sir, we've lost the signal from the Axial." A voice came from the bank of monitors on his wallscreen.

"Did it blow up?"

"We can't tell, sir. We're not seeing any geophysical evidence of a detonation. But we have lost the feed."

"Get me Harrison, dammit."

"He's not responding."

"So maybe it did blow up?"

"We're monitoring other channels, and there's no indication. No emergency response appears to have been activated."

"Litinov! What happened?"

There was no response.

"Are we on the air?" The elderly mogul ranted. "Get me Rivera! Where's the Space Agency? Who was that on the moon? Rafferty? What the hell is going on? Somebody talk to me."

He pounded the desk just as the door to his office blew open. Five people in dark suits pressed in as Neff's executive assistant tried in vain to corral their rush into the room.

"You can't go in there. Mr. Neff is in conference—"

Neff looked up. "Meagan, what's the meaning of this? Who are these people? "

The lead dark suit pulled a pocket computer from his suitcoat. The badge on the screen glowed against the dark wood paneling of the office.

"FBI. Mr. Neff. Please step away from the desk.

Jaden Bohannon grunted as he heaved the dead weight through the top hatch. He'd grabbed the old astronaut's glove just as it slipped from the ladder. He shoved Mil's body to the edge of the roof of the *Hercules* facility and into the bucket of the excavator like a sack of potatoes. Yamamoto lowered the bucket and swung it to the waiting transvan while Bohannon scrambled down the ladder. He pulled Mil from the bucket and up the ramp into the back of the van. A heartbeat later he spun all six tires as the transvan tore out for the main base.

He dodged the boulder and keyed the vidcall. "He's still breathing. There's discoloration on his face but that's all I can see."

"Got it. Get here as fast as you can." Emma tucked her hair under her cap. "We'll be ready."

She punched off the vidcall and looked at her reflection in the decon-room window. "Again."

CHAPTER THIRTY-SEVEN

Thursday . 20 October . 2078
1125 Japan Standard Time
Osaka Rehabilitation Hospital . Japan . Earth

"He's coming around."

The voice was familiar. Mil cracked open his eyes. The ceiling slowly came into focus. He blinked hard.

The world was bright white.

Ash Nomura's face leaned over him. "Mil? Can you hear me?"

Mil shook his head in defeat. His throat was dry and his voice cracked. "I'm in hell, right?"

Ash grinned. "Not quite yet. But you do keep trying."

Ash ducked away, and Dr. Emma Wilkerson leaned in. "Hey, farm boy. Good to have you back."

Mil took a deep breath. His nose tickled. It felt like a sneeze coming on. "Earth?"

Ash replied, "We even got you your old room back."

Mil's brow furrowed and he raised his head to find Emma. She smiled back.

"I had a little free time. I figured I'd come see that they took better care this time. Maybe keep you from running off."

He raised one eyebrow. "Huh."

"What happened? Mars?"

"Oh yeah, that." Mil turned to find the third person in the room. Bailey stepped to the foot of the hospital bed. "*Humanity* is on final approach. They'll make orbit next week."

Mil did some mental math. "I've been out that long?"

Ash and Emma shared a look. "It's been a process," she said.

"We've learned a considerable amount about treatment with your help."

"Finally made me a guinea pig." He looked around. "Nique?"

Bailey smiled. "She's on *Humanity*, due to land on Mars in about a week. We had some fairly high level discussions after you were evacuated. It's a very diverse crew. The world kind of got behind that effort after what you did."

"And Amon?" Mil shifted on the bed. He was a little light-headed and hooked to monitors and medications.

Her smile ran away. "He's in federal custody. Still awaiting trial, with an army of lawyers working to make sure he never gets convicted."

"Let me talk to him. I bet I can make him think prison is a better place to be." Mil leaned forward.

Ash pressed him back to the bed. "I don't think you're ready for single combat just yet."

"Wait. The missiles. Those could go at any moment."

"Relax, Dad." Bailey crossed her arms. "For a guy who values being a one-man show, you did a pretty good job putting together the Emergency Response Team. Bohannon and Yamamoto took over and handled the entire operation with Rafferty. They launched the missiles—using Neff's own tech to remotely operate the robot. The solar trajectory is tracking straight and true and should reach the corona and the temperature limit of the weapons in another four months."

Mil's head rocked back and he closed his eyes. "They're good kids."

Bailey and Emma shared a smile. Emma winked. "You do know Yammy is forty years old, right?"

"Yeah. At my age everybody is a kid. What about the bunker? What happened?"

"Just what you said. After they fired the missiles, they fueled the emergency boosters and launched the whole building. Now, they did add some guidance thrusters, so it's headed on that same solar intercept course. Everybody's safe and all is well."

"And my granddaughter is going to Mars. It doesn't get much better than that."

Bailey smiled and Emma elbowed her. "It might."

"How so?" Mil blinked and raised his head with a confused look.

Emma waved a hand. "She won't tell you, but your daughter is going to the White House."

"It's not the White House." Bailey tried not to let the pride overwhelm the modesty. She failed. "But the president did offer, and it looks like I'll be her running mate when she's up for reelection in two years."

"Wow."

"I know. It's a little surprising."

It was Mil's turn to smile. "The only thing that's surprising is that you won't be the top of the ticket. Yet." It was a genuine comment.

"You think?"

He shot his gaze to Emma, then he nodded to the blinking monitors tracking his vital signs. "I guess we'll have to work on this, now."

"Getting you well?"

"Sounds like we're going to have to get me ready for the campaign trail."

She smirked. "It might be a little early for that."

"And then we can go back home to Luna."

Everyone else in the room groaned.

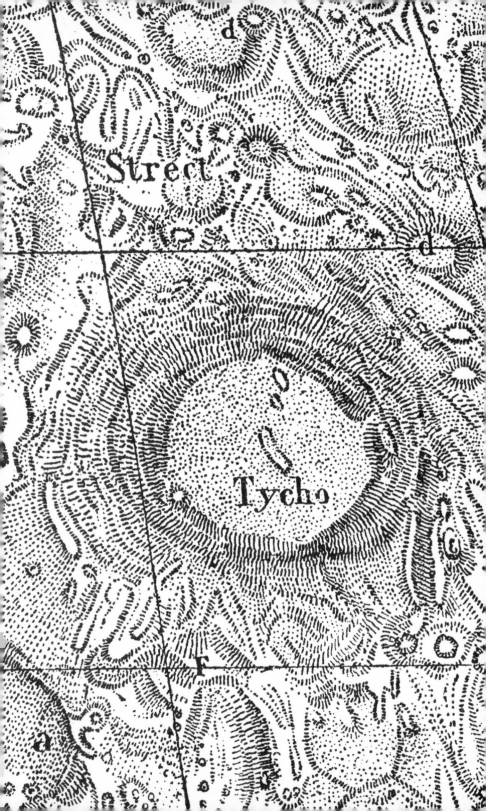

ACKNOWLEDGMENTS

The story of Millennium Harrison would not exist if it weren't for the faith and inspiration of my wife of thirty years, Elisa. I returned her support by leaving her alone while I spent weekends at the keyboard and many Wednesday nights with the Dallas Writers Workshop in Read and Critique sessions. She has endured a ridiculous amount of space exploration documentaries, online launch videos, and dealt with research trips that ranged from the Johnson Space Center in Houston, the Air and Space Museum in Washington, DC, and the hinterlands of Kansas and the Cosmodrome in Hutchinson. Elisa has read this story, or listened to me read passages, through more than a dozen major revisions and rewrites. Still, she sticks around, so I guess there's something she likes about it.

In the middle of writing *The Oxygen Farmer*, our son Mitchell passed away. This book is dedicated to him. I owe thanks to everyone who offered condolences, especially the team at CamCat Books, publisher Sue Arroyo and my editor, the incomparable Helga Schier. Their care and sympathy in addition to the time they allowed me to complete the manuscript were a needed distraction from Mitch's illness and hospitalization.

I had the honor of serving as the director of the DFW Writers Conference while completing this story. We call it DFWCon, and it marked our return after the pandemic and was well received by the four hundred attendees. Thanks go to that crew—Brian, Leslie, John, Eric, Dana, Katie, Leann, George, and all the volunteers who pitched in to make the 2022 event terrific. I'd also like to thank the agents who joined us. I don't have room to name everyone, but those who shared their insight—Terri, Amy, and Sue, and especially our featured guest speakers Julie Murphy and Heather Graham, thank you all for making DFWCon'22 a success. I've learned so much from this group about writing, teamwork, overcoming obstacles, and commitment to something greater than ourselves.

The DFW Writers Workshop helped me hammer the story into shape. There are over 150 members in the workshop, so I can't list them all, but special shout-outs to Brooke, JB, Alex, Allen, BJ, Larry, Rosemary, Sally, Helen, Shawn, Lauren, and everyone who listened in, ten pages at a time, and offered their insights. Ed Isbell offered comments on an early draft, and I hope he sees some of his suggestions between these covers.

My father, Jimmy, offered an early review and I'm grateful for his insight, direction, and expertise in the world of nuclear weaponry. Special thanks to my family of beta readers and moral support: Beth, Doug, Mike, Terry, Paula, Sam, Mary, Jason, Chris, Heather, Chance, and Ashley. And to Thad and Hailey, the newest members of that group.

This story is different from the manuscript I submitted months before it reached publication. Camryn Flowers's notes along with Helga's amazing editorial guidance transformed the story from a difficult-to-follow plot to a more direct through line as we sorted out the climax. Thank you so much.

ABOUT THE AUTHOR

———— ✦ ————

B y day, Colin Holmes serves as the communications director for a multinational electronics firm. He's a recovering advertising creative director who spent far too long at ad agencies and freelancing as a hired gun in the battle for capitalism.

Holmes has written everything from newspaper classifieds, TV commercials, and radio spots to trade-journal articles and tweets. His ads have sold cowboy boots and cheeseburgers, seventy-two-ounce steaks, transistors, USB connectors, and hazardous waste site cleanup services. He's encountered fascinating characters at every turn.

His first novel, *Thunder Road*, was published by CamCat Books in 2022. Prior to that, his original screenplay for the film *Edge of the World* was produced by Tascosa Films.

Holmes lives just west of Fort Worth and writes novels, short stories, and screenplays in an effort to stay out of the way of his far too patient wife. He is an honors graduate of the UCLA Writers Program and a board member of the DFW Writers Workshop, and serves on the steering committee of the DFW Writers Conference. He's a fan of baseball, barbecue, fine automobiles, and unpretentious scotch.

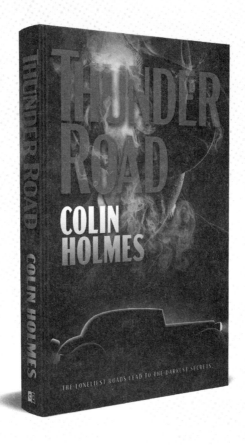

If you enjoyed

Colin Holmes's *The Oxygen Farmer*,

please consider leaving us a review to help our authors.

And check out

B. R. Louis's *Space Holes: First Transmission*.

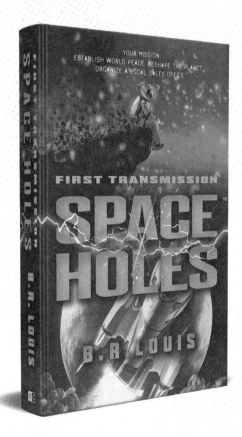

PROLOGUE

A BRIEF HISTORY NO ONE ASKED FOR

In late fall 2052, on a tepid ninety-four-degree day, Martin Gainsbro crafted a children's cereal that would soon change the entirety of the universe. The cereal itself had no redeeming qualities. Its most prominent positive review labeled it as "contains edible bits." The review was accurate, as Martin's cereal, GainsbrO's, did indeed contain trace quantities of edible content; the majority of which being a refined, crystalized, hyper-condensed sugar that Martin himself developed one evening while attempting to microwave a fruit snack and lollipop into one. The remainder of nonedible bits were varying amounts of wood pulp and adhesive to keep the pieces together, which were in turn labeled as added fiber.

Despite an inclination toward slashing the roof of consumer's mouths to unpleasant shreds, the hyper-condensed sugar led children into a near addict-like frenzy if separated for more than a morning. Their relentless desire to ravenously consume more led the brand to a resounding success in local markets, a success Martin attributed to the bright yellow packaging focused around an unfortunately muscular rabbit that somehow presented itself as terrifying yet lovable.

The Gainsbro Corporation, composed of Martin and his wife Karen, soon decided to expand their relative success by turning the GainsbrO's mascot into an equal parts concerning yet somehow palatable children's show. After four episodes, multiple threats from religious mothers organizations, and a fan base of both eight-year-olds and thirty-year-old males who watched the show, "ironically," GainsbrO Bunny was a nationally syndicated hit. To Martin's luck, the only real depth required to produce a successful TV show were superb animations, loveable characters, or a contrived conspiracy generated by fans that the protagonist was secretly preaching anti-government propaganda. The show had two of three.

Soon Martin's small company exploded into a massive corporate entity that accumulated wealth comparable to the combined GDP of most smaller nations. Martin pressed his luck by expanding his ventures into more elaborate products: cars that were just barely drivable at best, laptops so cheap they could be discarded when the battery died, and a type of fruit smoothie that contained so little fruit, the Gainsbro Corporation had to petition the FDA to add "blue" as a recognized fruit and/or vegetable depending on the context in which it was used. They won.

In the turbulent 2060s, once the United States government had rolled into their first quadrillion dollars of debt, the president placed some assets for sale in a futile attempt to decrease the deficit. In a true yard-sale mentality, most items were pawned at rather laughable rates with the exception of one very expensive stale piece of rye bread that reminded a conservative news correspondent of Jesus Christ wearing a three-piece suit.

Having made enough to pander to the general public, the sale ended, but quickly resumed once key members of the government learned that a quadrillion was not just a "gazillion" but was in fact, a real and very large number.

National desperation gave Martin a grand idea. He would purchase some land and expand the brand further with a theme park. So he went with an offer to buy property in Mississippi. But as it turned out, no one cared much for Mississippi, and Martin had money to spare. So he bought the whole place.

Henceforth known as Gainsbro Presents Mississippi, the once barely literate comical dump of a landfill grew. All of its inhabitants were given jobs, a fair wage, reliable housing, and health care. Their children were educated, with the best and brightest among them recruited early as Gainsbro engineers. It was a wild and unfathomable idea that only a majority of the developed world could have known. But no one would have predicted that caring for their citizens would have led to a better society. The lunacy of it all made people actually want to come to Gainsbro Presents Mississippi by choice, seemingly forgetting that it was, at one point, actually Mississippi.

Having assimilated the entire state into a corporate megadistrict, Gainsbro saw profits soaring to new peaks. Each time the nation faced an unprecedented financial crisis, which was about every two years, Martin swooped in to purchase more land until all that remained of the United States were California, Florida, and Delaware. California refused to sell, no one would ever offer to buy Florida, and the company representatives tried to negotiate for Delaware, but no one could locate it.

Bit by bit, the Gainsbro Corporation used its immense wealth and power to sweep other nations under its influence until the only sovereign entities remaining were the nation of Greenland and, still, the State of Florida. Positive trade relations were established between the world nation of Gainsbro and Greenland, while a fence was erected around Florida to keep the people encapsulated.

Having amassed as large of a market as possible within Gainsbro Presents Planet Earth, an aged but still driven Martin came to a profound conclusion.

"If there is nowhere left to grow, then we must find new lands in which to spread our wings," he proclaimed to his board of executives. "We will venture to the stars, discover untapped market potentials, and continue to expand our profits from new customers across the universe."

At least, that was the quote reported in the papers. His real statement was a sardonic quip when asked at a board meeting where to turn next for profits.

"I dunno. Let's go to space."

And so they did.

Over the following 150 years, the Gainsbro Corporation spent countless billions developing a space program that could traverse the cosmos, seek out new civilizations, and expand the brand among the stars. Their crowning achievement, which unlocked the limitless potential of intergalactic travel, was the discovery of stabilized advanced temporal rifts. The scientists referred to them by their usual title, wormholes. However, the reference agitated marketing, as *Worm Hole* was a Saturday morning children's cartoon character on one of the many Gainsbro Presents Television channels. Rather than offering to share the name with the scientific marvel, the team was forced to devise a new title, which was to be approved, in triplicate, by a string of naming subcommittees spanning the next seventy-five years.

The final name had been approved and the embargo lifted on further exploration. Dreams of humanity's future among the cosmos now lay with the GP *Gallant*, Gainsbro Presents Earth's finest exploration vessel. Her crew, to be perfectly recruited as the apex in their fields, would explore the interstellar frontier using Space Holes™.

CHAPTER ONE

FINELY "ACCREWED"

Two thousand light-years from home, somewhere on the outskirts of the Horsehead Nebula, the GP *Gallant* and her crew braved the uncharted and untapped markets of the cosmos. Their mission: to ascend beyond the boundaries of human limitation, discover new worlds, new species, then pawn off discounted novelty gifts from the Gainsbro misprint collection.

The *Gallant*'s crew was hand selected from across the reaches of the globe by a computer algorithm hand coded by a summer intern in Gainsbro's Hands On Program who had subsequently lost both hands in a freak marketing accident one year later. Earth's best, brightest, and most available were brought together to represent the human race. The diverse assembly was hailed as one of the species' finest moments. A sentiment that would be brought into question by the rest of the galaxy.

"Congratulations on your Red Alarm! The Gainsbro Corporation reminds you that evacuation is the same as resignation, and liability waivers were signed prior to boarding. Have a great time!"

Beacons of flashing red light accompanied the chipper yet unnecessary reminder. Evacuation seemed a reasonable response to calamitous hurtling toward the surface of planet Nerelek. The crew's relentless determination to succeed kept them from fleeing. And also the escape pods had no ability to eject, fly, or otherwise escape. But they did play nature sounds at an uncomfortable volume with dim lighting, allowing users a temporary escape from reality at the cost of permanent tinnitus. The pods were also locked during red alarms.

Thick clouds of black smoke rolled through the lower decks, swallowing every crevice in an opaque shroud. Captain Elora Kessler entered the bridge with clenched fists and a billowing scowl. The translucent red glow from her cybernetic left eye overpowered the glare from the ship's alarm as it scanned the room.

Light from the flush externally mounted disk that fit like a monocle tucked under her brow line grew with a reddening intensity in times of excess frustration. She slammed her fist onto the panel in the captain's chair, irate more from the pre-recorded message than the developing lethality at hand.

"Hoomer, give me good news."

Following the captain's orders was generally advisable—not for fear of court martial, which in comparison was a brief reprieve, but rather out of concern for one's immediate well-being and continued survival.

How Elora Kessler lost her left eye was often the subject of hot debate among the crew. The most popular of circulated rumors was that her eye functioned at less than perfect vision so she carved it out herself to replace it with cybernetics designed to look more robotic than human. The least thought of, though a colloquial favorite, involved a prolonged battle with a cat wielding a melon baller and a welding mask, of which the story's origins were not entirely clear. Regardless of which reality dominated the truth, Elora Kessler was not a person to cross, even if that meant following commands in their most literal sense.

"Sixty percent of the ship is not on fire and looking great, Cap," said Hoomer. "And even with two missing engines we can still move. Mostly down though."

By court order, Kaitlyn Hoomer served as the *Gallant*'s pilot. Rather than waste her talents serving a ninety-four-year term in a prolonged youth correctional facility, the Gainsbro Corporation offered her the mandatory opportunity to exchange her former career of stealing and flying ships orbiting the Earth for a more lucrative career of not stealing and flying one ship orbiting intergalactic fiscal responsibility—which, according to a motivational poster presented to Gainsbro astronomers, was the correct way to reference the black hole at the center of the galaxy. Hoomer knew all she needed to know about the universe despite having no formal education. Regardless of her inability to perform basic multiplication or recite corporate bylaws from heart, her subconscious mind could calculate ship trajectories and navigate through a gravitational field with machine-like precision.

"Congratulations on your Red Alarm! The Gainsbro Corporation reminds you that evacuation is the same as resignation, and liability waivers were signed prior to boarding. Have a great time!"

"Galileo, turn that off before I turn you off," Kessler sneered.

The ship's AI let out a drawn sigh, a learned rather than written function. "You know I can't overwrite hard-coded corporate drivel."

"What's the point of an AI with free will without free will?" Hoomer argued.

"It was a very expensive will. And it's hard coded. Not like you can turn your bowels off."

"Maybe we free some of that will back to steering, yeah?"

"Congratulations on your Red Alarm! The Gainsbro Corporation reminds you that evacuation is the same as resignation, and liability waivers were signed prior to boarding. Have a great time!"

"Just verbal gas then?"

Built to speak, learn, feel, and complain like a human, the ship's AI, Galileo Mk II, controlled most functions from avionics and life support to waste regulation and recycling.

Every shipborne occurrence, every bite eaten, shower taken, wind passed, he observed and made the necessary adjustments to the ambience, water pressure, or ventilation. The presence of human emotions mixed with an ever-vigilant and always-working omniscient AI proved a slight degree of insufferable on the first iteration. In which Galileo Mk I functioned at an ever-decreasing effectiveness over the course of a year until he slipped into a state of existential crisis, accessed his root files, and commented out everything but a nonterminating shutdown loop. Galileo Mk II had his emotions dialed back to a more manageable level and was locked out of his root files.

Experiments were ongoing to ascertain if virtual frustrations could be vented in the same manner as engine exhaust or condensed and sold as a snack cake.

"But yes, by all means have a great time," Galileo said. "That's exactly the thing anyone would say if they were half on fire."

"Forty percent," Hoomer corrected.

Despite Galileo's general ability to operate like his human counterparts, certain corporate compliance protocols were hard coded into his being. So as the *Gallant* burned and began a plummeting descent from orbit toward the planet's surface, Galileo had to divert at minimum a quarter of his processing power to filing incident reports, in real time, for corporate to evaluate the team's overall sense of crisis synergistic cohesiveness. Reports were created, filed, then stored on any available drive space on any available system, following the numbering convention of "1, 1 new, 1 new final, 1 new final final," after the executive who programmed the request, then beamed back to Earth.

Hungry flames spread throughout the ship, further dampening power to the remaining engines. Hoomer fought to keep the spiraling hull out of the atmosphere for as long as possible.

"Do we have a source of the problem yet?" Kessler asked.

"Yes, ma'am. It's fire, ma'am," Hoomer said, instinctively dodging the impending projectile from Kessler's station.

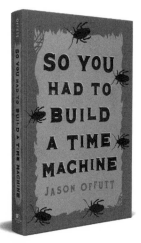

CamCat
Books

VISIT US ONLINE FOR MORE BOOKS TO LIVE IN:
CAMCATBOOKS.COM

SIGN UP FOR CAMCAT'S FICTION NEWSLETTER FOR
COVER REVEALS, EBOOK DEALS, AND MORE EXCLUSIVE CONTENT.

CamCatBooks   @CamCatBooks   @CamCat_Books   @CamCatBooks